NO ONE WAS SAFE

The street was still dark when Presidential aide Lattimere Spitz stepped out of the condo complex. There was a thin sliver of red-yellow to the east but overhead the sky was overcast and the wind was raw. There was a spit of rain and the limo driver was waiting, door open, collar up, hat pulled down to shield him from the weather.

"Good morning, Mr. Spitz," the man said, closing the door behind him. Spitz waited until he saw the driver walk around behind the car, slip in behind the wheel and turn the key in the ignition before he opened his paper.

That's when the car exploded.

RED WIND

R. KARL LARGENT

LEISURE BOOKS NEW YORK CITY

A LEISURE BOOK®

March 1998

Published by

Dorchester Publishing Co., Inc.
276 Fifth Avenue
New York, NY 10001

ISBN 0-8439-4361-0

Printed in the United States of America.

RED WIND

p972—u a AM-PLANE CRASH 10-31 0030
PM-PLANE CRASH
BULLETIN
MIAMI (AP)—A jet described as a military E-4 aircraft plowed into the ocean south and west of Point Sable and burst into flames shortly before 11 p.m.
    —Several witnesses said the plane exploded in midair.
AP-DN-10-31 0606 1114EST

Chapter One

Jacqueline Marceau could account for her time since she left her office. Not that anyone would question her—after all there was no reason to suspect her of anything other than the occasional indiscretions of any single woman in Washington. Nevertheless, she carefully jotted down each thing she had done and scribbled the approximate times between each.

For over a year now she had held the somewhat vague and uninspired title of "Asian Expert" in a largely clerical pool of language specialists assigned to the development department of the CIA. Even though it pleased Mao Quan, it was not what she had hoped for when she applied for the position. Rather it was a dreary day-to-day job that thus far had called upon her to do little more than translate from Chinese to English reams of shipping documents and cargo manifests monitored by the agency.

It was curious, she often thought, how the American government was willing to overlook the fact that she was a Cambodian nationalist by birth, for no other reason than that she read Chinese, and could call her superior's attention to articles of interest from *Renmin Ribao*. The *People's Daily* was still the official paper of the Communist Party.

She had left the office with two of her coworkers and walked to the parking lot with them. They had invited her to have a drink at the Navy Club, where they were meeting dates. She had declined based on the fact that she had an appointment with her hairdresser. From work to the hairdresser to home had accounted for a little over an hour and a half. She'd made a note about the traffic, *"heavier than usual,"* and at eight-forty-five she had called her friend, Julie Simon.

The two women had talked for almost thirty minutes when Julie informed her that she had to go. Jacqueline Marceau knew why—her friend had a date. It was not just any date, it was a date Jacqueline had arranged—with the very married senator from Iowa, Richard Crane.

At nine-thirty, she'd slipped down to the apartment complex's health center. She'd swum twenty laps, showered, and been careful to sign both in and out. Another hour was accounted for.

At ten-thirty she'd fixed herself a cup of tea and begun the wait.

Still later, with the inherited grace of her Vietnamese mother, Jacqueline Marceau moved about her apartment filled with the cultivated artifacts of her French father. Her recurring nightmares, a residue of the atrocities in the final days before the Chinese troops moved into Kampuchea, were now, for the most part, a thing of the past; a thing of the past consciously and carefully buried. Buried, she was quick to add, but retrievable. It was those nightmares that fanned the fires of her hatred.

The Americans she knew still talked about the brutality and savagery of the Khmer Rouge, but she had witnessed first-hand the cruelty and heinousness of a different army, that of the United States.

It was not the Khmer Rouge, but two American soldiers, that had raped her mother, cut out her tongue, and left her to die on a deserted delta cart path. And it was the Americans who'd condemned her father for conspiring with the Khmer Rouge after a sham trial that lasted no more than an hour.

Even now she could picture herself standing at the window of their burned-out home until she heard the shot. He had been executed by a young American lieutenant.

In the inquiry into her father's death, the American had testified that Gerrold Marceau, governor designate of the coastal village of Kampot Som, had tried to escape. Moreover, the lieutenant's superiors, six old men in stiffly starched uniforms with gaudy ribbons and decorations, had believed him. The young American by the name of Crane had been sent home a hero.

Jacqueline Marceau had convinced herself that the young American lieutenant had lied. Jacqueline knew her father too well. Gerrold Marceau would never have tried to escape. The Gerrold Marceau she knew would have stayed and faced his fate. Above everything, her father was an honorable man. Convincing Mao Quan that Crane should be one of the targets had been easier than she had anticipated.

As the thoughts of those early days faded, she paused to study her reflection in the mirror. Tall, slightly angular, with the ebony-colored hair and almond eyes of her mother, she relied more on the attributes she had inherited from her father to complete her mission. It was his cunning, his sagacity, his determination that endeared him to her. She likewise knew that it was her own shrewdness, deception, and subtlety that had caused Mao Quan to select her.

Now she waited to see if the second phase of Mao Quan's plan had gone as well as the first. The first call had come at eleven o'clock. It had been from the one Tonu Hon referred to as Liu Shao. As usual, their phone conversation was restricted; it took him less than thirty seconds to confirm that he had obtained the copy of Worling's report. She knew there was more, but even if there had not been the time restriction, Liu Shao was a man of few words who moved in his own shadows.

12

She had read Liu's dossier when Mao informed her of his plan. And it was Mao Quan himself who had warned her that Liu was a calculated risk—a question mark—a man prone to putting his own twist on any scheme. So far she would have to report he had followed orders to the letter.

She was still standing at the mirror considering what he had said when the phone rang.

This time it was Chen Po Lee. Unlike Liu Shao, his voice sounded hurried and edgy. Now there were two reports to file.

Time 2319LT:

Chen Po Lee cradled the receiver between his ear and shoulder while he lit a cigarette. He took two deep drags before he spoke, in Mandarin.

"It went exactly as expected," he reported, "and as we expected, there was much confusion."

"You are certain all of the American officials were on board?" Jacqueline asked.

"Records will show Airman Chow assisted with the luggage," Chen said, "and it was also Airman Chow who personally assisted The Undersecretary of State and his wife to seats aboard the aircraft."

"How many were aboard the aircraft?"

"Fifteen. You will recognize many names."

"You have done well," Jacqueline said, "but there is still much to be done."

Chen cocked the receiver under his chin a second time and checked his watch. There was still the matter of disposing of the real Airman Chow's body and getting rid of Chow's car. He told the woman it would take him no more than thirty minutes.

"Excellent," she said. Her assessment was followed by an abrupt click.

Chen placed the receiver back in the cradle, checked the now-empty military VIP corridor, headed for the nearest exit, and stepped out into the damp Florida night.

Twenty minutes later, he had driven south on 953 and turned onto the Dixie Highway. Finally, he came to an undeveloped and deserted stretch of beach south of Hemlock Park. He pulled Chow's aging Dodge behind an old bathhouse, stepped out of the car, and walked around to the trunk.

What had earlier been a light mist when they were loading Swelling's plane had now deteriorated into a steady rain. He took out his flashlight and traced the beam over the body of the young Chinese American whose identity he had used to gain access to the flight line. In death, Airman 1/C Chow had provided him with a fatigue uniform, a security pass, and the necessary credentials to mingle with the other TDY airmen from nearby Homestead. All in all, it had been much easier than Chen had expected.

Because of the rain, Chen hurried. He pulled Chow's body out of the trunk, dragged him around to the driver's side of the car, propped him behind the wheel, placed the small packet of plastic explosives in Chow's lap, changed back into his own clothing, placed the security badge and papers in the glove compartment, and walked back to the road.

The second car was waiting for him. He crawled into the passenger's seat, lit a cigarette, and looked at the driver.

"It is done," he said. At the same time he knew the young woman had no idea what he was talking about. Three blocks from where Chen had left the first car, he detonated the explosive.

Time 2351LT:

T. C. Bogner waited outside his former wife's dressing room while Joy finished dressing. From time to time he glanced at his watch and wished he had decided to meet her at one of their old watering holes instead of here at the studios.

"Five minutes," Joy shouted. "That's all it takes. Three minutes of airtime and two minutes of commercials. Then we can get out of here."

Bogner, seldom applauded for eloquence, grunted and fingered the gold bracelet in his pocket. Let the bracelet do the talking, he thought; the less he said until they were out of there, the better.

When she opened the door, Bogner knew it had been worth the wait. Joy Carpenter, formerly Joy Bogner, was still a stunner. He remembered how every head in the place had turned when she walked into the Officers Club at Pensacola twenty years earlier.

For the most part, things hadn't changed. She

still wore her sable-colored hair off the shoulder, and her Caribbean-green-blue eyes were as clear and inviting as ever.

She was trim, tanned, and enticing. It was easy to see why she was the hottest anchorwoman in Washington.

"You look great," he finally managed. Joy Carpenter knew that for Bogner that was extreme praise indeed.

Joy purred. "Why is it women get wrinkles with age and men get wisdom?"

Before Bogner could answer, their twosome had become a threesome. They were suddenly confronted by a nervous young man who handed Joy a piece of paper. "Just came in, Ms. Carpenter," he said. "We're using it as our lead. With any luck we'll have more by the time we go on."

Joy scanned the paper and handed it to Bogner. "Another plane crash," she muttered. While Bogner read it she straightened her skirt.

"Doesn't give you much to go on," Bogner said.

"I know, it's just breaking. By airtime we should have more." Joy blew him a kiss as she started for the set. Bogner grunted and reread the second paragraph of the bulletin.

Several witnesses said the plane exploded in mid-air. . . .

In the NBS newsroom, Joy Carpenter and Fred Napper, the news director, watched the second AP bulletin glide across the monitor:

p-1078—u a PM-Plane Crash 10-31 0030
PM-Plane Crash, 0050
Urgent Plane Crashes in Ocean—Miami Airport
CAPE SABLE, Florida (AP)
A plane crashed in the tidewaters off Cape Sable after takeoff, but there is no immediate word of casualities, a spokesman said.
"We are working on an alert 3. That is a crash," said Byron Combs, the spokesman for Miami Air Traffic Control.
No other details are available.

Napper hit the "print" key and handed the copy to Joy. "We'll have to go with this. You've got two minutes. I'll get it on the prompt. If there's anything else I'll hand you the copy on camera."

Napper turned and headed for the control room, while Joy made certain she had her facts nailed down. At the door he stopped. "One more thing. Stick around. We'll go right into *Night Owl Theater* after this, but I'll need someone on camera when this thing starts to unfold."

Bogner walked into the control room and took a seat. From where he sat he could see a bank of monitors, controls, the on-camera prompter, and the set. "We're getting an update," Napper informed the set. "We'll get you the copy during the opening commercial."

Bogner read it over Napper's shoulder.

p0031—PM Plane Crash 10-31—268—NOTE-PM-Plane Crash, 1st tv-write thru. A Boeing E-4B crashed

17

*in tidewaters off Cape Sable, Florida. URGENT
CAPE SABLE, Florida (AP)—A U.S. Military transport aircraft exploded shortly after takeoff at 11:31
p.m. 10/31.*

*"We are working on an alert 3. That is a crash," said
Miami Air Traffic Control spokesman Byron Combs.
Eyewitnesses in Cape Sable said the plane exploded
in flames and plunged into the tide waters five miles
off Cape Sable. There is no immediate report of injuries or fatalities.*

*Air Force officials were not immediately available for
comment.*

*"I was just approaching the bridge at Mercer when I
saw a huge explosion in the sky," Lester Main of Biscayne told WULD radio. "I never saw anything like
it. Then I saw pieces of something falling in the water.
I didn't know what it was."*

*The crash is the second involving a military transport
in the last five days. A similar Boeing E-4 crashed in
heavy seas off the coast of California on 10/26.
Secretary of the Air Force James Dunning died in that
crash.*

Napper hit the "print" key, and rushed out of the
room and onto the set.

Bogner sagged back in his chair and waited for
the inevitable. When Napper returned, he looked at
Bogner and shrugged. "Sorry, old boy, I know what
you and Joy had planned—but this is beginning to
look like it will take a while. I'll still need her even
after we get the network feed."

Bogner stood up and looked through the glass at

Joy, and she managed to give him a subtle shrug. He remembered the words of the judge in the Orange County courtroom. "I've seen the Navy wreck more than one marriage, young man. With the Navy, the mission comes first." It wasn't any different at NBS.

He walked out of the studio, got on the elevator, and rode down to the lobby. One of the security guards recognized him. "Thought you and Joy were off to Jamaica," the man said.

"Better turn on your television," Bogner said.

1 Nov: Time 0044LT:

Kent Peters was working the night shift at the ISA ops room. Recently transferred from California, he shared the responsibility with one of the agency's old-timers, Gordon Hatton. Peters was in his fifth year with the agency; Hatton was well into his twentieth.

Both men had spent the better part of the hour watching the CNN reports from the crash site off Cape Sable.

"So, what do you think?" Peters asked over his coffee.

"Who the hell knows," Hatton grunted. "All we know so far is the damn thing took off in marginal weather. And there were thunderstorms in the area—maybe it got hit by lightning."

Peters shook his head. "Helluva way to go."

"Yeah," Hatton agreed. "If this keeps up, the damn White House will have to hire a recruiting firm to fill the vacancies. First Air Force Secretary James Dunning and now Undersecretary of State William Swelling."

Peters was just starting to get out of his chair to refill his cup when the phone rang. As usual, Robert Miller's voice sounded as though he had just been dragged out of a dream; it was sleepy and halting.

"Don't you ever sleep?" Peters said, needling him. He winked at Hatton sitting across the desk from him.

"Just wondered if you guys had learned anything more about that crash down at Cape Sable," Miller said. "I'm surfing back and forth between the networks and they're all saying that there were some American diplomats on board. But so far no names."

Peters leaned across the desk and picked up the hard copy of the transmission they had received just moments earlier. "Lattimere Spitz issued an all-agencies bulletin less than ten minutes ago. Undersecretary of State Swelling was on that plane. The aircraft had filed a flight plan from MIA to LAX. From there they were flying to Beijing."

"Rumor is Swelling was carrying a letter of protest from President Colchin about recent Fifth Academy terrorist activities," Miller said. "Colchin wants the current regime in Beijing to put a collar on Mao Quan and his damned Fifth Academy."

Peters glanced around the room, checking for updates on the three monitors. The screens were blank. "Do you think we should call Packer and let him know what's happening?" he asked.

"Naw, let him sleep. If there's a problem, we'll all wish we had gotten a little extra mattress time."

"They're using the word 'explosion,'" Peters reminded him. "Think they mean . . ."

"That could mean anything," Miller assured him. He paused before he added, "Give me a call if anything comes through. Okay?"

"Will do," Peters said. By the time he had hung up Hatton had switched over to the Weather Channel, and a slender redhead was pointing to the spot on the map where the E-4 had gone down.

Now, in the area where the airline crash was reported earlier this evening . . . the Cape Sable Weather Station is currently reporting heavy rains, five-foot swells, one-half-mile visibility, and strong winds. At 11: 25 p.m., a United Airlines pilot reported a supercell with tops up to forty-five thousand feet forming some two hundred and fifty miles off the southwest coast of Florida. The pilot estimated the storm cell to be approximately ten to twelve miles in diameter and moving in a northeasterly direction.

The weather radars at both Marco and Naples have been picking up the storm in the last thirty minutes, and Naples has issued a severe thunderstorm warning effective until 4:00 a.m. . . .

Hatton switched back to NBS, where an attractive, sable-haired woman was conducting an interview on a split screen with one of the crash eyewitnesses. It was raining hard as the female eyewitness huddled under an umbrella.

"And then you saw the explosion?" "It was very dark—but it wasn't raining hard like it is now; just kind of a drizzle. We could hear the plane and it seemed awfully low. All of a sudden there was a bright flash and then what sounded to us like an explosion. It was to our left, out over the water. It came down in pieces—all of them were on fire."

"Is it possible that what you saw was lightning? Could the flash you and your husband saw have been the storm?" "I suppose it could have been. There was lots of thunder and lightning out over the gulf. . . ."

Peters leaned back in his chair. "Know what I think, Gordo?" he asked.

Hatton shook his head.

"I think that plane was hit by lightning."

Hatton stood up, stretched, and glanced back at the monitor. "I don't think so. Something in my gut tells me this place will be all asses and elbows in a few hours."

Time 0059LT:

When Bogner was in Washington, he shared a two-bedroom apartment with a longtime friend, Reese Smith, of the Associated Press. The two seldom crossed paths and when Bogner was in town, which wasn't often, Reese was usually out.

Bogner had been permanently assigned to the Naval Air Station at Pensacola for the past several years, and his forays into Washington were usually at the request of the President. His ISA assignments, all TDY, were Colchin's way of keeping him handy.

He parked, took the elevator to the third floor, and unlocked the door. He threw the luggage—containing the clothes he had expected to use in Jamaica while he and Joy got to know each other again—into his bedroom, then walked back into the living room, fixed himself a scotch on the rocks, turned on the television, and slumped down in a chair. It was, as Joy used to call it, pout time. He took a long sip of his scotch, and thumbed through the airline tickets he wouldn't be using.

"*. . . at this time there are no known survivors,*" he heard the reporter say. Bogner switched channels, purposely avoiding NBS and Joy. He surfed past an infomercial on selling real estate, a car dealer touting deals on "his overstock of certified used cars," and settled on a twenty-four-hour local news station in the Washington area. The reporter was talking about a shooting, and he muted the sound until he realized the screen was flashing pictures of his old Navy buddy, Robert Worling, now of the State Department.

Bogner turned up the volume.

Worling, forty-six, was last seen alive when he left his office late this afternoon. He was scheduled to be the featured speaker at the Webster Day dinner, but officials there reported that he was a no-show. Worling's wife found his body in his garage at their Alexandria home. He had been shot in the back of the head at close range. Investigators from the Alexandria hom-

icide squad said Worling had been dead for several hours when his wife discovered the body at 10:45 this evening. . . .

Bogner was still trying to digest what he had just heard when the phone rang. He knew it had to be either Packer or Joy. They were the only ones who knew Reese's phone number—and the odds were, at this hour, Packer was asleep.

He switched back to NBS, saw that Joy wasn't on the screen, and picked up the phone.

"Just how angry are you?" Joy began.

"Hell, you couldn't help it. You didn't blow up that damn plane." He was doing his best to sound conciliatory. Joy started to apologize, but Bogner cut her off. "Remember Bob Worling? He and Linda were stationed at Pensacola when we were."

"Sure, he's with the State Department now. I ran into him a couple of months ago; he asked how you were and what you were up to these days. Why?"

"Linda just found him dead, in his garage. Someone shot him in the back of the head."

There was a prolonged silence while Joy tried to regain her composure. "Do—do they—they know what happened?"

"It just came over the news," Bogner said.

There was another long interval before Joy broke the silence. "I'm sorry, Tobias, you know I am. Go to bed. Try to get some sleep. I'll be there in a little while. I'll wake you up."

Bogner hung up, sat there for several moments, and released the TV mute button. The first thing he heard was the news that Undersecretary of State William Swelling had been on the flight that crashed at Cape Sable.

Time 0139LT:

For the most part, the young woman and Chen Po Lee rode the last forty miles to the deserted marina on Toll Reef in silence. It was not the first time they had been together. Chen had made note of the young woman's reticence on every occasion that he had been with her. In each of his three assignments thus far, the woman had been called upon to chauffeur him from one location to another—and this time, as she had been in the past, she seemed totally unwilling to engage him in conversation or answer the simplest of questions.

South of Leisure City, the weather had deteriorated further, until there was frequent lightning in all quadrants along with occasionally heavy rain. Even the thunder seemed to be intensifying. With the storm came poor reception on the AM radio stations, and the FM stations all seemed to be carrying pre-recorded programs. When that happened, Chen Po Lee was no longer able to monitor the latest reports on the crash off Cape Sable. Agitated, he lit a cigarette, leaned his head back, and shut his eyes. What was the American expression he had heard Tonu Hon use? *Mission accomplished?* He had been successful, and he wondered if Liu Shao had been equally successful on his *"mission"* in Washington.

Turning off Hayward, the young woman pulled

down a side street, then turned back north on a sand road to the old marina. Two rusty Quonset buildings, one quite large, the other appreciably smaller, were all but concealed by invader grass, moss, and stickweed. Less than two hundred feet from the larger of the two buildings was a series of dilapidated old slips jutting out into the bay shallows. Only one of the slips had been repaired. Moored beside it was a boxy old wooden twenty-six-foot Bagadell. Two windows were out of the wheelhouse, it was sadly in need of paint, and there was obvious damage to the port-side hull.

Chen Po Lee pulled the collar of his jacket tight around his throat, shoved his glasses in his pocket, crawled out of the car into the rain, and sprinted for the larger of the two buildings. When he threw the door open, the old man was waiting.

His name was Tonu Hon, and he'd long been one of Mao Quan's closest advisors. Tonu was a slight man with obvious nervous energy who hailed from the island of Hainan. He spoke very little English, and what little he did speak was difficult to understand. Despite the fact that he had worked himself into a functionary's role in the hierarchy of the old Party, he was now forced to share the leadership role with the Marceau woman. He suffered this perceived indignity despite the fact that he had been involved with the Fifth Academy movement since his youth. Now his base of operations was in Cuba, and he awaited Liu Shao's report as well as that of Chen Po Lee.

Tonu Hon nodded and waited for Chen Po Lee to

speak. "You have news of the crash?" Chen asked.

"You have done well, comrade," Tonu Hon assured him. "Less than thirty minutes ago it was confirmed that Secretary Swelling was aboard the downed craft."

Chen Po Lee smiled, walked over to the small electric burner on top of the workbench, poured himself a cup of coffee, dropped down on a nearby straight-back chair, and lit a cigarette. "And what about Liu Shao? You have heard from him?" Chen asked.

"Under the circumstances, I do not anticipate receiving word from our comrade. When I hear of Liu Shao's success, I expect it to come from Mademoiselle Marceau. Nor do I anticipate much in the way of information from the American press until morning. The nature of our comrade's mission was, shall we say, slightly less newsworthy—would you not agree?"

Chen Po Lee glanced at his watch. He was tired. "We will leave soon?" he asked.

"Within the hour," Tonu Hon assured him.

Time 0238LT:

Homicide Detective Vin Suitland walked up the driveway of the two-story Worling house on Temple Street, glancing back at the curb, then at the garage. "Question: How far would you estimate it is from the curb to where Worling was shot?" he asked.

Suitland had directed his question at Glenn Rodale, a former patrol officer recently assigned to homicide. So far Suitland liked what he saw in Rodale; he was mentally agile and dedicated, two attributes Suitland considered vital in a budding homicide detective.

"Thirty—maybe thirty-five feet," Rodale estimated. "Why?"

Suitland frowned. He had a habit of qualifying what he was about to say with openers like, *"Question,"* or *"Is it possible,"* or *"Do you suppose."* Now he glanced back at the distance from the curb to where Worling's car was parked. "Do you suppose it would it have been possible for the assailant to have followed Worling, watched him pull into the garage, then jumped out and got to Worling just as he was getting out of his car?"

"If he did, how did he get him turned around and the muzzle of the gun pressed up against the base of his skull?" Rodale countered.

Suitland studied the chalk marks on the garage floor. They indicated the way Worling's body was lying when his wife discovered him. To Suitland they also indicated that Worling was still in the process of getting out of the car when he was shot.

"The assailant could have been waiting in the garage," Rodale offered.

"Maybe, but how did he get in? The garage door opens electronically. There's no access door, and Mrs. Worling is positive the door from the house to the garage was locked. She says she always kept it locked when she knew her husband wouldn't be coming home until late."

Rodale examined the lock on the garage door and

the one on the door leading from the garage to the house. "If whoever did it jimmied the locks, they were damn good at it, Vin. There's not a scratch on either one of them."

Suitland slumped back against Worling's car and shoved a stick of gum in his mouth. He was going through six or seven packs a day now that he had quit smoking. "All right, you know the routine; what have we got so far?"

Rodale leafed through his notebook until he found what he was looking for. He read it aloud:

Robert J. Worling, 47, 2721 Temple. Wife: Linda, no children. CIA. Body found at approximately 11:15 p.m. by subject's wife. Victim shot in the back of the head at close range, powder burns apparent. Assailant probably used small-caliber revolver; no evidence of exit wound. . . .

"Want more?"

Suitland shook his head. "Think robbery was the motive?" Rodale recognized it as one of Suitland's typical rhetorical questions. Rodale had worked with him just long enough to know his partner did not expect an answer. "Probably not," Suitland muttered, answering his own question. "Billfold intact, briefcase still lying on the seat of the car, watch, rings—all there. So why was he shot?"

"Maybe the lab reports will tell us something," Rodale ventured.

Suitland nodded. "In the meantime, what have we got on Mrs. Worling?"

Rodale studied his notes. "She says she was coming home from a Halloween party. She claims the only reason her husband didn't go to the party with her is because he was scheduled to speak at the Webster Day dinner. At any rate, she pulled into the driveway, hit the automatic garage door opener, saw her husband's car—and then saw him sprawled out on the garage floor beside the car."

"How do we know it wasn't her?" Suitland asked. It was another of his rhetorical questions, but Rodale answered anyway.

"On the surface, there's no motive. Besides, she has a pretty tight alibi, Vin. She left the party at ten-forty-five, arrived home at approximately eleven-fifteen and found the body. The medical examiner said Worling had been dead a couple of hours—which backs up the time of death to around nine-fifteen or earlier. We won't know for sure until we get the ME's report tomorrow."

Suitland unwrapped another stick of gum and threw away the old one. He studied the floor, the walls, opened the door of the car and studied the car's interior. Finally, he slammed the door.

"Dammit, it doesn't make any sense. This cat was slick as a whistle; no apparent motive, nothing taken as far as we can tell, and nothing left behind except a damn bullet buried in the back of the victim's head."

Rodale yawned and glanced at his watch. "Come on, Vin, give it a break. Maybe we'll find something in the morning. For all we know Worling was murdered because he works for the government. Hell,

I know a guy who works for the IRS I'd like to shoot."

Vin Suitland laughed, as much as he ever laughed, shoved his hands in his pockets, and walked out of the Worling garage. Two uniformed officers were standing by their patrol car, collars turned up against the cold. "No one goes near it," Suitland informed them.

Time 0310LT:

Bogner came out of a heavy sleep and rolled over when he heard Joy unlock the door to the apartment. He followed her footsteps down the hall into the bathroom, and heard her undress and shower before she came into the bedroom.

"Tobias," she whispered, "are you awake?"

When she heard the groggy response she knew he had been asleep. "What's the latest?" he managed to ask.

Joy turned on the small night lamp beside the bed. She was wearing a nightgown. "They think maybe there was a bomb on board Swelling's plane."

Bogner sat up, looked at the clock, and then at his ex-wife. "Bomb?" he repeated, still not alert. "Aboard an Air Force plane? How?"

"Less than an hour ago, a Dade County deputy sheriff reported an explosion on a stretch of beach south of Hemlock Park. When they got there they found a car in flames. Now get this, the car was registered to an Airman First Class Eric Chow."

"All right—connect the two for me." Bogner was yawning, still trying to sort through the haze and put the pieces together.

"I know this all sounds really bizarre, Tobias. But as it turns out, this guy Chow was stationed at Homestead Air Force Base and was assigned TDY to the Air Transport Command Support Detachment at Miami International. According to the duty roster, he was on duty tonight and he was assigned to assist in the loading of the E-4 that blew up over Cape Sable."

Bogner threw his feet over the edge of the bed and stood up. As usual, he was wearing boxer shorts. Boxer shorts were what he slept in for two reasons: He liked them and he knew Joy didn't— Joy preferred that he wear nothing.

"Where are you going?" she asked.

"Kitchen," he muttered.

"Kitchen? Why?"

"I'm awake, dammit. If I'm awake, I need coffee." Bogner shuffled down the hall toward the kitchen, switched on the coffeepot, leaned over, and stared out the window over the sink. "Know what I just figured out?" Joy shook her head.

"At three o'clock in the morning there isn't a hell of a lot happening—in here or out there."

Joy's face turned pouty. "What the hell did you expect, Tobias? Was I supposed to forget everything that happened out there tonight, come home, jump in the sack, and start playing tangle-toes? For God's sake, Tobias, that was a damn major disaster down there."

Bogner stared at her for several moments before he burst out laughing. "I guess we're not exactly getting this so-called reconciliation of ours off to a good start, are we?"

Joy started to say she was sorry, but he put a finger against her lips to silence her.

"So you think something sinister happened with Swelling's plane tonight," Bogner said a few minutes later, pouring each of them a cup of coffee. "Sounds like you've been hanging around Clancy Packer too much. That's the way he thinks. Clancy's the type who'll find something clandestine in a nursery rhyme."

Joy took a sip of coffee. "Think about it, Tobias. Last week it was the Secretary of the Air Force. Tonight it was the Undersecretary of State. And don't forget Bob Worling," she reminded him. "When I talked to him two months ago, he didn't actually say what his job was, but I got the feeling it had something to do with the current regime in Beijing."

"You're serious. You actually think that young airman that was killed down at Hemlock Park tonight might have had something to do with the explosion aboard Swelling's plane?"

Joy ran her finger around the rim of her cup and nodded. "It's too damn much of a coincidence, Tobias. The young man's name is on the duty roster. He's known to be assigned to the detachment working the military VIP lounge in the very building where Swelling and his entourage boarded their plane—and an hour or so later, the kid's car blows up just like Swelling's plane. In my book that's not a coincidence—that's a lead."

"Okay, so where do you go with your theory?"

"When we get up in the morning, I call the network. If they want me, I go in and I'll do some digging. If there's something there, I'll find it."

"And we reschedule our . . ."

Joy laughed. "As far as I'm concerned we're not delaying or postponing anything. It's just you and me until at least eight o'clock tomorrow morning. A lot can happen in five hours."

She took Bogner's hand and led him back down the hall toward the bedroom. In the background they could hear the phone ringing. "That has to be for you," Bogner said. "You're here, Packer is probably asleep, and—"

"Phone?" Joy asked. "What phone? I don't hear a phone. Do you?"

Bogner shook his head.

Time 0613LT:

Lattimere Spitz enjoyed the high-visibility role he played in the Colchin Administration. A lean, often gangly-looking man, he had a large nose, intense brown-black eyes, wide mouth, and very little hair. Long considered to be one of Colchin's two top aides, he was known as "the mouth" of the Colchin Administration, while his counterpart, Chet Hurley, a former philosophy professor at Harvard, was known as the "the mind."

Despite their obvious differences, the men had

two things in common: They were both fiercely loyal to David Colchin, and they were both Texans.

Now, sitting at the breakfast table in his Falls Church bi-level condominium, Spitz was keeping one eye on CNN for further news on the Cape Sable crash and scanning *The Post* with the other. His wife, Frances, in the process of pouring him a glass of grapefruit juice, had twice stopped to watch the search scenes from Cape Sable.

"Are they certain Bill Swelling was on board that flight?"

Spitz, already preoccupied with what he knew was destined to be a hectic day, only half heard the question, and he nodded without looking up from his paper.

"And what about Virginia?" Frances Spitz wondered. "Suppose she's all right? Suppose the kids are with her?"

Spitz shook his head as he stood up. He hadn't known Bill Swelling all that well; not half as well as he knew Jim Dunning. There was the dinner party at the Halls' the previous spring; Swelling was there. Swelling talked a lot; bragged actually. Spitz didn't like that. Dunning, on the other hand, was his kind of people. Lattimere Spitz and Jim Dunning both played in the "over forty" basketball league at the Falls Church Athletic Club. Spitz considered him a friend.

"I'll see what I can find out about services," Spitz said, folding his paper. Frances Spitz was used to it; she knew her husband was already absorbed in his schedule for the day and that he would probably forget to find out. Back in his routine, he kissed her on the cheek and started for the door.

The street was still dark when Lattimere Spitz stepped out of the condo complex. There was a thin sliver of red-yellow to the east, but overhead the sky was overcast and the wind was raw. There was a spit of rain, and the limo driver was waiting, door open, collar up, hat pulled down to shield him from the weather.

"Good morning, Mr. Spitz," the man said, closing the door behind him. Spitz waited until he saw the driver walk around behind the car, slip in behind the wheel, and turn the key in the ignition before he opened his paper.

That was when the car exploded.

He felt the car rock, saw the windows disintegrate and a maelstrom of purple-blue flame envelop the car's interior. He felt shards of glass rip through the smoke and gouge holes in his face, hands, and chest. In a world of instantaneous heat, acrid, choking smoke, and total chaos, Lattimere Spitz felt himself lifted up, then just as quickly pinned back by the force of the blast. The upholstery burst into flame, and he tried to claw his way up and out of the inferno. His clothing was on fire; his hands were already seared, and in a matter of seconds they had become ineffectual clumps hammering and flailing at the scorched world that surrounded him.

Finally, there was the smoke—and Lattimere Spitz, blinded and choking, lunged forward. The doors had been blown off by the blast, and he somehow managed to pitch his body out into the street. He felt the hard, uneven surface of the asphalt gouging out chunks of skin as he rolled over against the curbing.

From that point on, everything was instinctive. He was somehow able to shut out the crescendo of frantic voices, screams, and the swelling chorus of chaotic sounds. Still conscious, he could feel the stinging but welcome sensation of the cold rain poking needles into his cooked flesh. Then, in what to Spitz seemed like an eternity later, he spiraled into the terrifying world between light and darkness. Momentarily trapped, he heard the awful, and frantic, and pleading screams of his wife.

Then he heard nothing.

Chapter Two

Time 0817LT:

Bogner was still in that hazy twilight zone between sleep and reality when he heard Joy come back into the bedroom. His eyes were still closed, but he felt Joy sit down on the edge of the bed and he could smell the coffee.

When he opened his eyes, Joy was smiling. "Just like old times, huh?"

"Better," Bogner acknowledged. "Back in Pensacola, we couldn't lay around like this. I'll take the new over the old anytime."

Joy shook her head. "That's easy. We didn't have a dime to our name. Remember what they were paying you in those days? It's a good thing I was around. Ensigns in flight school had to live on love."

Bogner sat up, took a sip of coffee, and grunted. "We called it abject poverty—remember?"

"We couldn't even afford this," she reminded him, handing him the paper. "For your information, the Cape Sable crash is all over the front page. And I almost hate to tell you this, but your answering machine is lit up like a pinball machine."

"Did you check the messages?"

Joy held up her hand. "Whoa—not me. There may be something on there I don't want to hear. Who knows what kind of messages one of our town's most eligible bachelors gets. That's not the sort of thing the lady who has just spent the night with you wants to know."

Bogner frowned. "Like I keep telling you, three people know Reese's number: Reese, Clancy, and you. Reese is somewhere in the Orient, you, my dear, are here, and that leaves Clancy—and Clancy is under the impression you and I left for three fun-filled and erotic days in Jamaica. He wouldn't dare call."

"Wanna bet?"

Bogner got out of bed, stretched, pulled on a robe, and walked down the hall to the kitchen. The first two messages were for Reese, and Bogner jotted down the names: Barbara and Tammy. The third was from Packer. *"T.C., if you're there, call me. I'm at the office."*

When he turned around, Joy was leaning against the door frame, sipping her coffee. To his surprise, she was still smiling. "Hey, you knew it was going to happen," she said. "I'm just glad they got to you before NBS got to me—that way you're the culprit."

Bogner picked up the phone and punched out Packer's number at the Internal Security Agency. Packer picked up the phone on the second ring. "Yeah," he grumbled. He sounded out of sorts and harried; harried usually didn't come until later in the morning.

Toby Bogner lowered his voice. "You have reached the number of Toby Bogner. Captain Bogner is in Jamaica, remember?"

Packer barged ahead. "Have you got your damn television on?"

"They don't have television in Jamaica where I—" Bogner began, but Packer cut him off.

"Car bomb. Two hours ago a bomb went off in Lattimere Spitz's limo. It killed the driver, but Spitz is still alive—barely. They took him to a hospital in Falls Church."

Bogner was stunned. He sagged back against the breakfast bar and closed his eyes. The words came hard. "Will—will he make it?"

"Too early to tell. He's in surgery right now. Chet Hurley's called twice. The President is en route from San Antonio; he was down on his ranch for the weekend. We're calling in all our markers. Dunning's flight might have been an accident, but we're certain now it was a bomb on Swelling's flight out of Miami last night. Couple that with the Worling shooting last night and what happened to Spitz this morning—and we've got ourselves one helluva problem."

Bogner clamped his hand over the mouthpiece

and looked at Joy. "Someone set off a car bomb in Lattimere Spitz's limo this morning. Pack says he's in pretty bad shape. He's in surgery right now."

Time 0842LT:

Chen Po Lee watched the Toyota work its way up the rutted path from the access road to the abandoned marina. The storm had passed, the clouds had dissipated, and for the first time in days he could feel the warmth of the early morning sun.

The car came to a stop, and Liu Shao stepped out. Liu's driver was the same woman who had picked Chen up the night before. Even before Liu trudged his way up the hill to the Quonset hut, the woman had turned around and headed back toward the road.

Chen stopped his countryman before he entered the building. "You were successful?"

Liu nodded. "Like clockwork."

"You have the documents?"

Liu nodded again, holding up his briefcase.

"Tonu Hon will be pleased."

Inside, the two men waited for the man who had engineered the terrorist attacks. When Tonu Hon entered the cluttered room that had once served as the marina office, he acknowledged Liu's presence with a nod and a rare smile. "I trust your journey was pleasant as well as successful, my young comrade."

Liu nodded, sat down at the table, cleared away a stack of newspapers, opened his briefcase, and handed the nine-page document to his elder. Tonu Hon rapidly read through the report—he read English quite well—and intensified his smile. "It is as we suspected," he announced.

"I do not see what this accomplishes," Chen muttered. "Surely the Americans have many copies of these documents."

"Quite so," Tonu Hon agreed, "but now we know what they know. It is said that it is most advantageous to be familiar with the song the lark will sing. Such knowledge permits us to enjoy the lark's song even more."

Liu Shao leaned forward with his arms on the table. He knew Tonu Hon expected a full report. "The report indicates the American Naval Intelligence offices were warned two months ago of the possibility of an increase in terrorist activities."

"And the source of this warning?" Tonu Hon pressed.

Liu Shao shrugged. "One must assume the Americans have as many friends in Beijing as we have friends in America. The report you are holding was prepared by a man named Robert Worling. I am told by Mademoiselle Merceau that there was a lengthy meeting held only yesterday. It lasted much longer than anticipated; Worling was scheduled to be a speaker at a formal function of some kind last night. When the meeting concluded, instead of driving to his appointment, Worling drove to his home in Alexandria."

"And you?" Tonu Hon pressed.

"I followed him. When he pulled into his garage,

I noticed that the house was dark. The rest was easy."

Tonu Hon leaned back in his chair and read the report a second time. Now he knew how far Worling's investigation had progressed. There was no indication the Americans knew anything about the 5A staging area in the offshore islands north of Nueva Gerona in the area known as the De Pinos Aquiero. And even if there had been, Mao Quan's arrangements with the Cubans guaranteed secrecy by virtue of the around-the-clock patrols by the Cuban gunboats. All in all, the report pleased him.

"We must do everything within our power to insure that Colonel Mao Quan's objectives are met," Tonu Hon said. "Until the Fifth Academy assumes leadership in our country, it best serves our purpose if Premier Qian's regime in Beijing and the Colchin Administration continue to regard each other with an air of suspicion." Tonu Hon continued to smile. "And In the last few days we have given our American friends more than sufficient reason to regard our current leaders in Beijing with mistrust."

Time 1017LT:

Bogner found himself sitting across the conference table from the familiar core of the ISA Washington Bureau staff of Clancy Packer and his top strategist, Robert Miller. They had been joined by Peter Langley of Naval Intelligence's counterinsurgency squad. The three of them had been waiting for both Bogner and Millie Ploughman, Packer's assistant. The latter had temporarily left the conference room to field a call from Chet Hurley.

When Ploughman returned, she took a seat next to Bogner. "Surprised to see you, T. C.," she said. "According to my notes you're suppose to be in Jamaica."

Bogner looked out the window at the gray day and rain. "Don't rub it in," he grumbled.

Langley laughed and slid a stack of papers across the table in Bogner's direction. "Duty calls, T. C., Robert and Clancy have already had a chance to look at this, but it won't do any harm for all five of us to go through the highlights a second time. What you have in front of you is a copy of Bob Worling's report based on a tip we received from one of our operatives in Beijing two months ago."

Packer leaned forward. "A week ago when Dunning's flight went down off the coast of California, we pretty much assumed it was one of those misfortunes that could befall any one of us. We still don't know what happened. The FAA is on it, but since we still haven't been able to recover the flight recorder, we're still pretty much in the dark as to what happened."

Miller cleared his throat. "What Pack is saying is, for the moment, we can't say for certain that the Dunning crash has anything to do with what's happened in the last twenty-four hours."

"No, but we are starting to look at it in a slightly different light," Langley admitted. "Since shortly before midnight last night when Secretary Swell-

ing's plane went down, we've had two other incidents that give a helluva lot of credence to the
report from our operative in Beijing.

First, of course, is the shooting of Bob Worling,
who was working on this advance report of terrorist
activity, and this morning, the car bomb that nearly
killed Lattimere Spitz."

"How is Spitz?" Bogner asked.

"I just called the hospital," Millie said. "He's out
of surgery and in the IC unit. The hospital spokesman described his condition as critical."

"Which brings us around to Worling's report,"
Packer said. "Peter here spent most of the day yesterday with Worling going over the contents of that
report, so I'll let Peter take over."

Peter Langley, like Bogner, was a former Navy
pilot. He had moved into the Investigations section
of Naval Intelligence after he nosed his F-4 Phan-
tom into a Vietnam rice paddy and broke his back.
He was *too Navy* to turn down the assignment in
NI, and three years later Bogner had worked with
him in what was now known at the infamous Je-
hovah Hole incident that led to the assassination of
then-Russian President Zhelannov.

In addition to being a graduate of the Naval Academy, Langley's Washington status was enhanced by
virtue of the fact that he was the son of Massachusetts Senator Loren Langley, an acknowledged Capital heavyweight.

Bogner so respected him that he had tried to lure
Langley to the ISA—but the brass at NI knew they
had something special in Langley, and no less than

the Secretary of the Navy had thrown up the road-block that squelched the transfer.

"Okay," Langley began. "Obviously Bob's report isn't complete—but he has made considerable headway. Bob had been told, through channels, that we could expect an acceleration in terrorist activity from Mao Quan's dissident Red Army wing in Hainan. According to Bob's information, Colonel Mao was sending his number-one nightmare, a fellow Party hardliner by the name of Tonu Hon, to America to step up 5A terrorist activity. The FBI and the CIA were alerted the minute we got the report. Fortunately, we had a pretty good dossier on Tonu, and we took measures to be reasonably certain he didn't get into this country by slipping through the back door. But as you well know, that doesn't mean he didn't work his way in through some other hole in the fence."

Langley paused just long enough to pass out photographs. "This is our boy, Tonu, in a 1994 photograph with Deng Xiaoping. The second shows him some months later as part of a disarmament conference with President Jhiang Zhemin in Manila. Both photographs identify Tonu, but you'll notice that he looks decidedly different in each picture."

"Stands to reason," Bogner muttered. "And I'll bet now he looks a lot different than he does in either one of those pictures; that's the way Mao Quan's mind works. He's bound to figure we've got files on the bastard."

"Obviously, if we don't know what he looks like, there's a damn good chance he'll either slip through without being detected, or already has," Langley added.

"I assume there's more," Miller said.

Langley frowned. "There's more. Even before I heard about Spitz this morning, I drove out to Worling's place in Alexandria. As luck would have it, Bob and I had parked next to each other in the parking lot yesterday and we walked to our cars together after the meeting. I know for a fact that Bob was carrying a copy of the report with him. It was in his briefcase. He indicated there were a couple of things he wanted to clean up in the report before he turned it over to Jaffe this morning.

"When I got to Worling's place, the police forensics team was there. I told one of the officers who I was, showed him my credentials, and asked him if he could check something for me. I wanted to know if Bob's briefcase was still in the car. When they told me it was, I knew the shooting wasn't just a run-of-the-mill robbery gone bad. Why? Because he always carried his passport and an international letter of credit in his briefcase. Even a third-rate petty thief would have recognized the market value of those and taken them. Then I asked them to check and see if Bob's report was still in the briefcase. It wasn't. Any doubt I may have been harboring up to that point about whether or not his shooting had something to do with the investigation was gone."

Packer looked around the table. "All right, it's theory time. What do you think, T. C.?"

"It's pretty clear to me they wanted to know how

much we knew," Bogner said, "and they were more than willing to kill Worling to find out."

Packer lit his pipe. "Assuming you're correct, T. C., that only raises more questions; like how did they know Worling was involved in the investigation?"

"Maybe they didn't," Millie offered. "Maybe he was on the original hit list."

Miller shook his head. "I don't think so. Worling wasn't a prominent name in Washington—he pretty much moved in the shadows. If Tonu is behind this, he seems to be focusing on high-profile movers and shakers."

Packer put down his pipe. "Someone had to tip them off."

"Obviously, but who?" Miller said.

"So where do we go from here?" Langley pressed.

Packer leaned back in his chair and looked at the ceiling. "We start by learning everything we can from the Alexandria homicide people. Bogner can check that out. Then we talk to anyone and everyone that might know something about the limo that picked Spitz up this morning. Between Millie, Miller, and me, we can make some phone calls and find out what the people at the VIP lounge at MIA can tell us about Dunning's flight last night."

Miller looked at Bogner. "Toby, less than an hour ago I got a call from . . ."

Bogner grinned. "You got a call from Joy, right?"

Packer and Miller nodded.

"And she told you about a report that came over the AP wire last night. A car exploded on a stretch of deserted beach near Hemlock Park, Florida. Apparently the car was bearing license plates showing it belonged to some airman who was assigned TDY to the Air Transport Command Support Detachment at Miami International."

Packer was grinning. "She said she thought you were asleep when she told you about it."

"I made a mental note to check it out," Bogner admitted. "But it may be nothing more than a coincidence."

Packer pulled his papers together and looked around the table. "Coincidence or not, we better check it out. Let's get on it. Robert, pull in any of the field personnel you need. Peter says we can expect the full cooperation of NI, and Oscar Jaffe says he'll keep us apprised of anything his people come up with over at the CIA. In the meantime, say a prayer for Spitz; I'm afraid our old friend is going to need all the help he can get."

Time 1430LT:

At age seventy-five, the infrequent trips between south Florida and De Pinos Aquiero were difficult for Tonu Hon. To avoid detection by the American Coast Guard, Mao had arranged with Cabandra Marti, the one-time architect of Cuba's counterintelligence efforts, to use a little known partially completed Russian submarine base in De Pinos Aquiero. While American spy satellites had uncovered the construction of a Russian submarine base near Cienfuegos in 1970, it had failed to discover a smaller-scale support facility in the archipelagoes south of Peninsula de Zapata.

Now, despite the fact that the Russians had long since abandoned the project and the facilities had fallen into a state of disrepair, Tonu Hon had his base of operations. Cuban gunboats insured security, Cuban air-space was seldom violated except to the north, and the American military base at Guantanamo was at the far end of the island.

The facility included a short airstrip that accommodated an early-seventies Lockheed S-3 Viking purchased from a Chilean arms dealer and an arsenal of weapons obtained through Pentagon surplus sales by a Korean salvage dealer willing to do business with Mao Quan. While the oversized concrete repair berths for the Russian subs had never been completed, the network of underground bunkers, storage bins, and personnel accommodations were all in place. It had taken a handful of Cabandra Marti's *grufo obreros* less than three months to outfit the tiny base for Tonu Hon's purposes.

Now, after the trip from Florida, Tonu Hon gathered with his three lieutenants—Quin Lo Wan, Chen Po Lee, and Liu Shao in a small bunker set aside for their planning sessions.

Quin Lo Wan and Chen Po Lee's roles in Tonu Hon's master plan was simple. With rare exceptions, they were the ones who implemented the plan. Liu Shao, the man who had killed Worling and obtained the copy of the report, had a quite different role. Like Chen, he was an accomplished helicopter pilot. Unlike Chen, he was American-born, of Chinese descent, had graduated form UCLA with a degree in political science, and had served in the American State Department as a courier-interpreter before being recruited by Mao Quan. Perhaps the most important entry on Liu Shao's resume was that he was fluent in English and knew his way around better than his counterparts.

Liu Shao's real expertise, however, was his ability to make arrangements and contacts without the assistance of Jacqueline Merceau. He could obtain documents, make airline reservations, move money, and operate freely in the arena Tonu Hon had designated as the target.

The copy of Worling's report was again on the table in front of Tonu. "The Americans have been diligent in some areas and remiss in others," the old man began. "They have been alerted to Colonel Mao's intention to step up our activities in their country, but nowhere in this report do I see evidence of knowledge about our intended targets. They do not even mention the crash that took the life of Air Force Secretary Dunning."

"Nothing I have read would indicate they are even suspicious," Liu Shao confirmed. "They talk of being stymied until they find the black box."

"The unfortunate incident with the CIA agent Worling will heighten their awareness, I am afraid," Quin said.

"It was necessary to obtain a copy of the report," Liu Shao snapped.

Tonu Hon held up his hand. "Their awareness in

no way enables them to deter us. Nothing in the report would indicate they have organized their thinking. They do not know where to look for us. They do not know our targets. From what I read in this report, they appear to be quite inept in matters of this nature."

"The incident earlier today," Chen said, "how was it accomplished?"

Liu Shao's expression did not change. Still, he was more talkative than usual. "While our fathers embrace tradition, we embrace technology. Only yesterday, I was able to determine which of the limousines was scheduled to pick up the President's aide and the time the task was normally accomplished. The timer was a simple device designed to accomplish a simple task. When it detonated, I was already en route here."

"You have both done well," Tonu Hon said.

"Then we are to proceed?" Quin asked.

"There is no adversary quite so vulnerable as one who is off balance," Tonu said with a smile. "Most assuredly, we continue." He looked at Liu Shao. "The name of Richard Crane, long considered a proponent of closer ties with our decadent leaders in Beijing, is next. Mademoiselle Merceau assures me his demise will give Colonel Mao a great deal of personal pleasure."

"And the one called Langley?" Liu Shao probed. "I can begin to make arrangements?"

"According to the plan," Tonu Hon replied. "According to the plan."

Time 1630LT:

Gleason's Grill, three blocks from RFK Memorial Stadium, was one of Clancy Packer's favorite watering holes. Whether the Redskins were winning or losing, Clancy made it a point to always include Pokey Gleason's place in his weekly itinerary. In the off-season, Gleason's regular clientele, all Redskins faithful, met to evaluate trades, discuss players, and excoriate the Skins' front office. There wasn't a newspaperman in town who dared repeat anything he had observed or overheard at Gleason's. Pokey and his friends saw to that. At Pokey Gleason's Grill it was understood that everything was off-the-record—even the prices on drinks. Pokey had two prices, one for his regulars, and another for drop-ins.

At four-thirty in the afternoon, any day but a game day, it was common to see two, three, sometimes four people cloistered in one of Gleason's darkened booths engaged in discussions that affected commerce, legislation, and sometimes even the course of world events.

So when Joseph Albert "Rooster" Ricozy lowered his 280-pound frame into one of Gleason's booths, it was because someone had sent for him. Ricozy was an ex-Dallas Cowboy who had been traded to the Redskins in the twilight of his career, and had capitalized on it by establishing himself as a reliable conduit of information in and out of the Washington establishment. It was rumored that Ricozy had CIA connections, Mafia connections, even foreign government connections; but Clancy Packer was one of the few who knew the truth.

"So how's Sara?" Ricozy grunted, getting himself situated in a booth more suited to people half his size.

"As pretty as ever," Packer assured him.

"Same for T. C. and Miller?"

"Both fat and sassy."

"Tell 'em Rooster sends regards."

"I'll do it."

At that point it was obvious Ricozy had depleted his arsenal of social repartee and was waiting for Packer to get on with why he had called him.

"Something happened this morning," Packer began.

"You're talking about Lattimere Spitz?"

Packer nodded. "It comes on the heels of a nasty shooting last night."

"Worling?"

"Uh-huh."

"And you think what?"

"We have reason to believe those incidents are tied to what is being called an explosion aboard the plane carrying Undersecretary of State Swelling down in Florida last night."

Ricozy grunted and signaled for the waitress. A trim blonde wearing a Redskin jersey ambled over to the table and took their order. The Rooster ordered three Buds, two for him and one for Clancy. "So?" He was waiting for Packer to continue.

"Sometime ago we began hearing talk about a possible escalation in terrorist activities."

"By who?"

"Ever hear of a group called the Fifth Academy?"

Ricozy shook his head. He had heard—but he wanted Packer's version.

"It's a splinter faction of the Red Army headed up by a longtime Party dissident in Hainan by the name of Mao Quan. Mao Quan has a hard-on for the current government in Beijing because he believes the Party leaders have gone soft and are getting a little too cozy with the current U.S. Administration and the way Colchin's people think."

The waitress returned, and the Rooster managed to polish off one of the beers even before Clancy instructed the woman to run a tab.

"Keep going," Ricozy urged.

"Little known fact: Bob Worling had been assigned to look into all of this. He was scheduled to submit his preliminary report this morning. When he was killed last night, he was carrying a copy of that report."

"Let me guess. Now that report's missing."

"Exactly. And the conventional thinking is they hit him because they wanted to know how much we knew."

Ricozy grunted and reached into his pocket. Among his indulgences were large, dark, handmade Cuban cigars that would have looked obscene in the hands of a lesser man. He lit one and exhaled a massive cloud of pungent slate-gray smoke over the booth. "I hope we were smart enough to keep a couple of copies."

Packer nodded.

"So where do I come in?"

"The police are looking for the triggerman. I'm looking for a loose thread that might lead us to whatever."

Ricozy finished his second beer and shifted his weight, trying to get comfortable. "What does a *thread* look like? Act like? More important, what do they think like?"

"Can't help you. But I can guarantee you, somewhere, somehow, someone involved in Mao's scheme has made a mistake, dropped the ball, said something, forgotten to tie up a loose end—and when we discover what that is, we can throw a monkey wrench into their plan."

Rooster Ricozy looked at his watch, reached across the table, swallowed Clancy Packer's hand in a handshake, and stood up. Packer was convinced he heard the seat groan. "Got a couple of things to tend to, Pack—but I'll be in touch, okay? You know the question I gotta ask: Does the big man know we're having this little chat?"

"Jaffe knows."

The former Redskin tackle had taken less than two steps away from the booth when he turned back to face Packer again. "Any truth to the rumor that Spitz may not make it?"

Packer nodded. "It's touch and go."

Time 1711LT:

Bogner watched the attendant slide the oversized stainless-steel tray back into the bank of vaults and close the door. The entire room smelled antiseptic.

"Somehow you never picture yourself—I mean what's left of you when you die—stuffed into a four-ply plastic bag no bigger than a damn loaf of bread," Sheriff Bell said, opening the door and leading Bogner into the corridor.

Bogner shook his head. His stomach was still doing a slow waltz on him.

Bell led them into a tiny office, cleared away some papers on a cluttered desk, and offered Bogner a seat.

"Who found him?"

"One of my deputies. We got a report from one of the retirement homes on Sanderson Point. They said they heard an explosion and that there was a fire down by the old bathhouse on the beach. When he checked it out, he found Chow's car—burnt to a crisp."

Bogner looked at a handful of what he assumed were Chow's personal effects spread out on the table in front of him. "Have you got a positive ID on the victim?"

Bell opened a file folder and began to read:

Eric Chow, A/1C, USAF 18328849. Earl Park, Ohio. Born 4/6/74: Chinese American. Single.
Duty station: Homestead AFB, Homestead, Florida.
TDY: Miami International.

"Enough?"

Bogner nodded. "You said your deputy called you in. When you got there, what did you find?"

"Well, when I got there, the damn place was overrun with people. The local fire department had already dumped water on Chow's car and foamed it. We didn't know what caused the initial explosion and we damn sure weren't gonna stand there waiting to see if there was going to be another one. Half of the old farts in the community were there gawking. That's the most excitement most of 'em have had in years."

"I repeat, have you got a positive ID?"

Bell, as round as he was tall, started to laugh. "Hell, no. What you saw in that damn plastic bag in there is what I dug out of the wreckage with a damn kitchen spatula. The coroner told me what I salvaged was half-melted plastic, a couple of pieces of bone, and a handful of teeth. I called the air base and asked them to send over his dental records. They're bringing them over in the morning. Guess they wanta see what's left of the body. What's left of the car is out back. It had Ohio plates. From that we've been able to determine that the car was registered to one Eric Chow."

Bogner stood up, walked to the window, and looked out at the clouds gathering to the west. "Looks like you've got more rain moving in."

Bell grunted. "It's that time of year—happens damn near every afternoon."

"How far are we from Sable Point where that plane went down last night?"

"Ninety minutes, unless it's storming like it was last night—a real snake strangler. If you ask me it was lightning that knocked that damn plane out of the air."

Bogner looked around the room, finally turning to look at the sheriff. "Anything else I need to know?" he asked.

Bell shook his head. "Not unless you consider this important. It's a checkbook. We found it lying on the ground about three hundred feet from the car last night. I took it home and put it in my wife's clothes dryer to dry it out. Turns out that it belongs to Chow. Guess how much money he has in that damn checking account. Hell, he's got five thousand dollars just layin' around. Someone makin' the kind of money he was makin' in the Air Force has to live pretty damn close to the vest to save up five thousand dollars."

Bogner picked up Chow's checkbook and leafed through it. "Especially when it appears that he came up with all of it in one day."

Time 1837LT:

Early on, Robert Miller had learned the futility of fighting Washington's afternoon rush-hour traffic. At first, hanging around the office for an extra hour had been nothing more than a way to avoid traffic jams. Then it became a way to clean up a few extra reports. Eighteen years later, the Georgetown graduate and confirmed bachelor admitted traffic was no longer his concern; the ISA offices had unwittingly become both his bride and master. Now, seventy hours a week was the rule rather than the exception, and Miller saw no reason to do anything about it. Bogner had kept all of this in mind when Miller picked up the phone on the third ring.

"Where are you?" Miller demanded. "Clancy checked in less than thirty minutes ago. He wanted to know if I'd heard from you."

"I'm at the airport. My flight leaves in less than ten minutes."

"Was it worth it?"

"We hit the jackpot. The late Eric Chow deposited five thousand dollars in his checking account two days before he died. In addition, the duty roster shows he reported for his shift and assisted in the loading of Swelling's plane last night. At last count I've talked to seven different people who claim they knew Chow, but none of them actually recall talking to him last night. Six of the seven, however, recall seeing a Chinese airman wearing a fatigue uniform assist in the loading of that E-4. My guess is they just assumed it was Chow—no one paid any attention."

Miller let out a whistle. "Anything I can do on this end?"

"Call in one of your markers. Get someone over at the Department of the Air Force to crank up some of those state-of-the-art computers of theirs and run a background check on every Chinese-American enlisted man and officer stationed at any of their bases south of Interstate 75, Naples to Fort Lauderdale. Lets find out if that so-called airman was legitimate or someone that bought Chow's place on the flight line so he could plant a bomb."

"Will do, but where can I get in touch with you?" It was typical Miller; he wanted to know where his resources were at all times.

"I'll call you. Remember, I'm supposed to be on my second honeymoon."

Miller heard the telephone click, and he nestled the receiver back in the cradle. He was smiling. Bogner had no way of knowing, of course, but Packer had already given him the number to Reese Smith's apartment. "Millie," he shouted, "who do we know over at AIRCOM that owes us a favor?"

"I was listening in on your call," Ploughman admitted. "I'm already dialing."

Time 2112LT:

Liu Shao had rented a small, unpretentious, sparsely furnished bungalow on High Street as his base of operations. As far as his neighbors were concerned, he was employed in some capacity at the nearby Opa-Locka Airport. Other than that, they knew very little about the man. One neighbor had observed that he drove a Ford Probe with Mississippi license plates, and was seldom at home. Another had once commented to her hairdresser that he was "quite tall for a Chinese," and then voiced her opinion that he "seemed like a nice man."

The location and a cadre of non-interfering neighbors were exactly what Liu Shao wanted; anonymity in his line of work was a definite asset.

Now, less than an hour after making the journey to Florida from De Pinos Aquiero by way of a small airport south of Miami near Barnes Sound, he was making arrangements with his contacts in Washington.

While Liu Shao busied himself on the telephone, the young woman he had hired to serve as his housekeeper and driver occupied herself in the kitchen. Her name was Tian. She was a Chinese-American student at a local college. As far as Liu Shao was concerned, the arrangement with the young woman was working well. In exchange for her room and board, she gave him a dimension of convenience; she took and relayed the frequent fax messages from Mademoiselle Merceau, as well as taking care of both routine and non-routine chores—non-routine like seeing that Quin Lo Wan was picked up at Hemlock Park, site of the car bombing the previous evening, and driving him to the abandoned marina at Toll Reef.

Liu Shao had given her the job with only two stipulations. She was not to discuss what went on in the house at 112 High Street, nor was she to engage in conversation with any of his associates. Now, two weeks later, Liu Shao was satisfied that the young woman was following instructions. He had heard Quin complain earlier in the day that the woman had driven him all the way to Toll Reef without saying a word.

As the young woman spread her textbooks out on the kitchen table, Liu Shao dialed the second of the three numbers. The voice on the other end of the line was flat and void of emotion.

"It's Liu," he said in reply.

When Liu heard the phone being jostled on the other end of the line, he began immediately. He had no reason to suspect that his call was being traced, but he knew that the less time he was on the line, the less chance it would be. "We are ready to proceed," he said.

"When?" Mademoiselle Marceau asked.

"I will arrive in Washington early tomorrow."

"We will proceed then?"

"Yes."

As Liu expected, there was no response. He hung up and walked out into the kitchen. The young woman looked up from her textbook and smiled. "You will need me more tonight?"

Liu shook his head. "I will not," he informed her. "But tomorrow is a different matter." The woman did not question, nor did she expect an explanation.

Moments later, in his room, Liu Shao undressed, showered, and got into bed. His thoughts turned to the next day. This one would be different, if for no other reason than he had met Richard Crane, the senator from Iowa. He knew what he looked like, what his family looked like—had even been a guest in his home—as an interpreter during a State Department trade mission. The others—Dunning, Swelling, Worling, and even the latest, Spitz—were nothing more than names on a list.

He turned out the lights, and it took him no time at all to settle into a deep, untroubled sleep.

While Liu slept, Tian studied, waiting for the fax transmission confirming the day's activities.

Time 2137LT:

Massachusetts Senator Loren Langley was an older, only slightly less vigorous image of his oldest son, Peter. As the longtime Chairman of the Senate Armed Services Committee, he was a Washington fixture on both the political and social scenes. It was likewise well known that David Colchin had asked him to be his running mate when the lanky Texan decided to run for a second term in the Oval Office. But Langley, fiercely proud of his independent status, had declined because he wanted to avoid being thrust into the partisan role that serving as Colchin's Vice President would have entailed.

It had become a once-a-week ritual since then, when their schedule permitted, for father and son to meet in the Rose Room Grill of the Grant for dinner. During those times, their conversations ran the gamut from family matters to politics, with only an occasional foray into the seamy underbellies of Washington and their jobs.

Now, as the sixty-five-year-old senator pushed away an empty dish that had once contained a slice of the Grill's famous cheese cake, he frowned. "So far we've talked about everything except what we both know is uppermost on our minds."

Peter Langley took a sip of his coffee and shook his head. "Off the record?"

The senator smiled, "Of course. Nothing more than privileged conversation, father and son."

"Sometime back we were advised we could expect some kind of escalation in terrorist activity."

"Palestinians?"

Peter shook his head again. "Does the name Mao Quan mean anything to you?"

"Hainan? Fifth Academy?"

"Exactly."

"Aren't we a little off the beaten path for him? His beef is with the Party leaders in Beijing."

Peter nodded. "Uh-huh. But it seems our friend Mao thinks the Qian regime is getting a little too friendly with us—and he wants to put something more than a few ideological wrinkles between us and Premier Qian."

"I don't follow his thinking."

"It's a power struggle. Our people tell us Qian could go in there and take Mao Quan out anytime he wants to. But Qian is savvy enough to realize Mao Quan has built up quite a following. Qian knows there are a lot of his own people who think he and the rest of the current Party bigwigs in Beijing are getting just a little too cozy with the Colchin Administration.

"Our thinking is Qian can't afford a civil war—and we also think it's entirely possible he may take an appeasement route and invite Mao Quan to Beijing. But he won't do it if Mao Quan doesn't apply the pressure and keep the heat on. Bottom line, Mao Quan's way of making this happen is to step up his terrorist activity—terrorist activity Qian doesn't want and can't handle when he's trying to build bridges to Washington."

The senator took out a cigar, unwrapped it, lit it, and blew out smoke. The older Langley and his son had an understanding. Peter didn't tell his mother that the senator was still smoking an occasional cigar, and the senator neglected to inform Peter's mother that her only son was involved in clandestine and risky assignments with NI. "So, what's your involvement in all of this?" the older man asked.

Peter Langley leaned forward. "Apparently Mao Quan has a mole somewhere in Washington. That CIA agent that was shot last night was carrying a briefing that would have given his agency people an update on what Worling had learned so far. We've since learned that the copy of that report was the only thing missing from his briefcase."

"Surely there was more than one copy."

"That's not the point. Now they know what we know and they can cover their tracks."

The senator leaned back in his chair. "And you think . . . ?"

"We have reason to believe that the two planes that went down carrying Dunning and Swelling are Mao's work. The same goes for what happened to Worling and Spitz."

"Then they're operating here in the States now. It's already started."

Peter Langley nodded. "We're certain of it. But Mao's game is different this time—and his targets are different. Instead of oil rigs and opera houses, Mao appears to be getting up close and personal. So far he's picked off the Secretary of the Air Force, the Undersecretary of State, and today they took a shot at Lattimere Spitz. As for Worling, we think he was just plain unlucky—he happened to have something they wanted—but the effect is the same."

The elder Langley frowned and looked around the room. "This mole then—it could be anyone, anywhere." Peter had seen the expression on his father's face before. It was an expression he wore when he was putting the pieces together.

"For the time being, it's in the hands of a small task force put together by Hurley—no one agency—until we can find out where the leak is coming from. If I was at liberty to tell you more, I would."

Senator Loren Langley signaled to the waiter for another cup of coffee. He was mulling the word "terrorist" over in his mind. It had an ugly sound.

Chapter Three

Time 2145LT

Kent Peters juggled two cups of coffee and two day-old, plastic-wrapped tuna salad sandwiches as he waited for the elevator door to open. Hatton would be disappointed; he was expecting a ham and cheese, but the vending machines in the ISA commissary had been picked clean, and at 9:45 in the evening, it was tuna fish or nothing.

When the elevator finally settled and the door opened, Peters made his way past a series of cubicles: a maze of impersonal, aquarium-like glass workstations leading to the ISA inner sanctum and finally to the ISA situation room—a montage of phone lines, electronic gear, computers, and monitors that kept the Internal Security Bureau plugged into the outside world.

"No ham and—" Peters began before he realized Hatton was on the telephone.

"Let me read back what I've got so far," Hatton was saying. "The driver's name was Hon Winn and he was Korean, not Chinese. And you say you've been able to trace him because of his student visa—from Chicago? Was he a student there?"

Peters reached across Hatton's desk and turned on the call recorder. Then he pressed the speaker button. Hatton's caller's voice could be heard across the room.

"Affirmative. As near as we can determine, he left Chicago last Sunday. We were able to get through to a couple of people who lived in the same boardinghouse. They claim he told them that his grades were bad and he was in trouble—that his parents would be disappointed. Then he told some of the other students at UC that he'd come into some money and showed them his new chauffeur's license. He told them a man he knew had obtained a job for him in Washington. . . ."

Hatton was still taking notes when the voice paused to answer another telephone. He was back moments later.

"We talked to the dispatcher that assigned him to pick up Spitz this morning. He said he had to use this

Korean kid, who was originally supposed to do nothing more than ride along with Spitz's regular chauffeur this morning in a day of familiarization."

"Based on what you're telling me, it doesn't sound to me like the kid knew the car was rigged," Hatton said.

"Who knows? The dispatcher did mention one thing that was curious; he said the kid was carrying his lunch. When the dispatcher told him that wasn't acceptable, the kid told him that he didn't have any money to buy his lunch."

"I though you just said he told his friends he came into some money," Hatton pressed.

"Apparently he told the dispatcher the reason he didn't have any money was because he sent it all home to his parents in Korea."

"What about the regular chauffeur?"

"Haven't been able to locate him yet. We'll stay on it, though, and as soon as we come up with something we'll let you know. Okay?"

Hatton muttered something that sounded vaguely like "Thank you" and hung up. "That was Farley over at the FBI," he said. "Did you pick up on most of that?"

Kent Peters settled into a chair across the desk

from his coworker. "Jesus, Gordo, it sounds like the damn kid committed suicide."

Hatton nodded. "Five will get you ten that lunch sack the kid was carrying was the bomb—and he knew it."

Peters let out a barely audible whistle. "Did they say anything about trying to locate the man that got the chauffeur's license for the kid?"

"He said they were looking, but another five spot says the chauffeur's license was counterfeit. They got about as much chance of finding that guy that set this up as they have finding a self-confessed whore at a syphilis convention."

Time 2213LT:

Sara Packer managed to pick up the phone on the second ring, but her husband was already awake. As usual, Clancy Packer had thrown the recliner back and spiraled into a deep sleep less than half-way though the movie.

"One moment," she said, and handed her husband the phone.

"Pack, it's Rooster," the voice said on the other end of the line.

"I didn't expect to hear from—"

"I learned a long time ago to get on these things while the trail is still throwing off a stink. So far it hasn't cost you anything—but I got a hunch it gets expensive from here on out. The first part was easy."

"Let's hear it."

"First of all, what the hell is going on with your boys in the Pentagon?" Rooster asked. "Those silly bastards put a fifty-million-dollar padlock on the front door and the back door is standing wide open. They're selling everything but the kitchen sink and they don't seem to care who they sell it to. If I wanted one, I could buy a goddamn fully flyable A-6 Intruder with no questions asked."

"What the hell are you talking about?" Packer was still trying to clear away the cobwebs when he heard Ricozy unfolding a piece of paper.

"Ever hear of something called the DRMO?"

Packer had to think for a minute. "The Defense Reutilization and Marketing Office?"

"You got it. The problem is the DRMO has a problem—a big problem. A friend of mine who shall remain nameless tells me he can get damn near anything he wants in the way of weaponry—all he has to do is know the inventory. He showed me ten working machine guns and an M-79 grenade launcher he had stashed away in his barn. Not only that, he handed me the signed-off papers which showed that they had been 'demilitarized' and rendered useless."

"Your friend is blowing smoke."

"Afraid not. I got news for you, old buddy. Those things looked like they had just come out of the packing crate—brand-new—not a scratch on them—and they work like a Swiss watch. It's obvious there was no effort made to torch them."

"So how does this tie into—?"

"The word on the street is that a high-profile

South Korean scrap dealer has been systematically grabbing off some of these goodies and stashing them in a warehouse right here in Washington—not to mention a couple of other places just outside the Beltway. The word also is that our South Korean friend is well connected and has a string of clients that would make the feds cringe. A Lithuanian arms dealer by the name of Klaipent left town with no less than seven maritime shipping containers full—one contained the damn components of a Tomahawk missile—including the computer memory unit. My source tells me it's in the hands of the Chinese by now."

"I still don't see—we're talking terrorist activities. It doesn't take an arms dealer to supply explosives—any half-ass chemist can whip those up in his garage."

Rooster laughed. "Rhetorical question, Pack. What if the explosives weren't aboard those two aircraft when they took off? What if those planes were knocked down with a so-called sixteen-cents-a-pound-scrap-price handheld surface-to-air ANG-M4?"

Packer knew the ex-Redskin could be right. At this point, no one could afford to overlook any possibility—no matter how remote it seemed. "So, what are you suggesting?"

"At this point I'm not certain. Ever hear of a place called De Pinos Aquiero?" Packer shook his head even though he knew Ricozy couldn't see him. "Doesn't ring any bells," he admitted.

"Me neither, but it means something—it's

popped up twice today. We need to check it out. The question is, how much is the brass at ISA willing to invest to find out?"

Packer had anticipated the former Redskin's question. As Ricozy had said, information had a price tag. "What am I buying?"

"Walking money. I get my man, Shank. I give him the go-ahead and he starts asking questions. The man knows the market, he pays for what he gets. You evaluate what he comes up with and we respond accordingly. Deal?"

"Deal," Packer said. "Tell your man that the sooner we know something, the better."

"So where do I get in touch with you around noon tomorrow?" Rooster asked.

"Come to my office."

Ricozy hesitated. "Gleason's Grill is one thing, Pack. Strolling into your office, man, in broad daylight is something altogether different. Not good for my image. My contacts and the people I rely on might figure I'm getting a little too tight with the wrong people. Know what I mean?"

"There's a small bar on Ford at 27th. I'll be there at eleven-thirty. Be on the curb—I'll pick you up—and bring your man, Shank."

"I'll be there," Ricozy said. "Shank won't. He can't afford to be seen with someone like you."

Packer laughed—but he knew Ricozy meant what he said.

Time 2245LT:

Now Senator Richard Bellmont Crane was convinced his wife knew. He had answered the phone on an impulse because Julie had received three calls in the past week—crank calls. The first had come from a car phone. There were intermittent voids and periods of static, but she had distinctly heard a whispering voice use Crane's name. The latter two calls had come to the apartment late in the evening—"about now," Julie had indicated when he picked up the phone.

Still, the silence hadn't been what he'd expected. He interpreted the call as something more than it was, a silence full of discovery—the kind of stunned emptiness a woman might produce when her fears were confirmed, when she heard her husband answer the phone of another woman.

"Was it her?" Julie asked. It was the same small, frightened voice she had used the first time he'd met her. Crane shook his head. "No—at least I don't think so. I couldn't tell whether it was a man or a woman; they didn't say anything."

Crane had tried to sound convincing, but inside there was a gnawing feeling that the caller was a woman. More specifically, he was convinced it was his wife and that she knew. If it had been one of Julie's friends, there would have been no reason to play coy. He looked at the phone for several moments, and finally turned his attention back to Julie.

Senator Richard Crane, sixty-six, and Julie

Simon, forty-one, were having an affair. Crane was a four-term senator and former war hero from Iowa whose wife, Lillian, had become a popular talk-show host on a Washington television station. Julie Simon carried no such credentials; a divorcée, she worked in relative obscurity as an assistant in the Human Resouces and Public Relations Department of Washington General Hospital.

After ten years of night school and accomplishing what her mother had almost convinced her was an impossibility, Julie Simon had pocketed her business administration degree from Georgetown and made the decision to stay in the Capital after graduation. It was a decision she claimed to have regretted until she was introduced to the senator from Iowa. Until then, her only acquaintances had been the small handful of women she had met when she'd joined the Potomac Women's Club, some of the confirmed skirt-chasers at work who ignored the agency's "no fraternization" rule, and, of course, her good friend Jacqueline Marceau. It was Jacqueline Marceau who had introduced her to the senator from Iowa less than two months earlier.

It had taken less than those two months for the situation to become difficult for both of them. What had started as a one-night stand had become tangled, evolving into conversations about commitment and a "definite date" when he would leave his wife. Julie Simon had no way of knowing that Crane had no such intentions. Sooner or later, probably sooner, he realized, he would have to tell her so.

Still preoccupied with the call, Richard Crane got out of bed and studied the telephone. There was something strange about the call. If it had been Lillian, she would have said something. He thought he knew her well enough to know that. Lillian had a temper, a violent temper, and the vocabulary of a sailor when she was angry. If it had been Lillian there would have been outrage and indignation—never silence. "No," he decided, "it wasn't her. I'm certain of it."

"Then who was it?"

Crane shook his head, walked across the darkened room, and pulled on his trousers.

The woman followed him, and stood close to him. She was shaking her head. "I'm frightened—what if it's someone that knows about us? It could ruin your career."

Crane turned away from the woman and stared out the window. There was a cold rain, and an unseemly collection of leaves and papers swirled in front of the gate to the complex courtyard and the empty swimming pool. Julie was right. It could ruin him. He allowed his thoughts to dwell there for several moments before he turned back to her. She was holding his shirt out to him. "Here," she said. "I've seen that look before—you're getting ready to leave."

Crane started to protest, to tell her she was wrong, thought better of it, and put on the shirt. It

77

took another ten minutes for him to finish dressing, and she met him at the door.

"Love me?" she asked. Her face was concealed in shadows as she curled her arms around his neck and pulled herself to him. "I get panicky at the thought of something happening to us," she whispered.

Richard Crane held the fragile young woman close to him for several moments. He could feel the heat of her body and the pounding of his own heart; she was everything Lillian wasn't. But there was one exception—a very large exception. Lillian Baxter Crane had money and connections—and when he announced his candidacy for the Presidency, he was going to need every bit of both.

"When will I see you again?" she asked.

"Not tomorrow. Lillian's got that damn dinner party tomorrow night. I'll call you. Okay?"

Crane stepped into the outside hall and heard the door close behind him. He heard the lock engage and the security chain rattle as she secured it to the door frame. Moments later, in the deserted lobby, he passed the night manager's office and saw two young men bent over their books studying. Neither looked up as he passed.

When he stepped out, the wind brought with it an instantaneous chill. He shivered as he fumbled for his ignition key. Inside the car, still shivering, he started the motor and pulled out of the complex's parking lot. He had driven less than two blocks when his car phone rang.

"Richard?" Lillian's voice asked. "I called your office but they said you weren't there. Lucky I caught you. Just wanted you to know we're staying late tonight; we're running a segment on that downed E-4, the one with Swelling on it—and we're going over some tapes."

Crane started to say something, but she cut him off.

"See you in the morning, love," she cooed.

As Crane pulled on to Dempsey Boulevard he felt a sense of relief. He was convinced now that Lillian didn't know. If she had, she would never have been able to pull off that telephone call. Lillian Baxter Crane had never been one to mask her emotions— good or bad. Yet with that sense of relief came the disturbing realization that if it was someone other than Lillian, the calls Julie had been receiving could, in some ways, be even more dangerous.

Julie Simon took her cup of tea into the bedroom with her and sat on the edge of the bed. The loneliness was all but unbearable. She felt that old familiar ache, and knew the tears weren't far behind. Once again she was forced to face the fact that her relationship with Crane was . . .

That thought slipped away as the phone rang.

"I hoped you'd still be up," Jacqueline Marceau said. "I've been meaning to call you all evening but I thought Richard might be there."

"He left just a few minutes ago. Did you try to call me earlier?"

"No," she lied, and there was a pause before Jacqueline added, "If you don't have plans tomorrow night, I have tickets to a small dinner theater on Runyard. Interested? That is, of course, unless you're planning to see the senator."

"Unfortunately, no. He and Lillian are having a dinner party," Julie said, "but the theater sounds great."

"Well, if he's going to be home playing house with Lillian, then he won't know anything about it if I'm able to line us up a couple of dates."

"A date sounds like fun," Julie Simon admitted. "I'm game."

"I'll see what I can arrange," Jacqueline Marceau said and hung up. She penciled a note on the pad beside her bed: *"Confirmed. Crane will be home. Proceed."* Then she dialed a number and left the message.

2 Nov: Time 0031LT:

Blackjack Shank had once been what one Washington sportswriter called "a pretty fair country lightweight," but that was before his manager prematurely threw him into the ring against the number-one lightweight contender at the time, a back-alley hustler by the name of Slip Amena. It had taken Amena less than three rounds to turn a man with a promising career into a man with no future. They carried Shank out of the ring that night. He had been pummeled into submission, blinded in one eye, and had a brain so scrambled and swollen, it had taken fifteen months to return to its normal size.

Now he was the manager—a title given to him by the sympathetic owner—of a gym in a section of town that had no more future than he had. In a cluttered office filled with records of fighters and events long since forgotten even by the men who had crawled into the ring, Blackjack Shank watched Rooster Ricozy pull up a chair across from his desk. Ricozy opened an envelope and spilled twenty one-hundred-dollar bills on the desk.

"My client," Ricozy said, "would like to see you begin immediately. This should cover expenses. Plus, you should know, there's more where that comes from."

"Yer client's got deep pockets, huh?" Shank grinned. He had a bony face. Even his brow and cheekbones were sharp. When he talked, his mouth was crooked.

"My client," Ricozy said, "wants to know more about this guy Klaipent, the Lithuanian. And my client also wants to know more about that South Korean arms dealer you were telling me about."

Blackjack Shank picked up an old coffee can and spit in it. The spacing in his teeth allowed him to juice the can without opening his mouth. "What's he looking for?"

Rooster leaned back in his chair. "Anything that you think is interesting. Obviously, how you go about finding out is entirely up to you." Ricozy took time to light a cigar and take several puffs. "What's the word on the street?"

Blackjack thought for a minute before he answered. "I hear tell there's a couple of Chinks down in Cuba that are doin' a lot of buyin'. Nothing big, though—mostly small stuff: a couple of M-79 grenade launchers, a handful of machine guns. So far they're buyin' only Pentagon surplus pieces— they're staying away from the Russian stuff. Word is they're doin' most of their dealin' with an outfit by the name of Park Salvage Company. The owner is a former South Korean colonel by the name of Park Shin Ho. Somethin' you need to know is, this guy Park has lots of friends—real important friends."

"Where's the stuff going?" Ricozy pressed.

"He's cuttin' it into scrap, of course," Blackjack said, then laughed. It was a mulish sound, part hiss and part sucking wind. "What else? If you ask Park, he'd tell you he torches the stuff and sells it by the ton."

"Then what my client wants to know is who's buying the scrap and where they're taking it."

Blackjack nodded and glanced at his watch. "I'm gonna need some help. Someone to keep their eyes open and cover me while I get a look-see at the shipping records."

Ricozy repeated the offer. "Like I said, my friend, deep pockets—and the sooner the better."

Blackjack reached for the telephone. He punched out the seven digits and made no effort to conceal what he was saying. He spoke in his own jargon— the peculiar, uneven hitch of the street-savvy. Ricozy knew the lingo, but in the end he was able to catch only fragments of what the wiry little man was saying. From the urgency in his voice, however, it was obvious that Blackjack Shank had no intention of wasting the next few hours. The way Shank saw it, there could well be another opportunity by morning—and he wanted to be free of prior commitments to take advantage of whatever came down the pike.

"You're on," Shank informed him after hanging up. "By tomorrow mornin', you'll have it."

"Good," Ricozy said. "My client would like that."

Time 0037LT:

When Bogner stepped to the curb at Washington International to flag a taxi, Miller was waiting. Like everything else in the ISA administrator's life, even his car was unconventional. He drove an aging Simca with 200,000 miles on the odometer, and freely admitted that the odometer hadn't worked in years. He defended this by frequently stating that his father had impressed upon him that it was far more fruitful to collect interest than to pay it.

Bogner threw his luggage in the backseat, crawled in beside Packer's right-hand man, and loosened his tie. He leaned his head back and closed his eyes as Miller pulled away from the curb.

"How was Florida?"

Bogner looked out at the occasional flake of falling snow and shook his head. "If I tell you, you'll just feel bad. Now you tell me, to what do I owe the pleasure of this little late-night rendezvous?"

"First you say, 'Thank you for picking me up in this shitty weather,'" Miller replied. "Haven't you heard of the milk of human kindness?"

Bogner opened his eyes. "Come on, Robert, you didn't pick me up because you felt sorry for me dragging in this hour of the night. You've got something on your mind."

"So crucify me. The fact of the matter is, we've come up with some new information."

"First, how's Spitz?"

"Talked to the hospital less than thirty minutes ago. He's holding his own, but he still isn't out of danger. We did learn more about what happened this morning, though.

"As it turns out, the driver wasn't one of the limo service regulars. The driver that was scheduled to pick Spitz up this morning didn't show up for work. So they found a trainee who had been working there less than a week, armed him with a map, and sent him out."

"And the poor slug bought the farm, right?"

Miller nodded. "Witnesses said he got out of the car, assisted Spitz, closed the door, walked around the back of the car, crawled behind the wheel, turned on the ignition, started to pull away, and boom. One witness was across the street, the second was down three houses. They both had a pretty good look at what happened."

"Poor bastard," Bogner muttered.

Miller pulled up to a stoplight and held up his hand. "Maybe not. It turns out that the driver was just a kid—he came in from Chicago last week. He was a student, apparently one that wasn't doing all that well. According to his friends back in Chicago, he came into some money a few days before he left town, told them he was quitting school, sent the money home to his parents, came to Washington—and, as Paul Harvey says, 'Now you know the rest of the story.' "

"Let me guess," Bogner said. "The kid was an international student. Chinese. Right?"

Miller nodded. "Close. A Korean."

"Exactly what I found down in Florida. Same scenario, except Eric Chow was in the Air Force instead of being a student. Someone lathered his palm with major league money too; five thousand bucks to be exact—a helluva lot more than most young airmen could stash away."

"And you think . . . ?"

"It might be the first significant crack in the facade of inscrutability," Bogner speculated. "Indications are, all still to be verified, that Chow provided someone with his flight line pass and a fatigue uniform, and then that someone assisted in the loading of Swelling's plane."

"And planted the bomb?"

"Several people report having seen an airman of Chinese descent working out of the VIP lounge last night."

"Where the hell was security?"

Bogner shrugged. "It's obvious someone wasn't doing their job."

Miller turned onto Dowling Street. He was rolling Bogner's input over in his mind. "So instead of Mao Quan sending a goon squad over here, he's recruiting what he needs along the way."

Bogner looked out the window. "I wonder what the Chinese equivalent is for kamikaze?"

It was almost one in the morning when Miller dropped Bogner off at the apartment he shared with Reese Smith. By the time Bogner checked the mail, took the elevator to the third floor, and worked his way down the hall, he had decided to ignore any messages on the answering machine, take the phone off the hook, and not set the alarm clock. If Packer could figure out how to get through to him after all of that, more power to him.

He was halfway across the living room when he saw the light creeping out from under the door in the bedroom. When he opened the door, he saw Joy curled up on the bed, under the covers; she was asleep. Bogner undressed, showered, and crawled into bed. Awareness began to fade. The pillow was cool. Pellets of sleet pelted the window. In the distance he could hear the mournful sound of a siren, and then the sights and sounds of the day mustered for one final inspection. He thought about the young man that had died when Spitz's car exploded, about Eric Chow, and about the people aboard Swelling's plane. What had seemed clear and logical in the light of day became, with sleep setting in, nothing more than disarray and disorder—a mix-and-match collection of fragments and disassociated pieces.

Bogner's eyes were shut and the darkness was swallowing him up and pulling him down when he felt Joy's hand creep into his. "I'm awake," she said.

Her voice was husky and lazy—the words on the verge of blurring back into sleep.

Bogner put his arm around her. The gesture was more protection than passion.

"I'm glad you're home," she said.

Time 0203LT:

Blackjack Shank had long since learned to capitalize on the same moves he once had used in the ring—in the days when his career was still in front of him. He was still quick, moving like a dancer, each motion choreographed to achieve only one goal—the next objective. If asked, he could not have explained what he was doing; after too many years in too many gymnasiums, it was mostly instinct.

Parked in the shadows of a darkened side street along and outside the security fence of the Park Salvage Company in the Baton District in the earliest hours of the morning, he put on a mask and pulled an oil-stained canvas bag from the trunk of his car. Then he signaled to his companion, a man only slightly taller and older than himself. The man's name was Chew. Even Shank wasn't sure of Chew's last name.

Chew's qualifications for Ricozy's assignment were impeccable. A former Marine carrying a dishonorable discharge, he had been paroled after serving fifteen years for manslaughter; a nasty incident in which it was said he carved up his wife's lover with a hacksaw after catching them both in a delicate tangle of sheets and pillows. Chew, it was also said, moved in a world of night shadows, seldom appearing in the light of day. He had once boasted to Blackjack that his parole officer hadn't been able to locate him for seven years. Still, it was Chew's special qualification of having served a brief tenure as an employee of Park's enterprise that made him doubly valuable. As Blackjack had explained to Ricozy, Chew "knows where the bodies are buried."

Now, moving in tandem, the two men used the darkness to work their way to the scrap company's Third Street loading dock. It took Chew less than thirty seconds to pick the lock on the access door and hustle Shank inside.

"What about the guards?" Shank whispered. He was standing with his back pinned to the wall, a flashlight in one hand, the canvas bag in the other. The bag contained a camera with infrared film, a voice recorder, and some small tools. Chew carried their protection and muscle, a quad-column 9mm Spectre.

"There should be two of 'em. By now they're playing cards. They'll either be in the foreman's shed under the crane or the shipping office. We'll gotta get by 'em to get to the office area."

"What about dogs?" Shank asked.

"Shit, Park don't feed dogs. He says dogs are for eatin'."

Blackjack Shank motioned Chew to take the lead, and fell in behind him. They were in the warehouse and shipping area, and at this point it was obvious Park Shin Ho didn't believe in keeping the lights on when no one was in the area. With the exception of two small incandescent bulbs, one at each end of the bay, and a red light over an exit door, the staging area was a dark jumble of crates, barrels, shipping containers, and tarpaulin-covered monoliths.

"Look at all this shit," Chew muttered. "There's gotta be a damn fortune in here."

Shank paused just long enough to check the nomenclature of an open crate and mouthed the words as he read. "What the hell is a AN/AVS-6 goggle?" he whispered. But Chew was far enough ahead of him that he either didn't hear, saw no need to answer, or most likely, didn't know.

Silhouetted by the single light at the end of the building near the stairway, Shank saw Chew pause and motion for him to close in. "Unless I miss my guess," the ex-Marine hissed, "the guards are up there, top of the stairs, end of the hall. There's another door at the end of that hall that goes into Park's office area. To get in there, we gotta get past them."

Shank nodded, and waited while Chew maneuvered his way past a pallet of cartons and took the stairs, two at a time, with the Spectre ready. When he got to the top of the steel staircase, he dropped to one knee and covered the hall while Shank joined him. "Now's when the fun starts," he whispered.

Chew sucked in his breath, dropped to his stomach, and began working his way down the hall. When he got to the door of the room where he expected to find Park's guards, he could hear voices. So far he had been right on every count. He could hear two distinct voices, and in the background, the lower voices of a movie on a television. Again he motioned for Shank. By the time Shank caught up with him, he had managed to pick the lock on the door to the office area. "Cheap lock, piece of cake," he whispered.

Inside, with the door closed behind them, Shank turned on his flashlight and danced it over a latticework of glass and steel cubicles, most of which were equipped with an array of monitors, keyboards, and batteries of telephones. Park's operation was decidedly more high-tech than he had anticipated.

Chew positioned himself between two rows of file cabinets, propped the 9mm Spectre atop one of them, braced himself, and aimed back at the door they had just come through. "It's your show," Chew whispered. "Keep your eyes open in front of you; I got your ass covered."

Blackjack Shank had already formulated his plan; he would start at the top and work his way down. That meant going through Park's office and records first. It only made sense that if anyone in Park's organization was peddling what was supposedly the DRMO's inventory of surplus and no-longer-functioning weaponry, they were doing it with the old man's knowledge. That meant Park himself had to be involved. Even Blackjack Shank could figure out that making a market for an antenna on a Harpoon cruise missile had to be a helluva lot more lucrative than crunching metal to sell to some scrap processor.

He rummaged through Park's desk, found nothing, and turned his attention to the file cabinets beside it. The locks were easy. What he was able to learn from the reams of poorly organized files was less than he had hoped for. If Park was trafficking in illegal weaponry, and there were records of his transactions, it was a good bet they were buried under tons of conventional and very ordinary-appearing paperwork—documenting sales up and down the Eastern Seaboard. It had also occurred to him that any one of the so-called scrap shipments could have been a cover for the vital components to a Tomahawk cruise missile.

In the third cabinet he located a stack of printouts. One detailed Park's shipments for the month of October. While Park's market wasn't exactly global, the old boy had major customers as far away as Texas and as near as Groton, Connecticut. The printout detailed rail shipments, truck shipments, and even a couple of air routings. He recognized the names of some of the firms. Some he had seen on scrap cars in the railyards. Others were obscure, and some the names of companies that would have been recognized in most any household in the Capital. He tore off the printout, crammed it in his pocket, and reached for another file drawer to continue his search. That was when he heard the other door open.

Not even Chew had anticipated Park's men coming in through the front door. The lights went on, Chew blinked and wheeled, and Park's man managed to get off four shots from a .45 Chinketa before the ex-Marine could even pull the trigger. All four shots found their mark; the first gouged its way into Chew's throat, the other three were clustered in a tight pattern in his chest.

Chew died without Blackjack Shank ever learning his first name. He was dead long before he hit the floor.

Blackjack Shank didn't fare much better. The flashlight was no defense. Park's man only had to fire once. Shank slumped to the floor with the realization there was more sting in this than in the right cross Slip Amena had nailed him with that night in the Garden. Amena had pummeled him; this blow was sudden—and even more devastating, spiraling him into a black, lonely, terrifying void where he could hear his heart beat. He was choking and coughing. His mouth flooded with something thick and syrupy and hot.

If there had been someone to tell, Blackjack Shank would have told them that it wasn't like he didn't know what was happening. He did. He simply didn't know how long it would take. He closed his eyes and crawled deeper into his hole.

It was a little after three o'clock in the morning when a dark Blue Chevrolet panel van came to a rolling stop on a small access road under a rail bridge that crossed the Anacosta. Two men, collars up to protect themselves from a raw wind out of the northeast, got out, moved quickly around to the rear of the van, opened the doors, and pulled out their cargo. Two bodies, wrapped and bound in damp canvas, coated with frost, were unceremoniously rolled down the aging cement incline to the water's edge. It took several minutes, but the two bags eventually slipped beneath the sluggish black surface of the river.

Both men watched; neither spoke. Finally, one lit a cigarette. They stood there for several minutes assessing the merits of their work, and when there was nothing else to see, they walked back to the van. By then they had begun to discuss where they could get a good cup of coffee.

As the van pulled away, Jumanus Walker, homeless and, as on so many nights, less than sober, sheltered by the bridge's superstructure, was less than fifty yards from where the incident had taken place. He squinted, rubbed his eyes, messaged his numb fingers, and blew on them to get the blood circulating. Then he groped in his overcoat pocket for his bottle. Because there was usually no one to listen, Jumanus Walker had developed the habit of talking to himself. He took a swig of wine, rubbed his eyes for a second time, and studied the deserted ramp vacated by the two men. "What the hell was that all about?" he muttered.

Time 0327LT:

Gordon Hatton's eyes were heavy, a common malady for the early hours of the morning. The stretch from three o'clock until the morning crew relieved them at seven had always been difficult. He stood up, stretched, and looked across the room at Kent Peters busy filing the day's reports. Peters was wide awake. The difference between them was obvious: Peters was young—Hatton wasn't. "Youthful piss and vinegar" was the way Packer referred to it.

"We've still got the midshift security check at 0330," Peters reminded him.

Hatton glanced up at the clock, sat down again at the main console, and opened the line. A parade of five-digit clusters in patterns of seven began trailing across the screen. A green light flashed, and the first screen posted.

"Try 7-a, 7-b, 7-c, and everything from 7-k on," he shouted across the room to Peters. He could hear Peters's fingers skating across the keyboard, typing out the commands.

"Secure?" Peters called back.

Hatton checked two more lines with the same result, and scanned the monitors. "You showing anything since the hard copy on the Ringwald matter at 0151LT?"

Peters shook his head. "Wait a minute, we've got something on the WC line. Looks like inter-agency stuff. Want me to bring it up?"

Hatton nodded. "Log it in 'ndo,'" he said, and waited for the data to appear. When it did, it was an all-agency info sweep—a wrapup of the day. "Go slow—I don't show any copy on 56-d and 56-e," Hatton informed him. "A, b, and c are already in the previous day's file."

Peters glanced up and down the line of printers. "Shit," he muttered, "I must have inadvertently shut her down. Want to see what it is before I run a file copy?"

Hatton pressed the search and print keys. Then he leaned forward. "Talk to me, WC."

. . . filing a report from Santo Tomas, east and south of Ensenada, Baja, California (unverified) . . . . . . repeat . . .

"Hey, Peters, look at this," Hatton shouted. The younger of the two ISA agents crossed the room and looked over his shoulder.

(as reported) . . . MPL fuentes dentro Ojos Negros reportero mejicano policia haber descubierto componente (translation not verified) creer en esta um americano fabricar mano-helicoptero superficie an aire . . .

"What the hell does it say?" Hatton grumbled.

Peters read the screen a second time. "Looks like we're getting a second-line relay from the Baja. Someone's trying to translate for us and they're screwing it up big time. From what I can make out, some farmer reported finding parts of a weapon of some kind outside Ojos Negros."

"What kind of weapon?"

"Near as I can make out, they found parts of a damn handheld rocket launcher. My Spanish is pretty rusty, though. It may have been parts of a damned hair curler."

"Where the hell is Ojos Negros?"

"North of Ensenada, south of Tijuana. My wife and I used to drive through it when we went down to San Lucas."

Hatton still had no idea where Ojos Negros was.

Peters was still reflecting on their last trip down to the Baja Sur when it hit him. "Damn," he muttered.

"What's the matter?"

"Where the hell did Dunning's plane go down?"

Hatton thought for a moment. "According to the article in *The Post*, it went down about twenty-five miles off the coast of some damn place called Cabo Quintano."

"Make a copy of that screen, Gordo. Cabo Quintano isn't that far from Ojos Negros. That granjero just may have solved the riddle of what happened to Dunning's aircraft."

(copy)
NBS . . . 0730LT broadcast
Newsbreak . . .
Dateline: Santo Tomas, Baja California:

   A report this morning from Ojos Negros, Mexico.

   Authorities in this small Mexican village report that the body of a young Asian male along with several components of an American-made L-7 handheld missile launcher were discovered buried in a shallow grave, in a field south of Ojos Negros late yesterday. Ojos Negros is located north and east of Cabo Quintano.

   A Boeing E-4 carrying Secretary of the Air Force James Dunning exploded in midair as it was preparing to land at the U.S. Space Surveillance Station, October 24. Thirty-seven people died in that crash. . . .

Chapter Four

Time 0647LT:

Bogner's first impulse was to ignore the intermittent, annoying sound. He pulled the covers over
his head with one hand and groped for Joy with the
other.

"Want me to answer it?" she asked. To his surprise, her voice came from far away—perhaps as
far as the other side of the room—and he realized
she was already up.

Bogner snaked a hand out from under the covers,
picked up the receiver, sat up, and blinked. Joy was
dressed, sitting by the window, drinking a cup of
coffee. "Bogner," he muttered into the phone.

"You were right," Miller acknowledged.

"Right about what?" He was still in that groggy

half-awake, half-asleep zone where the temptation to hang up was almost as great as the inclination to listen. There was only one problem. Miller kept on talking.

"They discovered the body of a young Asian male and parts of an L-7 in a field down in the Baja last night—not far from where Dunning's plane went down."

Bogner was coming out of it. He shifted the phone to his other ear and sat up on the side of the bed. "You said Asian. Was he Chinese?"

"The reports are just coming in. Peters called me about four o'clock this morning and told me what was coming in over the wire. I got on the phone. I've talked to the Mexican authorities in Ojos Negros and the Base Information Officer at the U.S. Naval Air Station at Coronado. Coronado is sending a team down to Ojos Negros to identify whether or not it's actually an L-7."

"What about the Asian, dammit?" Bogner said.

"Nothing yet. When I talked to the people in Ojos Negros, they didn't know much. They did tell me they would have to send the body to Ensenada for an autopsy—the cause of death wasn't apparent."

"No ID?"

"Nothing. They said the body had been stripped. All he was wearing was a T-shirt. But I thought this was interesting. The shirt had a San Diego Padres logo silk-screened on the front."

"That doesn't mean much. He could have picked that up from any street stall in Tijuana. How soon will we know something?"

Bogner could hear Miller rummaging around on his desk. "I've got the name and number of the *pesquisidor* that will be conducting the autopsy—he'll let us know the cause of death as soon as he's finished. I did learn one other thing that may help us, though. The authorities in Ojos Negros think it's likely the victim spent a lot of time in the States. They said he had extensive dental work—and not the kind he would have been likely to get in Mexico."

"Does Packer know all of this?"

"That's the reason I called you. Packer wants us in his office at nine o'clock sharp."

Bogner clasped his hand over the mouthpiece and looked at Joy. "I have to leave in fifteen minutes," she informed him.

"I'll be there," Bogner said, and hung up.

"We've got two days left," he reminded her. "Are we making any progress? This isn't exactly Jamaica."

Joy crossed the room and sat down on the edge of the bed. "We always were good in bed, Tobias—that's never been an issue. When we started talking about this reconciliation thing, the question was whether we could make it work even with our two very different lifestyles. You've got your life and I've got mine."

"Packer versus NBS."

"Unfortunately, that just about sums it up. I love you, Tobias, and I don't doubt that you love me. If that's enough, we can make it work—but somewhere in the back of my mind, I'm getting that old caution signal. It's telling me to go easy—to proceed with discretion."

Bogner pushed the covers back. This time he swung his legs out over the edge of the bed and sat up. Joy had a way of making sense—even when he didn't want her to. She was doing it again. He knew she expected him to say something—and he wanted to—but it was the same old story. The words she wanted to hear were never there. "Will you be here tonight?" he asked.

"Do you want me to be?"

He nodded. "It'll be the highlight of my day," he said.

"I would hope so," she answered with a smile.

Day 2: Time 0811LT:

Bootsie Carter was a man of small rituals who lived in a cramped three-room apartment over his gym. A widower, he began every morning with a cup of strong black coffee followed by a fifteen-minute toilet routine. At age sixty-four, Bootsie was convinced that few things in life were as important as a good bowel movement.

He was thus occupied when he heard someone calling his name. "Be down in a minute," he grunted, and turned to the sports section.

Fifteen minutes later, unshaven, disheveled, still dressed in flannel pajamas and a worn terry-cloth robe, he made his way down the stairs. Instead of one of the young fighters who trained at his gym, Carter found himself confronted by two men, one heavy, one thin, both bundled against the cold Washington morning. The shorter and heavier of the two flashed a police badge as he snuffed out his cigarette.

"So what's the problem this time?" Bootsie grumbled.

"Name is Lieutenant Roberts. He's Detective Pace," the fat man said. "Are you Bootsie Carter?"

Carter nodded. He didn't like cops. He had a tattoo on his arm that said so.

"The name Blackjack Shank mean anything to you?"

Carter nodded a second time. His first inclination was to wonder what kind of trouble Blackjack had gotten himself into this time. "He works here on occasion," Carter lied. "Why?"

"When's the last time you saw him?" Roberts pushed.

Carter thought for a minute. "Last night. Why? What the hell is this all about?"

Roberts had already put out one cigarette, and now he was lighting another. "We just fished Shank out of the Anacosta. Someone put a bullet in him, wrapped him in a rubber coat, and dumped him in the river sometime during the night."

It had been said that nothing bothered Bootsie Carter, but this time his stomach did a slow pitch and roll before he regained his equilibrium.

"There was a second body," Roberts went on. "Same MO—but no ID. You don't happen to know where Shank was going last night or who he was with, do you?"

Carter shook his head. He was lying. He knew Shank was meeting Rooster Ricozy. He knew because he had loaned Blackjack a fifty and Blackjack had promised to pay it back after he took care of whatever chores Rooster had in mind.

While Roberts asked the usual questions, his lanky partner strolled casually around the gym conducting the obligatory homicide look-see. The way Pace went about it, it was a cursory inspection at best. Carter, who had seen it all before, wondered if the cops actually expected to find anything.

Each time Roberts asked a question, he made note of Carter's answer. It was a laborious process accomplished with a stub of a pencil and a pocket-sized notebook that was next to lost in Roberts's ham-sized hands. Finally he got around to the inevitable. "Where were you last night?"

"Where I am every night," Carter said with a sigh. "Upstairs, soaking my hands, fighting this goddamned arthritis." He held out his hands, exhibiting a fistful of gnarled fingers.

Roberts grunted, shoved his notebook in his pocket, and took one a look around the room. "Where did Shank keep his belongings?" Carter walked the two men to the locker area and opened Shank's locker, and Roberts rummaged through the contents. When he was satisfied, he closed the door. "Know anything about Shank's next of kin?" Roberts asked.

Carter sat down on a bench in front of the row of lockers. "None that I know of," he admitted. "This place was pretty much his life."

"We'd like to have you come down to the morgue and identify the body," Roberts said. He sounded bored. "It's a formality. I saw him fight once—gotta admit. I recognized him the minute we unwrapped that damn rubber wrapper."

Bootsie Carter still didn't have his act together. He stood with his gnarled hands shoved deep in his robe pockets watching the two officers move aimlessly around the gym. He had no idea what they were looking for, and he doubted if they did either. Finally he decided there must have been some kind of secret, imperceptible signal, because Roberts headed for the door with Pace close behind.

"Try to get down there today," Roberts admonished him. "We want to get this thing wrapped up."

Carter made certain he saw them get in their car and pull away before he picked up the phone and dialed Ricozy's number.

There were no pretensions in Ricozy's operation. He answered his own phone. "Ricozy here."

Carter had decided to forgo the prologue. "The cops were just here. Blackjack and Chew bought the farm last night. They were fished out of the Anacosta early this morning."

There was a moment of stunned silence on the other end of the line before Ricozy spoke. "Where are they?"

"The morgue. The cops want somebody to come down, identify the bodies, and pick up their personal effects—they want to know where to ship the bodies."

"I'll take care of it," Rooster said.

Time 0844LT:

Liu Shao parked the rented white Ford van half a block down the street from the Crane house, a two-story brownstone on the corner of Crawford and Benton Place. He double-checked the address the Marceau woman had given him and nodded at Quin Lo Wan. "This is the place."

Quin studied the location and looked across the street at the brown two-story Tudor. "There," he said, pointing. "That would be the best place."

"That is the one we were told about," Liu confirmed. "I am told that the people who own it are away for the winter."

"You have a plan?" Quin asked.

Liu nodded. He was still smiling as he pulled onto the Capital Beltway moments later. He would do exactly as Tonu Hon had suggested, but he would use Jacqueline Marceau's information to add a twist of his own.

Less than thirty minutes later, in a Belling Street motel room saturated with the pungent odors of years of abuse, Tonu Hon's lieutenants checked and double-checked each detail of their plan. As usual, Liu Shao had done his homework; that trait endeared him to Tonu Hon. It was the other side of Liu Shao that Tonu Hon questioned. Liu was headstrong, inclined at times to deviate from Tonu's carefully thought-out plans. Ultimately, Tonu Hon had once warned him, that trait would be his downfall. Still, they were a team; Liu did the planning, Quin did the implementing.

The next step was up to Quin; after sizing up the situation, Liu had decided that the house directly across the street from the two-story Crane brownstone gave him what he needed.

"We will have no trouble gaining access?" Quin asked.

"None," Liu assured him. "The house is owned by an elderly man and his wife. We are assured of what we need."

Quin closed his eyes. Liu understood the ritual. Quin had begun to prepare himself, envisioning the sequence of events beginning with the time when they entered the old couple's house until the time when the limousine arrived to pick up the senator. Finally Quin asked, "The senator is picked up at what time?"

"Six-forty-five," Liu answered.

"It will still be dark," Quin reminded him.

"There are streetlights on two of the four corners; some shadows are desirable." Quin laid the HK 94 9mm carbine on the bed, and closed his eyes again. Liu went on. "We will take possession of the house in the early hours of the morning—early enough that we will not be seen—the senator will suspect nothing."

Liu smiled. It was the added element of surprise in the assassination of Richard Crane that pleased him most. The Americans would get more than they bargained for. The dull-witted Americans would be caught off guard—taken by surprise. Even now he could see them focus on the reliability of both the car and the driver—conducting their safety checks, thorough point-by-point inspections of each limousine before it was dispatched.

The same would hold true for the use of any substitute driver. The method had worked once—it would not work again. Like the limousines, each driver would be checked and double-checked. Liu had thought of everything.

With the senator from Iowa it would be different. Quin would simply position himself in an upstairs bedroom of the house across the street. At that hour of the morning there would be little traffic. More important, Quin would have two opportunities. The first would come when Crane stepped through the front door and was briefly silhouetted by the light streaming through the door from his foyer. The second would come when the senator stepped down off the porch and was momentarily bathed in the yellow glow of the streetlights.

Liu unfolded a crude pencil sketch of the Oxon Hill neighborhood and laid it on the bed. "We will use the alley that runs behind the house. We will park behind the third house to the north. The house is unoccupied and listed with a realtor. I am told that others have been parking there—we will arouse no suspicion.

"When we have accomplished our mission, we will leave by the rear door, go to the car, and exit to the north. We will be safely out of the area before the police arrive."

Quin had been following Liu's plan each step of

the way. "Then we have nothing to do until . . ."

Liu Shao smiled, folded the sketch, and put it back in his pocket. "Correction," he said as he lit a cigarette. "It is you who have nothing to do. I have much to do in the next few hours."

Time 0913LT:

It was a typical Clancy Packer briefing session. Packer started on time, everyone knew what to expect, and everyone was expected to contribute. In addition to the regulars—Miller, Henline, and Ploughman—the ISA chief had brought in two of his logistics people and two outsiders, Peter Langley of NI and Jude Parrish of the Coast Guard's counterinsurgency group.

Parrish, like Langley, was a Naval Academy man who had been plucked out of the cockpit of an E-2c Hawkeye to conduct a twelve-month-long investigation of DRMO disbursement activity. Bogner had worked with him in the past. Parrish's credentials were impeccable.

"I think every one knows Jude and Peter, so we'll dispense with the formalities and get down to business," Packer began. "To get us started, I've ask Robert to give us a quick review of the report out of Ojos Negros earlier this morning."

Miller passed out copies of the update, and turned on the projector to display a map of the San Diego area and adjacent Baja region. "As you all know, Mexican authorities contacted our people early this morning to inform us that they had discovered the body of a male Asian and components of an L-7 handheld missile launcher. I'm afraid that set the tempo. Within hours, we were getting calls from every agency in the country. The question on everyone's mind is, is there any possibility that a handheld L-7 would be capable of bringing down something as big as an E-4? The speculation, of course, is that a missile fired from that L-7 discovered last night in Ojos Negros may have been what caused the crash of Secretary of the Air Force James Dunning's plane.

"Obviously we don't know the answer to that. But a couple of phone calls by Chet Hurley to the Commandant of the Coast Guard resulted in them springing Jude here to help us. You can take it from there, Commander."

Parrish, a tall and stern-looking man, wasted no time. "It's an interesting theory. There's no denying the L-7 has the range and punch, but we're talking an E-4 here, and my first reaction is that it would take one helluva lucky shot to bring it down.

"Let me put it in perspective for you. Dunning's plane was one of the first E-4s built. So that would make it circa 1974–75. Even at that, we're looking at an aircraft that weighs about four hundred thousand pounds, two hundred and thirty-some-odd feet long, and a damn wing span of close to one hundred and ninety-six feet. The only thing we've got in our inventory that's bigger is the C-5A Galaxy. All of which tells you that Dunning's plane was one big mama—carrying a damn second-generation electronics suite right out of an EC-135.

The Air Force likes to say things like it's been hardened against the effects of electromagnetic pulses attendant to nuclear explosion. In case that needs deciphering—Dunning's plane was carrying some extra protection.

"If you're still not convinced, let me carry it one step further. In an all-out nuclear war, this baby would have been up there as part of our National Emergency Airborne Command Post."

Bogner leaned forward. "Jude, are you saying an L-7 absolutely could not knock this thing out of the sky?"

"I'd never say that, T.C. But I would go so far as to say it would take a million-to-one shot. You'd have to hit her in just the right place—and have everything else on your side to boot."

Millie Ploughman rifled through one of her files. "Would everything else include IFR conditions; ceiling of three hundred feet, less than an eighth-mile visibility?"

"I don't think the weather had much to do with it," Parrish said. "We know the flight was off course, but not by much. Not even enough that there would have to have been computer corrections. Keep in mind, Dunning had a boatload of heavyweights from some of his top vendors on board. He's been known to instruct Captain Yost to fly off course just to demonstrate the multiple capabilities of some of that high-powered electronics gear his baby was packing. When you stop to think about it, flying through a thunderhead the size of those being reported that night off Catalina would enable a man to put on one helluva demonstration."

"According to the weather station at LAX, they had PIREPs of one supercell over Catalina with tops at forty-five thousand feet," Ploughman reminded them.

Parrish shook his head. "The way I see it, if Dunning had been in a chopper or a single-engine aircraft, I think the L-7 scenario would be a lot more acceptable."

Miller leaned back in his chair. "Are we chasing our tail trying to connect the two events, the Dunning crash and the Swelling explosion?"

It was Bogner's turn. "Pack, try this one on for size. We've tied into this Mao Quan before. We know this guy makes Machiavelli look like an Eagle Scout. Step back for a moment and ask yourself: If you wanted to bury something in the Baja that you didn't want found, how difficult would it be?"

"Not hard at all," Packer answered.

"A piece of cake," Langley offered. "Lots of nothing and plenty of place for it."

"That's my point, Peter. Same song, second chorus: Why did the Mexican authorities find the body of that young Asian and the components of that L-7?"

"Because . . . because someone wanted them to find it?" Miller guessed.

"Exactly. Mao had to figure someone like Jude here would know that it would take the perfect hit and an act of God to bring down an E-4, but he proved one thing while he twisted our tail—he proved he could position his people just about anywhere he wants, anytime he wants. Think about it. He blows up Dunning's plane on one coast, and Swelling's plane a week later on the opposite coast. We don't catch on fast enough, so he leaves a clue for us. He wants to make damn certain we know who's making our life miserable."

"T.C. may have something," Langley agreed.

Packer took time to light his pipe. He was playing with Bogner's theory. "It makes sense, T.C. If I was trying to plant the seeds of terrorism in your mind, I'd damn sure take credit for any misfortune that happened—whether I was involved or not."

"Let me back up for a minute," Miller said. "We've got two high-ranking officials in similar air disasters. Are we saying that we are reasonably certain it was a bomb that caused Swelling's plane to go down? Are we also saying that because we haven't found the black box, and didn't appear to be making much progress on our investigation into Dunning's crash, that Mao and his thugs threw us a bone—trying to convince us they blew the plane out of the sky with a handheld missile launcher?"

"That pretty well sums it up," Packer concluded. "I think we're also saying Mao and 5A could care less what we think, as long as we think both incidents are acts of terrorism and 5A is behind it."

"All right, bring it full circle, tie this in to the Spitz car bombing and what happened to Bob Worling," Miller pressed.

"My guess—Mao's work all the way," Langley said.

Bogner held up his hand. "But, I think we all agree, for different reasons. Worling just happened to be the guy carrying the report. They needed to know what we knew. It would have been the same if it had been any one of us.

"We're also saying Spitz is a different story. When Mao blew up Lattimere Spitz's car, he didn't give a damn whether or not Spitz bought the farm—he was merely demonstrating just how close he can get to the head shed any time he wants to."

Packer tried to sum up. "Even though I don't like it, it ties together. While we have every reason to believe all four incidents are the work of the Fifth Academy, Mao isn't demonstrating any one modus operandi."

"It's a bit like trying to anticipate the moves of a shadow in a round room," Langley agreed.

"What else have we got?" Bogner asked.

"At this point let's bring in our logistics people," Packer said. "That's why I invited Mike Janus and Dr. Leslie Marks up for this meeting."

Bogner had worked with Leslie Marks on the Lyoto-Straf investigation. The general consensus was that as a situational theorist she had few equals. Packer had once referred to the former National University professor as the only brain in town with less than one percent body fat. Mike Janus, on the other hand, was a former IAI and Pentagon operative who was forced in from the cold when his ticker went bad. Between the two of them, they had honed the art of situation analysis to a new zenith.

Dr. Marks spoke from where she sat while her colleague went to the head of the table. "When Clancy called me yesterday evening," she began, "we knew nothing of the events that have since transpired in Ojos Negros. But after hearing the discussion here this morning, I feel certain Mr. Janus would agree with me that discovery has little impact on the scenario we see developing. This morning, however, we think we can see some dimension to this over and above what we already know to be fact."

When Janus took over, he had a voice like a violin salesman. "In order for us to defuse 5A's efforts, we have to get inside their head. Five components of their operation need to be identified—components common to any clandestine scenario. In any terrorist operation you need defined targets, recognizing of course that 'random' may be the way you define your targets—and you need a way to accomplish your objective. Which is another way of saying, someone to plan—and someone to implement that plan. Then, on a lesser scale, you need supplies, if your operation is at all sophisticated, and, of course . . . a base of operations."

At that point Marks took over again. "I want to stress one thing here. Any clandestine operation must have access to classified or privileged information. Consequently, your first imperative is to identify the mole. But before we take on the issue of 5A's information source, let's deal with the other considerations. We can say with some degree of certainty that Dunning, Swelling, and Spitz were targets. And at this point I think it's safe to say we can assume they are going to use any means that suits their purpose. Assuming we're right up to this point, let's deal with their base of operations and their supplies."

Bogner leaned forward. "Have we got any clue to either?"

"Nothing we can hang our hat on, Captain Bogner. The supplies they've needed thus far would have been easy to come by. If we have any luck at all, we're most likely to find it when we discover their base of operations."

"Think like a terrorist," Janus advised.

Millie spoke up. "Neighbors that don't ask questions. Freedom to come and go as you please. What else?"

Langley leaned back in his chair. "How does the DRMO situation fit into all of this, Pack?"

Miller picked up the thread. "Peter may have something. Are we checking with the arms dealers? It would be easy to check their records."

"Legitimate arms dealers are one thing," Janus reminded them. "It's the ones that are operating on the fringe that we have to worry about. It's tricky. First we have to identify them. Then, when they stonewall us, we have to shut them down and subpoena their damn records. By the time we get that through the damn courts, Mao could be blowing up the White House."

"You've still got the problem of their mole," Marks reminded them. "Finding that mole has to be one of your top priorities. Let's face it, if they know what you know before you know it, we're all in for a long, ugly winter."

Time 1134LT:

Unlike his counterpart, Oscar Jaffe at the CIA, Clancy Packer had never been comfortable with a driver. Instead, he himself piloted the Crown Victoria the agency provided, and turned it in every two years, usually with less than twenty thousand miles on the odometer and smelling like Prince Albert pipe tobacco.

Now, as he edged out of the flow of noon traffic and over to the curb, he watched Bogner roll the window down. Bogner had ridden with Ricozy before; he knew what to expect. To Bogner's way of thinking, the EPA would have considered the combination of Packer's pipe and Ricozy's cigar a clear violation of the Clean Air Act.

"T.C." Rooster roared, "haven't seen you in ages. Where the hell have you been keeping yourself?" Before Bogner could respond, Ricozy was already in the process of opening the door and situating himself in the backseat. When he did, the brown Crown Victoria listed to port and the door slammed.

"Packer keeps me busy," Bogner said and Ricozy laughed, a perfunctory, otherwise preoccupied sound. Even though he liked Bogner, it was obvious the big man was only half interested in making or listening to small talk. Packer had once declared that Ricozy was the only man he knew who was less adept at the social graces than Bogner.

"Change in plans," Rooster announced. "We've got an appointment downtown. It looks like Park's boys laid some mean shit on us last night. About eight o'clock this morning, the cops fished my man Shank and one of his cronies out of the Anacosta."

It wasn't the kind of news Packer had anticipated. He flinched and waited for Ricozy to continue.

"After you and I talked last night, Pack, I cut a deal with Shank to find a way into Park's operation and have a look around. The police haven't put anything together yet—but from what Bootsie Carter tells me, it's pretty obvious what happened; our man Shank got caught with his pants unzipped.

"According to the police, someone pumped them full of lead, wrapped them in rubber blankets, and dumped them in the river. Fortunately for us, some damn derelict saw the whole thing and sobered up long enough to call the police. They're holding him downtown and the bodies down at the morgue."

Bogner heard Packer sigh. He knew what the ISA chief was thinking: He was getting too old for this kind of thing, and it was getting to be an old story— too much violence and all of it too close to home. He had lost his zest for the chase. On more than one occasion, the man who had recruited Bogner into the ranks of the ISA had expressed his growing distaste for the job that still had to be done and with no end in sight.

"That's where we're headed?" Packer asked. "The morgue?" There was a kind of futility in his voice.

Ricozy lit his cigar and belched a cloud of thick

blue smoke into the car's interior. "I told the cops I'd confirm their IDs," Ricozy said. "Let's hope dead men can communicate, Pack. Otherwise we're back at square one."

The attendant at Parkland was an untidy little man with bottle-bottom glasses and nicotine stains at the corners of his mouth. He had a habit of avoiding eye contact, and his voice was a monotone. "According to the preliminary report of the coroner, your friend here was killed by a single .45-caliber bullet. Most of the facial features were destroyed—which is understandable because the parietal bone, occipital bone, and the sphenoid bone were all smashed and shattered by the impact of the bullet. The Doc says his theory is the guy was turning away from whoever shot him when he was hit—like maybe he was getting ready to run."

Packer turned away.

For the first time the attendant's expression changed. Now there was a crooked yellow-toothed smile to contend with. "See this?" the little man said, holding up a clear plastic bag. "It's your friend's eyeball. Doc says it was probably blown out of the socket at impact." He pointed to the eye with a pencil stub. "This is the medial rectus muscle, this is the trochlea—"

Ricozy waved the man off. "I think we've seen enough."

The attendant grinned. Ricozy assumed it was more of a nervous gesture than a display of disrespect.

Bogner and Ricozy watched as the man pulled the sheet back over what was left of Blackjack Shank and slid the stainless-steel table back into the wall. "Is it who you thought it was?"

Ricozy nodded.

The man looked at his clipboard. "It says here on the viewing permit that if you recognize him you're supposed to go to Lieutenant Roberts' office on the third floor and fill out some forms. They'll talk to you about his personal effects up there."

The three men took the elevator to the third floor and found Roberts in his office: a cluttered, paper-inundated cubicle with two telephones, an out-of-phase monitor, and a half-eaten Big Mac and a cup of coffee dominating the only bare spot on his desk. Roberts was on the phone. When he finished, he rounded up three chairs from other offices and instructed them to take a seat.

"You must be Ricozy," Roberts said with a grin. "Saw you when you played against the Giants a couple of years back."

"Been more than a couple of years," Ricozy said.

"Anyway, according to Bootsie Carter, you may have been one of the last people to see Blackjack alive."

"As a matter of fact," Rooster said, "I saw him last night. I wanted to know if Blackjack was available to do a little personal training. I have a friend who's allowed himself to get a little paunchy. I thought maybe Blackjack could whip him into shape for me."

"What time was that?"

Ricozy shrugged. "When you're retired, who pays attention to the clock? All I can tell you is it was sometime after supper."

"Have you any idea where he was going after his meeting with you?"

Ricozy shook his head. "Not a clue."

Roberts took a sip of coffee and studied Packer and Bogner. "Who's your friends?"

"Redskin front-office personnel," Ricozy lied. "They were scheduled to have lunch with me. I asked them to tag along—neither of them had ever been to a morgue before. Thought I'd show them what might happen if they don't get us a division winner in here pretty soon."

Roberts smiled and handed Ricozy a sheet of paper. "How about an autograph for my kid. He'll love it when I tell him I actually had Rooster Ricozy in my office."

Ricozy scribbled his name on the scrap of paper and handed it back. "Question. Did Blackjack have anything on him when you found the body?"

Roberts shook his head. "Naw, they stripped him, but it was a half-ass job—they left this in his jacket pocket. It looks to be a computer printout of some kind." He handed it to Ricozy. "Mean anything to you? It probably means something to somebody— but for the most part it's just a bunch of names and numbers. We found it wadded up in his jacket pocket along with a pack of cigarettes and a couple of old fight stubs from the Armory. We figure whoever did it thought they took everything of value— including the wallet."

Ricozy glanced at the printout. "I'll pass this along to Bootsie Carter—it may mean something to him."

Roberts polished off the rest of his coffee, wadded the cup up in a ball, threw it in the direction of the nearest waste basket, and missed. Then he stood up. "Look, I know guys like you are busy, but if you hear anything or learn anything, we'd appreciate it if you'd pass it along. If and when we get an ID on the other body, I'll get back to you. As near as we've been able to determine, Blackjack doesn't have a family."

"When you're through with your investigation and are ready to release the body," Ricozy said, "give me a call. I'll take care of the arrangements."

Roberts nodded. "Oh—and one last thing," he said. "What with you guys being with the Redskin front office and all, you wouldn't know how a guy like me could get a couple of tickets for the Dallas game, would you?"

Bogner reached out and shook the man's hand. "Consider it done."

Time 1400LT:

Park Shin Ho had been educated in both his native South Korea and Great Britain, and had spent seven years with British Steel before deciding to seek his fortune in the United States. He had joined his uncle's company eight years earlier, serving in an apprentice-like series of positions before being rewarded with any real authority in the firm. Then, three years ago, he had assumed control when his uncle had died in what Park had described as "a most untimely and unfortunate hunting accident." Nothing was made of the fact that Park and a close personal friend had been the only other ones in the hunting party.

A major contributor to both the Republican and Democratic Parties, Park was said to have staunch allies on both sides of the aisle. And it was equally well documented that he moved in circles reserved only for the Capital's major movers and shakers.

Now he sat across from Liu Shao and studied the letter of credit from the Ministry of Trade in Beijing. "A most unusual request," he said, laying the letter aside, "and certainly far exceeding the scope of any of our transactions thus far."

"I assure you that the funds necessary to handle such arrangements are already on deposit in the Bank of America in Los Angeles," Liu Shao informed him. "As you well know, the draft you hold in your hand is a negotiable document."

Park picked up the letter along with the requested inventory and studied both documents for a second time. "I don't usually ask, Mr. Liu, but what is your purpose for this inventory? Items of this nature are normally only of interest to foreign governments."

Liu shifted in his chair. "I feel certain you realize I am not at liberty to discuss that," Liu replied. "From your hesitancy, however, I must assume that there are certain items your company cannot or is unwilling to supply."

Park tented his fingers in front of his oval face

and closed his eyes. As usual, in two readings he had committed the requested inventory to memory—verbatim. It was the second series of items that bothered him, items that could be traced directly to the ILS. If that was the case, the ILS could trace them to him if Liu or any of his people were caught. "All items you request in number one are specified as Code A, No Demil. It is the second series of items . . . handheld rocket launchers of the nomenclature you specify are usually classified Code D, Total Demil. A purchase of this nature might make you suspect in the event of—"

"I did not come here to play word games, Mr. Park. I came to purchase these items. We have done business in the past. I question why there is suddenly a problem."

Park sighed, stood up, and walked around to Liu's side of the desk. He was a much larger man than Liu, and he stood looking down at the man his sources identified as a representative of the Fifth Academy. Regardless of whether or not he was sympathetic to the cause of Mao Quan, this matter, if not handled properly and with extreme caution, could, in the long run, cost him dearly. "It was, of course, impertinent of me to inquire about your intentions, but please understand, Mr. Liu, I have concerns. Last night, our security was violated. Two men were discovered going through our files. This has never happened before."

"A robbery attempt?"

"Doubtful."

"And you suspect . . . ?"

123

"I suspect everyone, Mr. Liu—especially my government."

"You were able to stop them before they—"

"Rest assured, they did not leave with whatever they were seeking," Park said. "However, the mere fact that they were here may indicate that I and my company are under some degree of scrutiny. And as I'm sure you understand, I prefer to work without scrutiny."

Liu forced a smile. "Or perhaps they were merely trying to determine where you kept certain items of inventory."

Park sighed and clasped his hands behind his back. "We have not achieved our modest degree of success by being casual about such matters. It has long been my philosophy to assume the worst—and be quite pleased when I discover things were not as bad as I had first imagined. To do anything less would be foolhardy."

Liu waited while Park went back around to his side of the desk and sat down again. He had not expected reluctance on the part of the man that he knew dealt with all kinds of factions brokered through Israeli, German, and Dutch companies. "Is it because of your concern that such items may be . . . ?"

Park was surprised at the candor of the little man. "Have you not noticed," he asked, "the thoroughness and the tenacity with which our host country approaches the investigation of such events that they interpret to be a violation of their national security? The perpetrators of both the

Oklahoma City and World Trade Center incidents were incriminated and indicted on mere fragments, the tiniest pieces of evidence. It is quite a different thing to sell the multipurpose display of an F-117a Stealth, or a fire-control memory for the same aircraft to our friends in Iran or Iraq or Libya. They too have commerce to attend to. What they do with it after my transaction with them is complete is entirely up to them—and of course beyond my control. I will confess, the determining factor in all sales is the likelihood of these components being traced back to my inventory.

"On the other hand, the indiscriminate disposal of a handheld grenade launcher and its subsequent discovery only a few days after its suspected use in an event so close to my base of operations—disturbs me."

Liu cleared his throat. "The components of the rocket launcher found in Ojos Negros were planted—they had nothing to do with the cause of the crash of that airplane."

Again Park was taken back by how much the man was willing to reveal. "Perhaps—but I find it curious that I find my security violated within hours after its discovery. Would you call that chance, my friend? Or, if you were me, would you exercise added caution when you conduct business?"

Liu stood up. Park was still holding the letter of credit and the inventory request. "I suggest," Liu said, "that you consider our request. It would take nothing more than a phone call to locate other—"

It was Park's turn to smile. "True, Mr. Liu, but none so convenient nor with whom you have already established a dialogue." He looked at the list a second time, folded it, and laid it on his desk. "Call me tomorrow, Mr. Liu. In the meantime I will see what I can arrange."

Moments later, in the front seat of the van driven by Quin Lo Wan, Liu Shao, normally reticent, seemed eager to elaborate on his meeting with the Korean.

"He is reluctant to sell us the two L-7s?" Quin demanded.

"His reluctance is measured and cautious," Liu answered. "It appears that Mr. Park needs time to satisfy himself that there is no way the units can be traced to him."

"And how will he do that?" Quin pressed.

"It would be a simple matter to manufacture documents that show the units had already been shipped elsewhere. Then he would have to insure that the units he supplies us have been properly processed."

"Removing all nomenclature and military identification numbers?"

Liu nodded and leaned back in his seat. He could hear the rain pelting the van's roof and the slap of the windshield wipers. As was his practice, he was cautiously going over every fragment of his conversation with Parks and every detail of how the escalation in their activities would be accomplished. Finally, he took out a small notebook and began scribbling notes. When he finished, he put the book away and reflected on the matter of Senator Richard Crane.

Crane's name had not been on the original list, and it perplexed him if for no other reason than it was the first time the Marceau woman's role in their plan had become apparent. She had somehow been able to convince Mao Quan that the name of the senator from Iowa be included. Unlike the others, all considered to be influential in spearheading the evolving policy with Premier Qian in Beijing, Crane played no such apparent role. Nevertheless, he was next on the list—a list that had now grown shorter. Already he had been able to cross off the names of Dunning and Swelling. The President's aide, Lattimere Spitz, was still a question mark. Even there, there was reason for hope; periodic news bulletins from the hospital indicated that he was still in critical condition. As for Worling, the CIA agent, he was not even on the list. Yet there was merit in that as well—it served to demonstrate how successful they had been in penetrating the Washington security net.

Gradually Liu turned his attention away from what had been accomplished to what still had to be done. In a matter of hours, Crane would no longer be an issue. If all went well with Crane, only two tasks remained for him before returning to De Pinas Aquiero and, eventually, Hainan. There was still the last name on his list, the Chairman of the Armed Services Committee, Loren Langley. And, of course, making certain that Jacqueline Marceau was prepared to take the last step in Tonu Hon's plan, the assassination of the American President, David Colchin.

Chapter Five

Time 1603LT:

Bogner and Miller, along with Mike Janus of ISA Logistics, had been poring over the computer printout for the last hour when Packer walked in. "Come up with anything?"

"Couple of possibilities," Miller concluded, "but nothing definitive. Show him what we've got, T.C."

"Blackjack knew what he was looking for," Bogner admitted. "We've got a list of just about everything Park shipped out of his three locations for the past three weeks. What we don't have in most cases is a good description of what he shipped."

Janus pushed the printout across the table to Packer. "We took each entry and broke them out by shipping direction, shipping location, section of the country, the buyer, where indicated, and which ones were shipped to transfer agents. Then we broke each of these categories down by whether or not they fell into one of the alphanumeric classifications as it relates to one of the five condition codes, A through E."

"Here's what we've come up with," Miller declared. Code A accounts for items sold 'as is' without any demiling requirements. Most of these are items sold to folks with clean skirts. We had Millie and Janus get on the phone to check these out whenever we thought we saw something. So far all the Code A shipments appear to be clean."

"Then we put the Code B items, the one where you have to have a license to ship them overseas, into the computer," Marks added. "Parks made two shipments in the last two weeks. The customs people and the shipping agents both claim they were in order."

Packer scanned the original printout. "If we're going to find anything, we'll probably find it in the 'Key Point Demil' classification. Did he ship anything in Code C?"

"How about some Maverick antitank missiles, a couple of Sidewinders, and a handful of 40mm grenade launchers?" Janus said.

Packer let out a whistle.

"Our friend Parks shipped four Mavericks, three Sidewinders, and no less then twenty 40mm grenade launchers out last week—all by rail, all to one purchaser, Estrada Electronics in Miami," Millie said. She leafed back through her notes until she found what she was looking for. "I called an old friend down in the Dade County Sheriff's Department and asked them to check out Estrada Electronics for us. They got back to us in less than thirty minutes. It turns out Estrada Electronics is a one-room office on Purcare Street with two telephones and a couple of fax machines—no other facilities—not even a warehouse."

"Which proves Estrada is nothing more than a shill, a front to move along the purchases to God knows who," Miller said.

"Wait a minute," Bogner said. "Estrada. That name rings a bell. Wasn't Gerardo Estrada tied in with Cabandra Marti?"

"Damn it," Miller said, "I knew I had heard that name Estrada somewhere. Cabandra Marti was the one that led that aborted attempt to blow up the desalination plant at Guantanamo in 1965 after Castro shut off the base's water supply."

"And," Millie added, "he was the one reported to be helping the Russians build a submarine base near Cienfuegos when we finally got the Russians to back off."

Packer leaned back in his chair. Bogner knew the old man was pleased—but a long way from satisfied. "All right, that tells us something," Packer said. "So far we've got a pretty good indication that Park's Company is selling some heavy Code C items to Estrada Electronics in Miami. And we know Estrada and Marti have connections. Reasonable assumption: Park's shipments are probably destined for Cuba. Then the question becomes: Are the Cubans selling them, using them, or acting as a front for someone?"

"Like Mao Quan?" Janus suggested.

"It's not out of the realm of feasibility," Miller assured him.

"Run over that list again, Mike," Packer said.

Janus repeated the contents of the shipment. "Four Maverick antitank missiles, three Sidewinders, and twenty 40mm grenade launchers accounts for most of it—but there were several crates identified only as 'excess or outdated weapons parts—grade 2-ms,' which in Pentagon parlance means strictly scrap."

"You buy that, T.C.?" Packer asked.

"I hate to bite the hand that feeds me," Bogner admitted, "but all of you remember that classic old apple story. The Air Force was shipping apples from a base in California destined for an Air Force base in Washington—only to have the crew that loaded that plane go down to the other end of the flight line and unload a shipment of apples from a base in Washington bound for the same base in California. Bottom line, it happens too often. The left hand doesn't know what the right hand is doing— especially at the Pentagon."

Janus was the only one who laughed. The others had all heard the story before. Even so, Bogner had made his point.

"So what's our next move?" Miller asked.

Packer began directing traffic. "Miller, you get hold of Baker or anyone that will cooperate over at CIA and get Marti's files updated. I want the whole shooting match, full dossier, a record of his comings and goings over the past two years, the latest photographs available."

"What about using Jude Parrish?" Miller suggested. "We wouldn't have to do any explaining. Baker might start asking questions. Lately he's been exhibiting that old territorial-prerogative syndrome. Maybe Jaffe doesn't like the way he's been cooperating with us without Jaffe's prior blessing."

"Good idea," Packer said. Then he turned to Bogner. "T.C., you know what to do. I need background info. Get in touch with Peter Langley. See if he can arrange for you to sit down with his father. It's been a while. As I recall, Loren Langley was a green-as-grass senator at the time, but he was involved in the senate hearings on that Russian sub base debacle in Cienfuegos. And while you're at it, see what he knows about Marti."

Miller was already on his feet, preparing to leave when Packer held up his hand.

"One more thing," the ISA chief said. "Just before I came in here, I got a call from Lucy Spitz. You'll be glad to know, she says that Lattimere is holding his own."

As Packer walked back into his office, the phone was ringing. "I was hoping I'd catch you," Ricozy growled. "I delivered a couple of Redskin tickets to your friend Lieutenant Roberts. While I was there I asked him for a peek at Shank's report. He gave me thirty seconds' worth. The guy that contacted the police and reported the incident is a rummy by the name of Jumanus Walker. I had one of my people locate him."

"Where is he?"

"He's taking a bath and puttin' on some new duds at the Clayton Motel on Livermore, second floor, Room 212. I think it's the first decent meal and bath he's had in a couple of months. At any rate, he's waiting for someone to contact him. I told him to stay sober and try to remember everything he saw, that someone would be coming to talk to him."

Packer scribbled down the address.

"Oh, and one other thing. I told him the guy that was coming to talk to him had a C note for him."

Packer hung up and looked up. Bogner was waiting. "Looks like you've got a full plate this evening, T.C. Check out this guy Jumanus Walker and then work on Langley."

Time 1713LT:

Forty-one year old Rita Stern turned off her workstation, cleared her desk, took out her purse, and applied her lipstick. It had been a long day, and at last it was over.

"Heavy date tonight?" Jacqueline Marceau asked, peering across the top of their cubicle.

"Yeah, right." Rita nodded and laughed. It was a sardonic laugh void of mirth. "No, I've got really big plans. First a stop at Feldman's supermarket. Big purchase of the day is some cat food—and, if I think I can afford it, maybe one of those imitation seafood salads." She put on her coat, took her keys out of her purse, and locked her desk. "Such is the fast-paced, thrill-a-minute lifestyle of a single girl in Washington, huh?"

"You could have more dates if you weren't so choosy," Jacqueline reminded her.

"No, thanks, I like my men single." Having said as much, she was hoping Jacqueline wouldn't start pressing again. She liked Jacqueline, and knew she was only trying to help, but on this particular day, she was tired and her cohort's small talk was more annoying than usual.

"We could stop and have a drink at Buster's," Jacqueline offered. "Dish the dirt, talk about men . . ."

Rita Stern declined, made certain she had everything, and started for the door. True, she had no plans for the evening, but even a hot bath sounded better than sitting around the table at Buster's talking about their jobs and men.

The last thing she heard Jacqueline ask was, "Are your parents still in Florida?"

"Yeah, I called them the other night. It looks like they'll be there till spring," she said over her shoulder. "One of these weekends I'm going to fly down and see them. When I do I'm going to spend three whole days laying on the beach soaking up the sun."

Jacqueline Marceau waited until the door closed and she heard the elevator. The smile had already faded. She walked to the telephone, picked up the receiver, and called the lobby. "She's on her way down. The coast is clear. The house will be empty."

* * *

By the time Rita Stern got to the lobby, she was already engrossed in her own thoughts. So much so, in fact, that she failed to notice the two young Chinese men standing by the newsstand. She went through the revolving door, stepped out into the chill and rain, glanced at her watch, and wondered if the metro was on time. She had just shoved her hands back in her pockets when she felt something hard pressed into the small of her back.

"Say nothing, move slowly," the voice said, "act as if nothing is wrong, and you will not be hurt." The words were hisses, sometimes indistinct, and barely audible. She felt one of the man take her arm, begin steering her toward the curb and a white Econoline Ford van. One man opened the door and the other pushed her in. There was no seat, just an empty cargo space, and she fell, skinning her knees and tearing her hose.

Too stunned at first to protest, she started to scream, but the same man who had pushed her jumped in behind her and clamped his hand over her mouth.

"No talk," he ordered, and pushed her back against the side wall of the van. The other man had already scampered around to the other side of the vehicle and crawled in behind the steering wheel. He put the key in the ignition, started the van, and edged his way into the stream of traffic.

"Now, Miss Stern," Liu said softly, "you may scream if you wish. But I assure you there is no one to hear you, nor is there anyone to come to your aid."

In the darkness, Rita Stern reached down and tested her knee. It was bloody. She winced. She felt the man take his hand away, but at the same time she saw the gun. It was pointed directly at her and he was smiling.

"L-ook," she stammered, "if it's money you want, you can have everything I've got." She tried to hand the man her purse, but he let it fall to the floor when she loosened her grip. "If if you don't want the money, what do you want?" she screeched.

Finally, he said, "You are about to become involved in a small intrigue. Tomorrow, when the newspapers you Americans cherish so highly hit the streets, your name along with others will be spread all over front page. You will be very famous. Do you like that idea, Miss Stern?"

Rita Stern found it impossible to answer. Her throat was dry and she was having trouble breathing. Instead she felt the van turn and slow for traffic. She saw the lights of the bridge in the distance and the red, garish, almost surreal passing of storefronts. Occasionally she would hear a horn honk, and there would be the sound of a car passing or the van would gain speed.

Eventually, the lights faded and the world beyond grew dark. When they passed an infrequent streetlight, the interior of the van was momentarily lighted and she could see the face of the man holding the gun on her. He was Asian; thin, exceptionally thin—almost to the point of being emaciated. There was no expression on his face, and he seemed not so much interested in her as much as he was in the task of keeping her at arm's length.

"Where—where are you taking me?" she finally demanded.

"You will see soon enough," Liu informed her.

Instead of lacing together some sort of coherent thought process, Rita Stern's mind was racing, tumbling over itself in fragments of anxious and chaotic fancy. What were they going to do? Where were they taking her? She felt herself sweating. She remembered that Oscar Jaffe had once applauded her resourcefulness with one of his sometimes clumsy, left-handed compliments. He had called her "street smart," and complimented her on her survival skills: social, financial, and otherwise. At the time she had thought his remark uncomplimentary and demeaning—but now, she actually was thinking survival. She was trying to be "street smart." Surely there was a way out, or was there? She told herself she could handle one of them—but not both. They didn't want money, that was obvious now. If they were going to assault her, wouldn't the one with the gun have already tried? She drew her knees up, wrapped her arms around them, and tried to regulate her breathing. The first thing she had to do was get hold of herself—think straight— plan. What did they want? Her captor seemed not at all inclined to talk to her other than to warn her.

For what seemed like long intervals, she closed her eyes—trying to shut out the reality—trying to form a plan. The initial anger had at first turned to fright, but now it had evolved into unmitigated terror.

The van coasted to a stop and she opened her eyes. It was a stoplight—the first in some time. When the light changed, the van eased ahead again. She remembered reading an article about a woman being kidnapped and how the woman kept track of time, constantly listening for clues and mentally making note of certain landmarks along the way. How did the woman do it? How did she keep her wits about her? Rita had already lost track of both direction and time. Worse, fear made everything a blur. She tried to concentrate on her breathing again. Her father had always warned her to be careful—she thought she had been.

Then the van slowed again and she saw more lights: neon, red, blinking on and off. The vehicle came to a stop and the driver turned off the ignition. She heard him open his door and his footsteps. Finally, the side cargo door opened and she saw that he too had a gun. Neither man spoke, but the one who had been riding in the cargo area with her used the barrel of his automatic to prod her toward the door. The rain pelted in and she felt the wind. Rita Stern was no longer just sweating. She was on the verge of hysteria.

Time 1803LT:

Jumanus Walker moved about the room with an unsteady gait, he trembled, and more often than not displayed a great deal of difficulty holding on to a thought. His skin was a dusky brown-black, and it was obvious the shoes Ricozy had bought him hurt his feet.

He looked at Bogner with evident distrust. "That big man"—Jamanus hesitated—"said—said you would have something for me."

Bogner threw a new pack of Marlboros on the bed, and watched the man tear the package open, take out a cigarette, and light it. His hands were shaking when he inhaled. The shaking had diminished somewhat by the time he exhaled. He worked up an expression of gratitude, coughed, and looked at Bogner.

"You—you the guy that the big man wanted me to talk to?"

Bogner nodded. "I'm the one."

"You a cop?"

"No." Bogner shook his head. "Not a cop. But like the big man told you, I'm going to ask you some questions."

Jamanus finished his cigarette and lit another. He used a match, and it was still lit when it hit the carpet. It went out without Jumanus paying any attention to it. "Is this about what I saw last night? 'Cause if it is, I already told the cops everythin' I know."

Bogner sat down across from the man. Jumanus was sitting on the edge of the bed, kicking off his new shoes. "Do you remember what happened last night?" Bogner pressed.

"You mean about what I saw?"

"About what you saw. Tell me everything."

Jumanus Walker preened as much as a man without teeth can preen; he suddenly appeared to be enjoying his newfound importance. Here he was, with clean clothes and a bath, and people with suits on, people who smelled good and talked like they had manners, were actually looking to him for information. It was something he hadn't experienced in a while.

"I ain't always been like this," Jumanus explained, "I used to be somebody. I was in the Army. I had two stripes. Then this bitch—"

"I'm told you were sleeping under a bridge over the Anacosta on River Road," Bogner reminded him, "and you saw something. I want you to tell me everything you saw."

"Don't—don't know what time it was for sure," Jumanus explained. "I usually don't sleep so good—lots of stuff wakes me up. Sometimes the rats gets to runnin' around, settin' up such a racket in all that junk layin' around down there, makes it hard for a fella to—to sleep."

"Go on," Bogner prodded.

"Well, I'm layin' there and I hear somethin'. It ain't the traffic on the bridge. It ain't none of the usual stuff—so I lay real still. I don't want none of them kids to find me—damn kids, they won't leave a body alone. Two years ago—"

Bogner tried to pull him back. "What did you see, Jumanus? That's all I'm interested in. What did you see? I'm not interested in anything else."

Jumanus squinted as though he was trying to peer back into a murky, uncertain darkness full of shadows. "There—there was a car—no—bigger than a car. I don't—I don't know for sure. . . ."

"You told the police you saw two men. . . ."

"That's it, two—two men. They was drivin' a truck—not a big truck—not a big truck. It—it was the kind—the kind that opens up—opens up in the back." Suddenly Jumanus began to cry. He ran the tip of his tongue over his lips and rubbed his eyes. "Gotta blow my nose," he said.

"Would it help if you had something to drink?"

Jumanus nodded. There was even a crooked smile. It was the most animation Bogner had seen him exhibit. "I need a drink," he admitted. "You got one?"

Bogner nodded, got up, went into the bathroom and got Jumanus a drink of water. When the old man saw what Bogner meant by a drink, he looked disappointed. He took several swallows, handed the glass back to Bogner, leaned forward with his elbows on his knees, and stared at the floor. For a moment or two, Bogner thought the old man was going to be sick. "Do you remember what the two men did?" Bogner pushed.

"They—they—they opened the door at the back of the truck. . . ."

"You mean a van, a cargo van of some sort?"

Jumanus looked at him. Bogner knew he was trying to think of a word. "A del-del-delivery truck—the kind with doors in—in the back . . ."

"Then what?"

"They—they pulled out these long—these long things. They wasn't—wasn't careful—just sorta threw 'em on the ground. Then—then they kicked 'em so they'd roll down the hill—down the hill into the river. All the time I was—was rubbin' my eyes on accounta I wanted to be sure—sure I was seein' what I was seein'. . . ."

"Could you hear what they were saying?"

"I could hear 'em, all right," Jumanus said. "They was a-jabberin' at each—sorta like they were congratulatin' each other. Don't know for sure what they was sayin', though; couldn't—couldn't understand them—they was speakin' foreign-like."

Bogner pushed himself back in the chair. "Good. Good. You're doing great, Jumanus. Is there anything else you can tell me?"

Jumanus squeezed his eyes shut again and shook his head. "Can't think of nothin'."

"Can you remember anything about the truck or van? The color, the way it sounded, anything?"

Jumanus shook his head and looked down at the floor again. "Nope," he finally said. "Too dark . . . 'cept maybe I should tell ya I saw one of them guys before. The big one—the big one, he's the one what run me out of the yard over at that scrap company—he caught me sleepin' in one of them wrecks they got—you know, the ones they got piled up back in that big—big fenced-in yard out behind."

"The Park Salvage Company over in the Baton district is just seven blocks from the bridge. Is that the one you're talking about?"

Jumanus had to think for a minute. "That's the one," he confirmed. "Damn shame too—a fella can get real cozy and keep real dry in the backseat of some of them cars." He searched Bogner's face for some indication that Bogner understood the magnitude of his problem—keeping warm and keeping dry. When he was satisfied that Bogner was with him, he reached for another cigarette. This time there was some force behind the way he exhaled. "Any—any of that help ya? Is that whatcha wanted to hear?"

Bogner smiled. "It helps, Jumanus," he said. "It helps more than you'll ever realize." He got up, walked over to the nightstand beside the bed, and dialed Miller's number.

Miller scooped it up on the first ring. When he heard Bogner's voice, he asked him how it went.

"Nailed it," Bogner said. He reached in his pocket and turned off the tiny voice recorder. "I've got the entire thing on tape. Now it's up to you. Get somebody over here and lets get our friend out of here. Put him someplace nice and dry—real dry. If it gets to the point where we can haul Park's ass into court on murder charges, we're going to want one very healthy Jumanus Walker on our side. His testimony won't hang Parks, but it sure as hell won't do him any good."

"I'll have Peters or Hatton over there in thirty minutes," Miller assured him. "Can you hang on that long?"

Bogner grunted and hung up the phone. By the time he had walked back over to where Walker was sitting, he had taken out his billfold and was handing the man a fresh new one-hundred-dollar bill.

Jumanus Walker's hand was shaking when he reached for it.

Time 2010LT:

In the two hours since Bogner had walked into Jumanus Walker's room at the Clayton Motel, he had conducted Walker's interrogation, contacted Miller to arrange for ISA to hide the old man, waited for a replacement, made two phone calls, one to Joy—she was on the air and not available— another to Peter Langley to confirm the meeting with his father, Senator Loren Langley, then raced across town, and arrived at the Union just in time to make their eight o'clock meeting.

Now, while the senator sampled his martini, a Rose Room Grill specialty, Peter and Bogner congratulated each other on pulling off the meeting on such short notice.

The senior Langley looked across the table at his son and smiled. "I have no doubt that your mother will be calling here in the next hour just to make certain I'm not sitting here sipping tonic with some office floozy," the senator joked. Then he looked at Bogner. "When I told her I was having dinner with Peter two nights in a row, she wanted to know what kind of clandestine things we were cooking up."

"I appreciate you taking the time to talk to us on such short notice, Senator," Bogner said. "As it turns out, Peter and I are working the same scenario."

The senator's son raised a glass in toast. "Looks like the ISA can't get along without me," Peter quipped.

"Fine organization," the senator confirmed. "Now, how can I be of service?"

Bogner took a sip of his scotch and water and set it down. "Bear with me, Senator. I'd like to play a little word association game with you. All I want you to do is rattle off the first thing that comes to mind. If we spark something, then I may ask you to come back and elaborate. Okay?"

Loren Langley nodded. "Sounds like an interesting way to spend the evening. Let's see what happens."

"Park Shin Ho?"

The senior Langley looked around the room before he answered. "Too many friends in high places—or would you rather I confined my response to one word? If so, the word 'disturbing' is as good as any."

"How about Cabandra Marti?"

"Give me a second," the senator pleaded. "I have to dredge back through nearly twenty-seven years of flotsam for that one." He repeated the name. "Cabandra Marti, huh? Well, the first thing I think of is the way that two-faced son of a bitch twisted our tail at the conference table when we were negotiating with the Russians on that damn sub base down in Cuba."

"What else?"

"He had a nickname, the Butcher of Bomentos, because he massacred a whole village said to be loyal to the cause of Fulgencio Baptista—and this was in 1961—two years after Castro took over. Marti was a young firebrand in those days—the son of some sugar baron—pumped full of the Communist doctrine. He could spew it out like venom. It was said he would step on anyone, anytime when it came to Party concerns."

"He has to be getting up in years by now," Peter ventured.

"You would think so, but that's not necessarily the case," the senator speculated. "I do remember that he was younger than Che Guevara—and Guevara was still a relatively young man when he died in a 1967 guerrilla operation in Bolivia."

"Let's try another one," Bogner said. "Cienfuegos?"

Langley smiled. "I was involved with that one. That's where they were going to build the Russian submarine base and that's where all the attention was focused . . . but they almost caught us with our pants down."

"What do you mean, Senator?"

"Cienfuegos is located on the southern coast of the island, on a natural harbor just west of the Sierra de Trinidad. But if you look approximately two hundred kilometers or so directly west, you'll see something called the Archipelago de Los Canarreos. The crown jewel of the area is a place called Isla de Pinos, or Isle of Pines. Roughly translated, the whole area is known as the Islands of the Canaries. In many ways it's a lot like our Keys."

"Go on."

"What we discovered," the senator said, "was that Cienguegos wasn't the only place the Russians were doing construction work. What we discovered was they were building a another facility south of Peninsula de Zapata; not as big, but nevertheless, a real go-to-hell sub base. We discovered it on satellite recon photos after the fact; 82.5 degrees west longitude, and 23.5 degrees north latitude. It's hard to forget that one—the committee really had egg on its face. In an area we figured was mostly shallows and reefs, we learned there were a couple of natural deep channels and plenty of places to hide a sub. We gave it a name but it was after the fact; we gave it a code name, *rojo aqujero*—the Red Hole."

"What came of it?"

"Nothing, that I know of," Langley admitted. "As far as our government was concerned the Russians packed their bags and walked away from both Cienfuego and *rojo aqujero* at the same time. From the satellite photos, we were able to determine that both efforts pretty well came to a halt after that."

Bogner settled back with a perplexed look on his face. He looked at the senator and then his son. "Suppose for a moment that you were Mao Quan and you wanted to set up a base of operations in this part of the world. Where would you set it up?"

"If they didn't have to do too much construction, Cuba would be a natural," the senator volunteered.

Peter thought for a moment. "That's right. Quan, or anyone else for that matter, could run a slick terrorist operation out of damned near any second-floor walk-up or old warehouse here or in Cuba."

"Peter's right," the senator said. "Most terrorists have it down to a science. All you have to do these days is mail a bomb in from anywhere—at any-time."

"I'll agree, up to a point," Bogner said. "If all I was going to do was plant a few plastic bombs, I could run it out of any basement or back-alley shop in the country—but this is Quan's show, and I know Quan; he thinks big. Remember, this is the same guy that had the Ukrainians shipping him missiles with Libyan bio-warheads on them, the same guy that planned the terrorist attacks on the Royal Opera House in London, and was singularly successful in getting a Russian SU-39 out of Russia right under Aprihnen's nose. My guess is he's thinking bigger than what we've already seen."

"So what you're saying is, you think Dunning, Swelling, and Spitz may just be foreplay to the main event?" Peter asked.

"I'd be willing to bet the farm on it," Bogner said.

"Then just exactly what is it you need from me, T.C.?" the senator asked.

"I need old photos," Bogner said, "satellite photos, recon photos, and copies of your files. We need photos of every damn nook and cranny in Cuba—especially the sites of those two partially constructed sub bases. Then I want to go over your files and compare them to what we have now. I want to make certain we haven't overlooked something. I'm playing a hunch, Senator. The fact that Cabandra Marti's name pops up on Park's shipping records makes me doubly suspicious. There isn't any reason to believe those shipments stopped in Miami."

"It'll be easy enough to get those old recon shots,"

Peter assured him. "A phone call to the right people in NI will get that accomplished."

"And I can round up copies of the hearing's files," the senator added. "How soon do you need them?"

"The sooner the better," Bogner said.

"Have someone stop by my office first thing tomorrow," the senator said. "They'll be ready."

Time 22:17LT:

Even though the doors were shut, the hangar was cold and drafty. Liu Shao could still feel the chill of the night wind, and he continued to shiver. The call from Park's office had not been expected, and in his haste, he had not dressed warmly enough. He had driven straight from the motel to the aging hangar to meet the man Park called Quinto.

The Armenian quickly paraded him through a maze of crates, barrels, and wooden containers to the far side of the hangar, rambling on as he went. "This is the one Park said I'm supposed to show you," Quinto said. "He said he thought this one would fill the bill. She's the same make and configuration as the ones most of the hospitals in the area are flying now. We stripped and upgraded two of 'em for a firm in New Jersey just two months ago. You're smart. It's a helluva lot cheaper to convert one of these babies than it is to buy a new one."

They came to a clearing in what Liu considered to be little more than organized clutter, and Liu frowned. He had expected something different. The helicopter was covered with dust, mud, and bird

149

droppings, with two canopies thrown over it; one covered the cockpit area, and the other covered the two engines and part of the rotor. Quinto was holding a piece of paper in his hand. "As I recall, we bought this for a firm in West Virginia, painted it, got her ready, and then they couldn't come up with the money." Then, as an afterthought, he added, "Sound as dollar, though, used in the Air Weather Service down in Florida." Finally Quinto asked, "What hospital are you with?"

"We are not a hospital," Liu said. "We have obtained a contract to provide emergency service for two small hospitals in Maryland."

The Armenian nodded. "By the way, Park says to tell you we'll need a couple of days to get it checked over and bring the maintenance records up to snuff. There's all kinds of regulations on how these things are supposed to be outfitted."

Liu knew it would only prolong the conversation if he admitted that he was already familiar with the aircraft. Quinto appeared to be the kind who could talk all night. Still, he knew questions were expected of him and he had rehearsed. He compared the craft to the one in the photograph. He was relieved to find that the aircraft looked like the ones in the pictures supplied by Jacqueline Marceau.

"It is still capable of performing as it was designed?" he asked cautiously.

"In her hey-day she could clip off one hundred sixty MPH plus, with a range of over four hundred miles."

"The craft is capable of that now?" Liu asked.

Quinto shrugged. "You've got the word of the Navy. We take the Navy's word and we show you the mission papers and maintenance logs. Park bought this little gem at a DRMO depot in Florida a little over three months ago, and his man flew her here. Like I said, she flies."

Liu circled the aircraft a second time. When Tonu Hon had given him the assignment, he'd realized how carefully he had been trained. The Kaman was identical to the one Mao had provided for his training. As he walked, he tried to picture where he would stow what was needed the night of the mission. "I will require an opportunity to familiarize myself with the aircraft," he said.

Quinto had seated himself on a nearby crate. He seemed not at all interested in encouraging Liu. If anything, he seemed impatient. "Park said you were in his office earlier today and that this is what you wanted. After you hand over the money, you can do anything you want with this little gem, for all I care. If you ain't gonna fly it, bring your man by. Won't take more than thirty minutes if your man knows what the hell he's doin'."

"I will conclude my arrangements with Mr. Park in the morning," Liu said. "How soon then will we be able to arrange a familiarization flight and delivery?"

Quinto grunted and spat. "Anytime you're ready. Like I said, you can do anything you want to once Park tells me it's a done deal."

Liu circled the craft a third time before Quinto escorted him back to the small office. Along the way, Liu took note of the man's inventory. There were two oversized crates housing GE T58-GE-8 engines, another containing a Ryan APN-130 Dopler unit, and an entire bay of homing torpedoes and depth bombs. He would, he decided, relay this information to Tonu Hon.

Moments later, as Liu stepped through the door and into the raw night air, he had shifted his thoughts to the more immediate task that lay ahead of him and all that would transpire in the next twelve hours. He pulled his coat collar tight around his neck, got into his van, and drove back to the motel.

Rita Stern drifted in an out of her nightmare world only half aware of what was happening around her. Despite the fact that her hands and legs were bound, she had been heavily sedated, and as a consequence she felt little, if any, discomfort. In her periods of awareness, she was vaguely conscious of one man and sometimes two. The one that she was aware of now was short, slight of stature, and engrossed in his task.

There was a small container on the adjacent bed and he seemed to be packing. For some reason she was conscious of the fact that he had changed clothes. Now he was wearing black—a black turtleneck sweater and black trousers. He seemed to be paying meticulous attention to a weapon of some sort; she would have called it a rifle or a shotgun. Rita Stern wasn't sure she knew the difference between the two.

On one occasion she had told him she was thirsty and asked for a drink of water. The man had laughed at her—and though he'd made no effort to get her a drink, she had drifted back into her dream world of half shapes and moving shadows. In that world, nothing was distinct and any anguish she felt when she was awake subsided. In that dream world there was only one problem; she had begun to identify a terrible pattern—a pattern that eventually vaulted her back into the reality of that dreary motel room and the realization that she was being held captive.

She awoke again when the door opened and closed. There was a rush of chilled air, and suddenly there were two men again. Their conversation was a tangle of gestures, hurried glances in her direction, muted sounds, and hushed whispers. There was a series of metallic clicking sounds and the smell of cigarette smoke. But even with their methodical, almost marionette-like movements, there was a distinct sense of urgency and schedule.

Finally she realized that one of the men was standing beside the bed looking down at her. She squinted, unable to make out any of the man's features. As he looked at her, he asked the other man a question. To her surprise, the second man answered in English. "I think she is beginning to come out of it," the man said. "The sedative appears to be wearing off."

Liu Shao's voice was only half intelligible as he bent over her. He grabbed her, jerked her into a sitting position, and pulled her legs around until she was sitting on the edge of the bed. When he finished, he stepped back and she felt as though she was going to be sick again. Her mouth was dry, her head was light, and she was convinced she would faint.

Finally Liu took out a knife and she watched through a haze as he cut the tape on her hands and ankles. When he did she felt the sudden rush of blood into her numbed hands and feet and there was a searing, burning sensation. "Everything is ready?" Liu asked.

The other man nodded. Rita Stern tried to remember if at any time prior to this she had actually understood anything they said. Was she too frightened? Too rattled? She couldn't be certain. She couldn't remember. She tried to think about that woman she had read about, the one who had been abducted. That woman remembered; she was even able to tell the police what kind of dialect her abductors had. Rita Stern knew now that she would not be able to give the authorities that kind of assistance—she knew only that her abductors were Oriental. They had not referred to each other by name. Their fragments of conversation had been minimal. For all she knew they could have been Chinese, Japanese, or even Korean.

"Stand up," Liu demanded.

She hesitated, and he grabbed her by the arm and pulled her to her feet. She was unsteady and there was a burning sensation in her feet and fingers.

"Stand," Liu repeated. She was aware now that he was holding a gun and that he was motioning her toward the door. She tried to take a step, wavered, grabbed for the nightstand to support herself, and struggled to remain standing.

"Give me a moment," she pleaded.

While Liu Shao continued to watch her, she was aware that the other man had taken the container from the bed and left the room. He returned moments later and indicated that everything was ready.

"Very good," Liu assessed. He lowered his voice. "And now, Miss Stern, whether you care to or not, you are about to become tomorrow morning's headline."

Chapter Six

3 Nov: Time 0117LT:

While Quin Lo Wan maneuvered the white van through the maze of narrow and ice-coated streets of the prestigious Oxon Hill section of Brighton Heights, Liu Shao accomplished the dual tasks of checking out the neighborhood and keeping an eye on the Stern woman. As always with Liu Shao, everything was accomplished according to a carefully executed plan. With Liu Shao, nothing was left to chance. If the first route of escape was blocked, Liu, because of his planning, could be certain there was an alternative.

Quin Lo Wan continued to drive, and Liu made doubly certain there were no impediments and no last-minute surprises. If Liu Shao prided himself on how carefully the plan was thought out, he was equally proud of his thoroughness in implementing the plan. He continually tried to anticipate where the plan could hit a snag—where something could go wrong. He checked and double-checked for unexpected street closings, street repairs, the timing of traffic signals, even the placement of stop signs.

Finally, after Quin had made three passes through the neighborhood, he was satisfied.

As Quin turned on to Lafford Street, one block east of Benton, he slowed. The steady drizzle, light most of the day, had turned to sleet as the temperature hovered near the freezing mark. Now the situation was compounded by the fact that the wind had diminished and an ice fog had begun to settle in. Instead of being alarmed at the change in the weather, Liu had decided the deteriorating weather conditions, such as they were, could work in his favor.

He had likewise noticed that at 201 Benton Place, only two cars remained from what had been the dinner party held earlier that evening—and even then, the lights in the vestibule of the Crane house revealed that the last of the Cranes' guests were about to depart.

Quin turned the corner and drove past the Crane home for the final time, and Liu motioned for him to turn north again.

"Turn here," he said. "You know where to park."

Quin Lo Wan pulled into the alley behind the house across the street from the Crane residence, and drove to the garage area behind a vacant house two houses east of the McMillans' two-story brick house. Then he turned the van around, backed it in to a narrow area between the garage and a sheltering stand of ice-crusted pines, got out, and covered the windshield with a piece of cardboard.

From there on, it was a routine that had been rehearsed repeatedly. The two men donned masks, and Quin slipped the rifle into a carrying case and grabbed the metal container. Liu shoved the Stern woman, now gagged, out of the van and prodded her ahead of them with the barrel of his Beretta. They used the shadows created by a series of security lamps to move quickly down the alley to the rear of the house across the street from the Cranes'. There they paused under the overhang at the rear of the garage just long enough for Liu to insure that they had not been noticed.

At the rear entrance, Liu instructed the woman to unlock the door. Rita Stern, with hands shaking and Liu Shao holding the Beretta to her head, complied. Ten seconds later they were inside and Rita Stern was in for a shock. The house was warm and there was a night-light burning in the kitchen; her parents had returned home unexpectedly. If they had tried to call her, she hadn't been home, and now the gag prevented her from calling out to warn them.

Quin Lo Wan froze, waiting for Liu Shao.

Liu was quick to size up the situation. He moved quietly up the hall, and looked into the first-floor bedroom. It had taken him less than ten seconds to formulate his plan. The Stern woman's parents were a retired couple in their mid-sixties. There were no domestics and no dog. It would still work. Disposing of the elderly couple would be both easy and necessary. Jacqueline Marceau, posing as a health-care investigator for an insurance company, had confirmed through a visiting nurse service that Rita Stern's father, because of a stroke, had a bad heart and had been confined to a wheelchair for the last three years. He had minimal use of his arms, had difficulty speaking, and was dependent upon his wife of nearly forty years for most of his needs. His wife depended heavily on her divorced daughter and a visiting nurse service to take care of her husband and the home.

Rita Stern was prodded upstairs, bound, gagged, and again sedated. Quin, following Liu's instructions, moved quickly from the kitchen down the hall to the couple's bedroom. He locked the silencer on the barrel of the Beretta, covered the woman's face with a pillow, reached under, buried the barrel against her head, and pulled the trigger. There was a muffled, momentary explosion, and then he moved to the other side of the bed. Roger McMillan was awake, unable to move, staring up at him. Quin clamped his hand over the man's mouth, jammed the barrel against the old man's temple, pulled the covers up around the weapon, and fired a second time. The entire episode had taken him less than thirty seconds.

In the meantime, Liu, checked out the rest of the house, returned to the kitchen, lit a cigarette, and rummaged around in the elderly couple's liquor cabinet for a suitable toast.

It was the sound of the two men moving furniture that pried Rita Stern out of her drugged lethargy into a state of semi-awareness. Awake for the first time in hours, she realized the passage of time had not altered the dream—the nightmare was continuing.

She remembered thinking, hoping—even praying—that when she awakened, the ordeal would be over. But there they were again—the same two men that she had been with in the motel room the night before—the same two men that had forced her into the van—and the same two men that had pushed her ahead of them down the darkened alley, forcing her to unlock the door. Now, as she lay there, she noticed something that she had never noticed before. The house that she had grown up in now smelled of mildew and medicine.

With the passing of time, her thoughts had finally become more organized and returned to her parents, when one of the men opened a window and she felt an icy blast of air. She shivered—or was she trembling? She could no longer tell the difference. She tried to order her thoughts again, struggling to return to a rational plane. Where was she? Yes—she was home—but what was happening? What would that abducted woman she had read so much about do now? Would she plead for her life? Would she cooperate with her captors? Would she stoically accept her fate? Her thoughts, disconnected, were

160

ricocheting, like a stone skipping across the surface of water.

Finally, she pulled herself together; she rationalized that it would be safer not to move, safer not to let her captors know that she was awake. But how long would she have to stay that way? She had lost all track of time. Beyond windows glazed with ice she saw a streetlight, and there was a pale, almost ethereal kind of light coming into the room. There was something familiar about it. That's it, she told herself, now she knew—she was in the bedroom on the second floor, the guest bedroom.

Now that she knew that much, she tried to think—to scheme—to figure a way out; but that seemed fruitless—her thoughts were disjointed, little more than a montage of chaos—little more than fragments of terror. Finally, she closed her eyes again, hoping the darkness would somehow bring the terror to an end.

Some inestimable time later she heard one of the men close the window and speak briefly to his colleague. That was followed by more commotion as they moved furniture again. Most of it was accomplished in silence, buy when they did speak it was clearly in a language she did not understand. She heard metallic sounds that she could not identify, followed by infrequent but excited exchanges between the two men where one word seemed to be attached to another. Ultimately it was all a series of unintelligible fragments amounting to little more than further confusion.

Finally, when she dared, she opened her eyes

again. The two men had moved out of the room and they were standing in the hallway. They were smoky images, propped with their backs against the wall, silhouetted against an overhead light, occasionally and nervously glancing at their watches.

Since she could make nothing of their infrequent fragments of conversation, the woman tried to concentrate on their actions. One, she decided, the one with the gun, seemed more excitable. He smoked more. He talked more. He moved like an agitated cat. The other seemed more contained, more aloof or perhaps the word was elusive—almost as if he wasn't really there.

Finally, one of them glanced at his watch, and she heard him say something she couldn't understand.

Both men smiled, and Rita Stern felt her eyes begin to close again. She was spiraling back into her world of escape.

Time 0611LT:

Gordon Hatton stood at the second-floor window of the lounge, staring out at the early morning traffic creeping down off of the ice-crusted interstate onto 14th Street. From his vantage point more than a block down the street, the intersection at M and 14th was pure ice. Cars were having a difficult time of it. Moments later he saw flashing yellow lights and a salt truck approaching from the south. There was a God, he decided, and what's more, there was hope he might make it home—especially if the day crew could make it in and he got lucky enough to find a route that had already been salted. Yes, sir, he decided, he just might make it home.

At this point, though, all he could realistically hope for was improvement—even a modest improvement. If the ice didn't turn back to rain by the time Ploughman and Miller made it in, Washington's morning rush-hour traffic would be a monumental snarl.

Hatton paused long enough to straighten his tie looking in the glass on the coffee machine, took one last look at the traffic, and started back to the situation room. He had long since decided that anyone born and raised in Florida as he was should, under no circumstances, be expected to drive on ice like these crazy Northerners.

He slipped his ID card into the S lock, waited for the scanner on the C-1 to read his thumb print, and opened the door. After a long night of virtually nothing to do for either of them, his colleague on the night shift, Kent Peters, was busy logging in a transmission.

"It's from NI," Peters said, glancing up. "They want an ID confirmation. They're ready to transmit some high-resolution Air-Obs photos. Source not identified."

Hatton slid into the chair behind the keyboard and typed out the call-up code. The letters JCALS appeared on the screen and demanded an access code. Hatton entered the ISA night watch pandect: Gh/45-45/3.

Hatton looked at Peters. "We're hooked in—it's coming in from Joint Continuous Acquisition and

Lifecycle Support's initiative. It might be the data Bogner said he had requested from Naval Intelligence."

Peters had already pulled up a chair next to the monitor.

The words *"image," "transmit,"* and *"downlink authorized"* blinked intermittently on the screen.

Hatton's code was requested for audit reverification, and he entered the Gh/45-45/3 a second time. The transmission appeared and Hatton leaned foreword in his chair.

> *NI-6678/234: 06:15LT-0915Z*
> *MSTI: Sequencing photoreconnaissance:*
> *Data bank: 4-06-34-55, a1 a2 a3 a4-file*
> *Profile reference;*
> *Data bank: 4-06-34-55, r1 r2 r3 r4-file*
> *File: KH-11 643-649-7854ab*

Coordinates began to appear. "What the hell are we looking at?" Peters asked.

"That, my boy, is Cuba. See the highlighted area in green? The square to the east is the location of the aborted Russian sub base in that inlet near Cienfuegos. I was here when that happened. The other one is on the western side of Isla de Pinos in Zapata Bay. Don't ask me why they're highlighting that."

"There doesn't appear to be anything there," Peters remarked.

"On the contrary, look at that cluster of red spots.

Those indicate heat-sensor activity—every damn one of them."

"What are they?"

"Who the hell knows," Hatton grunted. "One thing for certain. The early rf shots indicate there's nothing going on there up until the 05/ab image. We'll have to check back in our files. That would be early this spring, April maybe." Hatton compared the two photos. "Okay, now look at the 05/cd and 05/mn. We're getting something different—see the clusters? I don't know what, but they're sure as hell telling us something is going on—if for no other reason than they're giving us a different color; see how the color has intensified between cd and mn?"

Peters squinted at the first printout. "I still don't see what—"

Hatton leaned back in his chair. "That's the archipelagoes—the Canaries. If those were fishing boats, we'd ID 'em as such. My guess is those are Cuban gunboats. The question is, why are there so many of them and why are they deployed all through that particular region?"

Peters shook his head. "Hell, you're the expert."

"Under normal circumstances we would expect to find them on the north side of the island," Hatton said. "If they weren't there before—and they weren't according to the photos—how come they're so damn thick down there now?"

Kent Peters was still studying the screen when the transmission ended. Hatton logged in his code for a third time and confirmed reception. The authorization was being repeated on screen while Hatton studied the printed images.

"So what does it mean, Gordo?"

"That was Bogner's code," Hatton said. "Maybe he knows."

Time 0629LT:

As had become his custom of late, Senator Richard Crane finished his shower, shaved, and dressed without waking his wife, Lillian. Out of habit, he checked his answering machine, turned off the mute, listened to the two messages, neither of which he determined would impact his day, and went downstairs.

The Cranes' housekeeper of seven years, Miranda, had awakened early and was busy cleaning up after the previous evening's dinner party. Crane had developed a fondness for the forty-seven-year-old woman who always greeted him with a smile and handed him the morning newspaper.

Miranda Jose reciprocated those feelings. Unlike her former employer, Senator Hastings Avery, her present employer was usually cheerful and not nearly as formal or demanding. Richard Crane, unlike Avery, who expected a full-blown breakfast served in the Avery dining room, wanted little more than what he called "quiet time" to skim over the morning paper, sip his coffee, and drink a glass of juice.

During the last seven years the routine had become a ritual. "A breakfast meeting this morning?"

she would ask. The senator would nod and she would usually inform him about the weather. "The streets are very bad this morning—very icy. Your car may be late."

Crane glanced at his watch, nodded, and took a sip of coffee. As they did almost every morning in this quiet time, his thoughts turned to Julie Simon. He wished there was a way he could warn her about the icy streets. Lillian, still asleep, wouldn't know— but Miranda would even if she pretended not to be listening. It was a risk he dared not take. He would call Julie, of course, either from his car or as soon as he got into his office. She would be expecting his call.

"So what's the news this morning?" Crane asked. It was his way of teasing her. Miranda usually had a juicy tidbit of neighborhood gossip, and more often than not, she was eager to share what she knew.

"The Fremonts are selling their house," Miranda said. "I talked to their maid. She says they're moving back to Georgia."

"Nice people," Crane muttered, "hate to see them go." An observation of some kind was appropriate, but he had quickly decided that if that was the best Miranda could come up with on this icy morning, the neighborhood scuttlebutt was a little on the thin side.

Miranda glanced up at the clock as she poured him another cup of coffee. "Your car will be here in fifteen minutes," she reminded him.

*   *   *

Liu Shao had nodded off momentarily, but he came out of it when he heard Quin Lo Wan stirring. Quin had slept earlier, and now, still in the darkness of the upstairs bedroom, Liu could hear Quin checking the clip in the .308 Steyer SSG and shouldering it. "The woman," Liu whispered, "you have checked on her lately?"

Quin nodded. "She is awake."

"Get her up," Liu ordered.

Quin Lo Wan laid the rifle across the foot of the bed, shook the woman, and pulled her up on the side of the bed. Her hands were still tied and she was still groggy.

Liu looked at her. He spoke in a hollow monotone. "I would assume there is no need for me to inquire if you are familiar with the one known as Senator Crane," he said. "After all, you lived across the street from him for years. Perhaps even, your paths have crossed at one time or another—not so?"

Quin took the gag out of her mouth, but she refused to answer.

"He is, I am told, a rather superficial man, but that is neither here nor there. And since there is nothing particularly noteworthy about the Senator, it is debatable whether even those who will appear to mourn for him will be sincere in their gesture."

Rita Stern's brief struggle ended when Quin spun her around and pushed her back down on the bed again. This time she fell on her back. "Stay," he ordered, as though he were commanding a dog.

For the briefest of intervals she thought about

Crane. She had heard the rumors—mostly from Jacqueline Marceau; rumors about an affair between Crane and a woman Marceau had introduced him to. The thought was transitory, and she turned her head to watch Liu as he opened the window again. Instantly she could feel the fresh blast of frigid air. The tranquilizer had started to wear off, and she was beginning again to give order to her thoughts.

For hours now she had been drifting in and out of her nightmare. There were brief glimpses of reality interwoven in a fabric of amorphous images. But the reality was brief. In truth, she knew nothing more than she did when the ghastly episode began. There were questions, dozen of them—half formed—but the words were trapped in her throat, muffled before they could escape.

She watched the one who appeared to be the younger of the two men, the one who seldom spoke, lift the rifle, check the clip, and position himself next to the open window. She could tell there was some kind of sighting device on the weapon, but she knew nothing about such things. He brought it up to his eye several times, and appeared to be adjusting something. When he wasn't sighting it, he polished the weapon constantly—rubbing a cloth over and over the same area. It was almost as if he was caressing it. She hated herself for not knowing the words—for not being able to describe what was happening. The authorities, when the marathon nightmare was over, would want to know and she wondered if she would be able to tell them.

She had just closed her eyes again when she felt herself being jerked into a sitting position and the one she now knew as Liu began unbuttoning her blouse. He held her with one hand, wrapped two wires around her chest, and concealed them by tugging the bottom of her bra down over the wires. Then he shoved her back on the bed and inserted the ends of the wires into a tiny black metal box about the size of a film cartridge. She tried in vain to twist away from her captor, but the pointless struggle ended when Liu brought his open hand crashing down across her face. The blow momentarily stunned her and dislodged the gag. She tried to scream, but Liu was too quick. He stuffed the rag back in her mouth and the cry for help never materialized.

Richard Crane checked his watch and shoved the remains of his second cup of coffee back across the table as he stood up. "It's time to pay the devil his due," he announced. Miranda smiled and handed him the Thermos of coffee, and he started toward the closet in the hall to pick up his coat and hat.

"Will the senator be here for dinner tonight?" Miranda asked. "Mrs. Crane won't be home. She is attending. . . ."

Crane slipped into his coat. He really didn't care where his wife would be. But if she wasn't going to be home, it might be an opportunity to see Julie. "Chances are I won't be early enough for dinner," he said.

* * *

Frank Will prided himself on the fact that in the twenty-one years he had been a driver for Capitol Limousine Services, he had never been late or missed a pickup. But the icy streets as he pulled into the Oxon Hills section on this particular morning were putting that record in jeopardy. He slowed the Lincoln as he prepared to make the right turn onto Benton Place, and edged the big car over to the curb. He gave a sigh of relief when he realized that the porch light at the senator's house was still not on. He reached for his hat and started to get out of the car when the light came on.

For Frank Will, the thought of getting out of a warm car and standing in the icy rain to hold the door for the senator wasn't all that appealing; he had been nursing a cold, and this wasn't going to help. But he could see the senator in the vestibule, so he walked around, opened the door, and waited.

In the darkness of the upstairs bedroom, illuminated only by the streetlight on the corner, Liu Shao watched Quin Lo Wan wipe his fingerprints off the rifle one last time, don the thin goatskin gloves, and inch the barrel of the rifle through the open window. Across the street, Quin could see the car edge carefully to the curb and the driver open the door. The driver was bundled against the rain and cold. A porch light came on at the Crane house, and he saw two figures talking just inside the front door.

Finally, Crane opened the door and stepped out on the porch.

Quin adjusted his position, somehow finding a way to inch closer to the window, and sighted. Liu estimated the distance at no more than forty yards—if that.

The Stern woman was fretting again, and Liu looked down, momentarily distracted. Quin inched forward again—holding his breath.

Then, as Richard Crane started down the steps, Quin Lo Wan squeezed off the three carefully planned rounds. The result was three rapid-fire, whip-like explosions—followed by the predictable eerieness that pays allegiance to shattered solitude. The icy silence returned.

Liu watched as Crane's body pitched backward, slammed against the single porch pillar, twisted, and plummeted down the steps toward the sidewalk. The body lay motionless.

Liu knew they did not have the luxury of assessing Quin's marksmanship for any length of time. Nevertheless, he waited until he was certain. When he was satisfied, he reached down, took out the woman's gag, pried her mouth open, and poured her mouth full of tranquilizers. As a final gesture, he knotted a small wire into the edge of the blanket, activated the small sensor on the metal box strapped to Rita Stern's chest, and threw a blanket over her.

Within moments after the shooting, the two men had made their way down to the first floor, escaped through the back door, and raced to the van. While Quin peeled the ice-coated cardboard off of the front window, Liu started the engine.

Several minutes later, by the time Liu Shao heard the first indication of sirens, they had managed to get more than a mile from the Crane home.

Time 0737LT:

Homicide Detective William Andrews had commented to one of his colleagues earlier that morning that the ice storm could be a blessing in disguise. "It keeps the crazies off the street," he remembered saying. Now he was thinking how wrong he had been. The night had been slow enough that he had been able to finish up a backlog of paperwork, and he could now say that his desk was cleaner than it had been in months. He had even signed out thirty minutes early.

So much for a long night and a clean desk, he thought; the dispatcher's call had come through when he was less than eight blocks from home.

Now, twenty minutes later, he was edging his car in between two patrol cars and stealing a glance at an ugly montage of garish red-blue-yellow lights and men milling around a crime scene. It was a scene he had seen all too often.

He sat in his cruiser for several moments, finishing his coffee and wadding up the paper cup, before crawling out of his car.

Forty-nine-year-old William Jefferson Andrews already knew this wouldn't be just another case and it wouldn't be just another day. The dispatcher had been filling him in as he drove to the scene. This time the victim wasn't some pusher or back-alley nobody with no name. This one was a big shooter. In Washington, senators came under the heading of big shooters. Everyone from the commissioner on down would have their fingers in this one.

The victim's name was Richard Crane. Crane was the senior senator from Iowa. Andrews, born and raised in Washington, would have been embarrassed if he thought about it, but he would have had to admit he wasn't even certain he knew exactly where Iowa was—except to say it was somewhere out there in those farm states that from 22,000 feet up in the air all looked the same. It was a thought that occurred to him every time he flew over them on his way to see his sister in California.

He tiptoed his way over the ice to a group of uniformed officers waiting while two other men examined the scene. "What happened?" he asked.

"The housekeeper claims he just stepped out on the porch and whammo, three shots," one of the officers volunteered.

Andrews nodded, shouldered his way past the three men, stopped long enough to lift the blanket that had been thrown over Crane's body and study the body momentarily, and proceeded up the steps to the porch where two other detectives were questioning two women. Both women were in tears, the blonde slightly less than the woman wearing a uniform. They were introduced as Lillian Crane, Crane's wife, and Miranda Jose, Crane's housekeeper. Andrews recognized Lillian Crane from her television talk show.

He waited several minutes, apologized, and

pulled one of the detectives aside. "What have we got?"

The detective checked his notes. "At the moment, nothing more than a bunch of bits and scraps. The housekeeper claims that Crane stepped out on the porch and she heard shots. When she looked out, Crane was lying on the sidewalk. She's the one that called. Mrs. Crane was still asleep when it happened."

Andrews walked to the edge of the porch and looked at the crowd of people milling about. The temperature had gone up a couple of degrees and the sleet had turned to a steady drizzle. One radio station had already arrived, and a television crew was setting up.

"Any idea who fired the shots or where they came from?"

The detective shook his head. "One thing for certain, it wasn't a drive-by. Whoever did this one knew exactly what they were doing. Three shots, all clustered in a six-inch area. Any one of them did the dirty work. Probably the first one. My guess is Crane never knew what hit him."

Andrews backed away from the edge of the porch out of the dampness and studied the area. "Do we have a good fix on the time?"

"Close to it. That guy down there in the chauffeur's uniform is the limo driver that was supposed to pick him up. He said he was scheduled to pick the senator up at six-forty-five. He claims he was on time, and the housekeeper corroborated his story. We talked to the driver as soon as we got here, but he was pretty shook. He did tell us he thinks the shots came from somewhere behind him."

"Where was he when the shooting occurred?"

"He showed us where he was standing: car door open, with his back to the car, facing the Crane house."

"That means the shots could have come from across the street," Andrews said.

The officer nodded. "I had one of my men go over there. He says the ground all around the front of the house is covered with ice, no sign of tracks. According to the Cranes' housekeeper, an old couple"—the detective checked his notes—"by the name of Roger and Florence McMillan live there. But the house is closed up; she says they're in Florida."

"Have you had your men check the house?"

"Like I said, it's locked up tighter than a drum."

Andrews looked up and down the street. "What about these cars?"

"If any of them have been moved, they moved between the time of the shooting and the time we got here. I had Phillips close off the street at both ends of the block. Nothing has moved since. The only thing that's different is the patrol cars and the media people."

Andrews lit a cigarette and walked back down the steps to where the limo driver was standing. By the time he got to the curb, the drizzle had put out the cigarette and he threw it away. Andrews introduced himself and began asking questions.

Frank Will was more nervous than cold. He shivered and kept his hands in his pockets. "Hey, I told the other officer everything I—"

Andrews held up his hand. "Relax. Detective Henderson said you thought the shots came from behind you."

"Hey—I don't think they did, I know they did. Senator Crane was coming down them steps and all of a sudden his body goes backward—and I mean like something slammed into him. Whatever hit him was pretty damn strong. I was in Nam and I saw men get hit by a slug. This wasn't anything like that. Whatever this cat was usin', it was a helluva lot more powerful."

"How many shots were there?"

"Three. Ain't no mistakin' that. There was three of them—sorta like a burp gun."

"An Uzi maybe?" Andrews kept testing the water. Did the limo driver know what he was talking about?

"Naw, this wasn't no Uzi. No one I know can squeeze off just three shots on an Uzi—and I heard three distinct shots—but all together, like bambambam, with no space in between."

"And you say the shots came from behind you?"

This time Frank Will nodded.

William Andrews walked out into the middle of the street and looked back at the Crane house. There was a thin crust of ice on everything: the street, the curb, the grass between the walk and the street, the sidewalk, the McMillans' steps, and the porch. He lit another cigarette. This time he kept it cupped in his hand. He signaled for Henderson to follow him, crossed the street between the two houses, and trudged around to the rear of the Mc-Millan place. Henderson was right—nothing. Nothing, that is, until he tried the rear door; a twist of the knob and he was in.

It took him less than five minutes to sift through the downstairs. He found the bodies in the first-floor bedroom, and returned to the kitchen. Henderson was just coming up the back steps. "Look's like Crane's housekeeper was wrong. Check the first-floor bedroom."

Henderson brushed past him and started up the hall.

In the semidarkness, Andrews fumbled his way up the stairs to the second level. From the landing at the top of the stairs he could see into three of the five rooms: a sewing room and two bedrooms. One of the closed doors led to a bath, while the third led to a room at the front of the house.

He tried the door and it opened. The room was cold and, unlike the rest of the rooms where everything was carefully in place, this one was cluttered. The floor was littered with cigarette butts, and the furniture had been moved around. Even more important, there were still what Andrews called *vibrations*. This was it—where it happened; after twenty-two years in homicide, he could smell it, feel it, and taste it. What had at first appeared as though it might be difficult case, a drive-by shooting, now looked like a careful setup. Crane's killer had left a trail a mile long and a mile wide. He kicked a pile of covers aside and there it was—the rifle—lying on the floor beside the bed along with three spent cartridges. He made note of the fact that there was still moisture on the inside windowsill. He tried the window. It was not completely closed, nor was it locked. It was almost as if the assassin had intended to leave a trail.

The detective bent down and peered out the second-story window at the front of the Crane house. Whoever shot Crane, he decided, had the ideal setup—the angle was perfect. The plan had worked about as well as could be expected.

William Andrews slumped down on the edge of the bed. Only then did he hear the muffled sounds coming from the tangle of blankets. He reached over, grabbed the corner of the blanket, and started to peel it back.

The explosion shattered windows in houses two blocks away.

NBS . . . 0813LT broadcast
Newsbreak . . .
Dateline: Washington: BULLETIN (alert network stations)

> *This just in from* Dateline *news and the NBS news center.*
>
> *Police have cordoned off a seven-square-block area of the Oxon Hills area in Doran Springs, Maryland, this morning after an explosion in a home at Benton Place. Police report there are casualties.*
>
> *The explosion occurred at 7:48 a.m. The site of the blast was directly across the street from where police are conducting an investigation into the fatal shooting earlier*

this morning of Iowa Senator Richard Crane.
No further details are available at this time.

Stay tuned to WNBS for late-breaking news twenty-four hours a day. WNBS is your news leader in the nation's capital.

Chapter Seven

Time 0837LT:

The ice fog had begun to settle in, and Patrol Officer Gerald Mayer was less than two hundred yards away when he spotted a man standing beside his car, waving frantically. Mayer radioed his location to control and informed his dispatcher he was stopping to assist a motorist.

"Down there, Officer, down there," the man screamed as Mayer opened his door. "The driver lost it. The people are still in it."

Mayer crawled out of his patrol car and peered down into the twenty-foot-deep drainage ditch. A white Ford van with the engine still running was lying on its side. "Did you see it happen?" he shouted as he started to work his way down the embankment.

The motorist was trying to keep up with him, scrambling through the weeds, slipping every few feet. "Yeah," the man panted. "The damn fool tried—tried to pass me coming down off—the ramp. He—he was going—too fast. I knew—he wouldn't make it—then he lost it. I know it rolled once—maybe twice."

Mayer slid the last few feet, but finally regained his footing. The man was right. The van had rolled over and was lying on its side. The engine was still running when Mayer shimmied up over the undercarriage and peered in. Both the driver and his passenger were cut and bleeding. The driver appeared to be conscious but dazed. His passenger wasn't as lucky. Mayer could hear the man gasping for air, but his head was twisted grotesquely to one side and he was vomiting blood.

"Can you hear me?" Mayer shouted. The driver, an Asian, was moving, and when Mayer shouted a second time, he managed a nod.

"Can you move? Can you reach the ignition?"

The driver shook his head.

Mayer reached through the broken window in the driver's door, managed to roll down what was left of it, and was able to get a grip on the driver's arm. "How bad are you hurt?" Mayer asked. "Think you can crawl out?"

The driver nodded, reached for the steering wheel with one arm to brace himself, winced, and hesitated. The other arm was hanging limp. He managed to prop one leg against the passenger seat, and started to crawl out.

Mayer knew it was a gamble. The van, with the engine running, could erupt in flames at any minute. Still, he reached in, grabbed the driver under the arms, and lifted.

Liu Shao's face was covered with blood from a deep gash over his left eye, and he was still partially stunned. Nevertheless, with Mayer's help, he was able to inch his way along and crawl out of the window until he could pull his legs through.

"You," Mayer shouted at the motorist who had stopped him. "Get back up to the road and stop someone. Tell them an officer needs assistance. I got the driver out, but the other one is bleeding badly."

With the driver out of the way, Mayer was able to work his way back into the driver's area, reach around under the steering wheel, and shut off the ignition. Then he reached down, captured Quin Lo Wan's wrist, and tried to get a pulse.

Liu, no longer dazed, watched the motorist claw his way back up the icy hill toward the road, waiting until he had made it to the top before he crawled back up on the side of the van. By then, Mayer had managed to worm his way halfway into the driver's compartment, still trying to get a response from Quin Lo Wan.

Liu Shao didn't hesitate. He slipped the .45 out of his pocket, released the safety, reached over the officer's shoulder, inched the barrel under the officer's collar, buried the barrel at the base of Mayer's head, and squeezed the trigger. At that range, Mayer's protest was nothing more than a brief convulsion. His body went limp.

Without hesitating, Liu reached down, grabbed the dead officer by the hair, and pulled his head out of the way. Then, with the same deadly efficiency, he fired two more shots into Quin Lo Wan's already bleeding temple. This time there was an instantaneous paroxysm of flesh and bone shards that gave Liu Shao no alternative but to close his eyes. It did not matter. Liu Shao had seen men die before. He did not have to see the devastation to know what had occurred; he could feel it.

With typical methodical implacability and unhurried efficiency, he reached into his coat pocket, took out his handkerchief, and began wiping off the .45. When he was satisfied the job was complete, he crawled down from the overturned van, put the automatic back in his pocket, and climbed the hill.

The motorist who had stopped Mayer was two hundred yards up the road on the crest of the hill, still trying to stop traffic, when Liu Shao crawled into the man's car and drove off. He had already formulated his plan. He would leave the car in the parking lot at a shopping mall less than two blocks from the motel. If he used the alley, he could make it. He was confident it would be hours before the police located it.

Time 1030LT:

By the time the meeting at A1-RT was scheduled, Clancy Packer had already marshaled his troops through one briefing during which Miller and Peter Langley had conducted an assessment of the satellite photos received from MSTI early that morning.

It was the police discovery of the wrecked van in a ravine off of the Ross Road intersection that carried them into the second session at the briefing center in the NI wing at the Pentagon. This one was Chet Hurley's meeting. With Lattimere Spitz only just off the critical list, Colchin had turned the matter over to his other senior aide.

When Bogner entered the room, it was already crowded. Of the twenty or so people in the room, he recognized only a handful: two from the FBI, Jude Parrish from The Coast Guard, Tom Clevenger from the Secret Service, and the other members of the ISA contingent. He took a seat next to a slim, slightly angular woman wearing a CIA ID. Her name was Jacqueline Marceau, and her ID bore the title "Asian Expert—Language Specialist." Bogner nodded, but the woman ignored him.

"All right," Hurley began. "It looks like everyone's here, so let's get started. We've got a lot of ground to cover and not much time to cover it.

"You're all here, of course, because of developments in the last forty-eight hours. In that time the situation has seriously escalated, and the President wants action.

"I talked to President Colchin less than an hour ago, and he has asked me to impress upon you that this is no time for inter-agency territorial squabbling. He wants your full cooperation, and he has instructed me to inform you that he has put Clancy Packer of the ISA in charge. Each of you in this room will report through your section head to Packer until this situation is resolved. Is that clear?

"Now to get us started, I've asked Clancy to bring us up to speed on what his people have come up with so far."

Bogner watched his longtime friend and bureau chief put on his glasses, stand up, and walk to the lectern at the end of the table. This time there was no pipe and no sign of the usual irascible smile. Richard Crane had been a friend of his.

"As Chet indicated, an already critical situation has become even more so in the last forty-eight hours—but if there is an upside to this unfortunate situation we find ourselves in, it is that we know a whole lot more about what's going on than we did two days ago. However, before I get into that, let me bring those of you who have just been called in to this briefing up to speed.

"As most of you know, it was less than two weeks ago when Secretary of the Air Force James Dunning's plane crashed on final approach to the U.S. Space Surveillance Station east of San Diego. And it was less than sixty hours ago that Undersecretary of State William Swelling's plane exploded off the coast of Florida near Cape Sable. Whatever we may have thought the cause of these two misfortunes were at the time, we are now reasonably certain that both incidents are the result of carefully planned and executed 5A terrorist activity.

"While I feel certain most of you are familiar with

5A, some of you may need a brief refresher course. The Fifth Academy is a highly volatile and decidedly dissident faction of the Chinese People's Army headed up by an Army colonel, Mao Quan. We have been following Mao's activities for some time now.

"Mao is at odds with Premiere Qian's Beijing regime and Qian's efforts to establish closer diplomatic and economic ties to the Western world. Bottom line on Colonel Mao is, he is an isolationist, a pure Party hard-liner—and he wants no part of us, our democratic form of government, or our allies."

"Do we know for a fact that 5A is behind the two crashes, Pack?" The question came from the far end of the table.

"Sometime ago we were tipped off by our contact in Hainan that we could anticipate an escalation of 5A activity. Based on that tip, the CIA assigned one of their agents, a man by the name of Robert Worling, to look into the report. And as most of you know, Agent Worling was shot and killed after drafting his preliminary report the night of the thirty-first. Unfortunately, 5A now knows what we know—and that gives them the opportunity to either change their plans or step up their activity. From what we've seen in the last two days, the latter seems to be the case.

"We now know that their attempt on the life of Lattimere Spitz shows just how close they can get to some very key people."

Packer paused just long enough to rummage through his briefcase for another document.

"What we've seen so far is the kind of terrorist activity we are all familiar with. A terrorist operation of this kind can be run out of any back-alley garage or one-room walk-up anywhere they choose to set up. At the same time we are also aware that Colonel Mao, in the past at least, has been given to somewhat more flamboyant tactics than 5A has exhibited so far. Over the years he has demonstrated that he likes to operates on a decidedly bigger stage and do a little tail-twisting in the process. You will recall that two years ago he was instrumental in stealing that SU-39 right out from under the noses of the Russian military. Last year he attempted to purchase some surplus Russian missiles from the Ukraine and tie them to bio-warheads built in the Middle East. We were successful in aborting both efforts—but I can assure you, it was pretty dicey for awhile. That slowed him down. But now he's back.

"Our best thinking now is that what we've seen so far is only the tip of the iceberg. In other words, Dunning, Swelling, Worling, Spitz, and the attack this morning on Senator Crane is just the beginning. All signs point to more of the same and in all probability, if possible, something a whole lot bigger."

This time Packer took a sip of water when he paused.

"In the meantime, we've been trying to do our homework. We have ascertained that one of the largest arms dealers on the East Coast, a man by the name of Park Shin Ho, has been making sizable shipments of some supposedly demiled military equipment purchased through the DRMO to a location in Miami. We have since learned that those shipments are being rerouted from the original manifest destination in Spain to an as-yet-unidentified location in Cuba. But I can tell you that the name Cabandra Marti has popped up several times in our investigations.

"As recently as three hours ago we began to assess MSTI photo-reconnaissance shots taken over the archipelagoes between the Zapata Peninsula and the Isle of Pines at the southwestern end of Cuba. While we don't have anything to hang our hat on at this moment, we have reason to suspect that there is some as-yet-unidentified activity in what has heretofore been an area of little concern. In view of this, we have been in touch with MSTI to see if we can come up with something more definitive. If we learn anything, we'll keep you posted."

Packer picked up his papers, sat down, and nodded at Hurley. The President's aide stood up, cleared his throat, looked around the room, and frowned. "This is your chance. Are there any questions?"

Bogner looked at Miller. He remembered the first time he had attended one of these briefings as a scrub-faced young officer recently assigned to the ISA. That first time he hadn't known what to expect—this time he did. Miller would be the one to tap the resource people, like the Marceau woman sitting beside him, if and when they were needed. Clancy Packer, on the other hand, was a man who relied heavily on instinct—a lone wolf and a strong believer in keeping his operations lean and taut. It was the first commandment, Packer liked to say, of the control freak.

The room was still clearing when Hurley motioned for Packer and Bogner to follow him.

Hurley ushered them into a small room off the briefing room. It was dominated by an Oriental rug and a scarred oak desk. With three lounge chairs, it was anything but military. The man waiting for them was barrel-chested and smoking a cigar.

"Gentlemen," Hurley said, "this is Police Lieutenant Sam Churchill. Sam has the somewhat delicate job of keeping the White House informed in matters that fall outside the realm of official city-federal government liaison. He's a master at walking on eggs."

Bogner watched the man get up out of the chair. He moved and looked more like a bear than a man, and was, in all likelihood, just about as strong. Churchill stuck out his hand and repeated their names. He communicated in a series of wheezes and grunts.

"I've asked Sam to bring us up to speed on the Crane shooting earlier this morning," Hurley said.

If Churchill needed any prompts, Bogner couldn't tell. He squatted down with half of his weight on the arm of the chair. "At 0837 this morning, one of our patrol officers stopped to assist a motorist at the Ross Road interchange. The motorist informed him that he had seen a van slide off the road down into the Ross Road drainage ditch.

"The officer investigated, and based on what the motorist tells us, the officer assessed the situation and instructed the motorist to flag down passing traffic to call for assistance.

"Our dispatcher logged that call-in at 0846. We dispatched one patrol unit and a Medic 1 unit. By the time they got there at 0854, the motorist informed us a man who the motorist believes may have been one of the occupants of the van had managed to crawl up the hill and drive away in his car. The responding units reported that they found the body of the officer wedged in the driver's seat of the van. He had been shot in the back of the head. They also discovered the body of a young Asian male who was, we believe, a passenger in the van. He had been shot twice. Both shots were to the temporal region at close range."

Bogner leaned against the desk. "And you think this is somehow related to the Crane shooting?"

Churchill puffed on his cigar. "Can't say for certain at this point, but we think there is a strong probability. We're working on two angles. First, the Oxon Hill's community employs one of those private security firms to patrol their area, and at 0413 this morning, one of their patrols reported a Ford van parked at 209 Benton Place. It was parked in the alley behind the house. The security patrol wasn't overly alarmed because they said neighbors had been using the area to park their overflow for quite some time. The house at 209 is empty and listed with one of the local realtors.

"Nevertheless, the security people took down the license plate, and they checked it out to see if the plate was registered to anyone in the neighborhood."

"Was it?" Packer asked.

Churchill shook his head. "No, the plate was stolen. But here's your kicker. That was the same van in which the officer was shot."

"Were you able to ID the passenger?" Bogner asked.

"No wallet, no papers, no nothing . . . except for a pack of cigarettes and a book of matches. The cigarettes carry a Maryland tax stamp, and the matches come from a place called the Kopich Motel on Elizabeth Street. We're in the process of checking that out now."

"Anything else?" Bogner asked.

Churchill reached in his battered briefcase and pulled out a .45 automatic. "This," he said. "We found this. It was in a carrying bag in the van along with three ammo clips. It was packed in an old World War II kerealene bag. It was military issue and apparently never used, according to our ballistic experts. They tell me this is the way these little gems were shipped from the manufacturer. We're attempting to put a trace on it, but it's a long shot at best."

"Who would have something like this?" Bogner asked.

Churchill shrugged. "A collector maybe. Nothing sophisticated or out of the ordinary about it. For all we know, it may have been lying around some old arms depot or armory and someone just picked it up."

Packer picked up the kerealene bag and held it up to the light. He remembered qualifying with a weapon similar to it in OCS. "This thing would put a hell of a hole in someone," he said.

Churchill grunted. "That's why we think we're on to something. Whoever killed the officer and that young man in the passenger seat did exactly that; the killer put one hell of a series of holes in the victims."

Miller picked up the bag and studied it. Then he looked at Bogner. "Let me chase it down," he said. "It'll be a cold day in hell when I can't trace a damn gun."

Time 1231LT:

The Kopich Motel turned out to be something straight out of the sixties: chenille bedspread, blond furniture, and a bathtub with claw feet. Churchill looked in every drawer, behind and below every piece of furniture, ran his fingers over every shelf, and shoved his small penlight down the drains in both the basin and the tub.

"Looks like we're a day late and a dollar short," he grumbled. "Nothing. Looks like our man fled the coop." He looked at Bogner, then at the motel's manager.

The manager had turned out to be a small woman who regarded Churchill's movements with an air of obvious suspicion. Maria Kopich was the widow owner who insisted on apologizing for her English. In many ways she was a woman who defied description. Everything about her was plain, and Bogner had decided her most distinguishing characteristic was the fact her dentures were loose and she had a habit of periodically adjusting them with her thumb.

The woman hesitated for a moment before thumbing back through the pages of her ledger until she found what she was looking for. "He stay here three weeks ago, and again just a week ago. Each time just a short time. Then he register again two days ago."

"Can you describe him?" Bogner asked.

The woman shrugged and adjusted her dentures. "He is tall man. Understand? Very slight, but tall— maybe Chinese, never no trouble. Mr. Pan always pay in money, no credit cards."

Churchill sat down on the edge of the bed. "What about the phone? Did he use the phone a lot?"

The woman nodded. "Many calls." Churchill glanced at the telephone. They were in luck. It was obvious the motel's phone system hadn't been replaced in years. It was the kind where all calls went through a switchboard in the motel's cramped lobby. "Do you keep a record of all calls?" he asked.

The woman hesitated. Bogner could tell she was reluctant to answer. Obviously she regarded Mr. Pan as one of her better customers—if not her best. The Kopich Motel didn't appear to be the kind of place that had a steady or well-heeled clientele. "Yes," she finally admitted. "Mr. Pan give me number. I dial and keep track of time. I must do this in order to know how much to charge him for calls."

"Where do you keep your records?" Churchill said.

"Next to switchboard. When I receive telephone bill, I compare."

"We'd like to take a look at your phone log," Churchill said.

The woman led them down a flight of stairs to the motel's office, complained several times about the weather, and handed Churchill a clipboard with a tattered yellow tablet. Several pages were filled with dates and telephone numbers. Several more were crossed out.

"Which ones are Pan's calls?" he asked.

Maria Kopich took the stub of a blunt pencil and underlined the calls. "This one Mr. Pan makes many times." She pointed to a number with a Florida area code. "Calls are long," she added.

Bogner jotted down the numbers each time the woman underlined one.

Churchill continued to scan the list.

"Here is another," the woman said. "Yesterday he make many calls—mostly in morning."

Bogner again jotted down the number. Miller could chase them down in a matter of minutes; he had a system.

"And you say he checked out less than two hours ago?" Churchill asked.

The woman nodded and adjusted her teeth.

"Did he say where he was going?"

"He said nothing," she said. But after considering

her answer for several moments, she added, "That is not true. Mr. Pan said he had a slight accident and he needed to see a doctor. I gave him the name of the clinic where I go. It is not far from here."

Churchill turned, looked at Bogner, and smiled. "Let me assure you, Captain, it normally ain't this easy. Now you're going to get an up-close-and-personal look at what we call legwork."

Time 1331LT:

Miller was still waiting for Bogner to pick up the phone when Packer walked into his office. "Located him yet?" As the day had worn on, Packer's voice had deteriorated into a semi-growl.

Miller nodded. "The woman who answers the phones at the Rosewell Clinic says he's there but he's in a meeting with the clinic's director. She says she won't interrupt them."

"Try again," Packer grunted.

Miller did, and the response was the same. "Do you wish to hold, sir?" the receptionist asked. For the third time Miller declined, gave the woman his number, hung up, and picked up a piece of paper. "We're making some headway, though, Pack. T.C. came up with some phone numbers, and we're in the process of checking them out. In the last two days our friend Mr. Pan made four calls to a house located at 112 High Street in Bunche Park, Florida. Each of those calls was lengthy: ten, twelve, nine, and fourteen minutes in duration. I checked back with the woman who runs the motel, and she said

Pan always spoke in some foreign language, when he made these calls. I asked her what language, and she said she didn't know but that it sounded like Chinese."

Packer had propped himself on the corner of Miller's desk. "What about the other numbers?"

"This is where it gets interesting. Three of the calls were to the Park Salvage Company."

Packer smiled. "Bingo."

"The third number puts a whole different dimension on what this guy Pan may be up to. He made two calls to a company by the name of Quinto Aircraft. The company is located at a private airport just outside of Creighton, Virginia. I did a little checking around, and it turns out that Quinto Aircraft has ties to—guess who?"

"Wouldn't be Park Shin Ho, would it?"

"Good guess."

Packer loaded his pipe and let out a whistle. "Park, huh? That'll blow the socks off a few folks around here."

Time 1332LT:

As far as Bogner was concerned, Doctor Horace Spielman had demonstrated a reluctance to cooperate. A tall man with a pompous attitude and silver hair, he was willing to admit only that a patient who'd identified himself as Frank Pan had visited the clinic earlier in the day. But that admission was where he drew the line. "In reality, gentlemen, under law that is all I am obligated to tell you. Now, unless we have a situation where Lieutenant Churchill here feels the need to get the appropriate legal documents, I feel certain the lieutenant realizes that the nature of Mr. Pan's visit is privileged information. I'm afraid it's that old doctor-patient thing, which I'm certain is most annoying to the Police Department. Nevertheless, it is the law."

"I have ways of getting the information," Churchill reminded him, "but it doesn't need to come to that. A little cooperation on your part can save us both time and money. I'm sure you understand what I mean when I say *money*, Doctor."

"What Lieutenant Churchill hasn't told you, Doctor Spielman," Bogner said, "is that in all probability, the man who visited your clinic and called himself Frank Pan is the same man who shot and killed a police officer and another man this morning."

"You're talking about that Ross Road shooting?"

Churchill nodded. "One and the same. Now how about cooperating before I start throwing around terms like aiding and abetting."

Spielman considered his next move for several seconds, then left the room and returned with a manila file folder. "Let's see. According to this, Mr. Pan was treated for contusions to both his face and legs, a sprained shoulder, and there were two deep lacerations on his right leg just above the knee. Both required stitches." Spielman squinted at the report as he turned over the page. "And according to one of my staff members, while the man was being treated, he exhibited a high degree of agitation and was quite nervous. Doctor Andrews attended to Mr. Pan, and he notes the patient spoke both English and Chinese, and several times expressed the fact that he was in a hurry. We advised him that the pain medicine we had given him would make him drowsy and advised him not to drive. Our receptionist informs me that he asked her to call a taxi."

"Did he tell her where he was going?" Bogner asked.

Spielman shook his head. "He did not. And with that, gentlemen, I've told you everything I know. Now if you'll excuse me, I have a waiting room full of people."

"One more question, Doctor," Churchill said. "Did Mr. Pan tell you how he got those cuts and bruises?"

Spielman opened the folder a second time and scanned the report. "Ah, here it is. Mr. Pan said he had been in an in a minor altercation. He did not say what kind."

Time 1421LT:

Clancy Packer waited until Bogner finished reading Miller's notes. When Bogner laid the piece of paper back on the table, he had a good idea what would happen next. "Want me to guess?" Bogner asked.

Packer took a sip of coffee.

"Washington's love affair with Park Shin Ho is about to come to an end, I take it."

"I've already talked to Senator Loren Langley. He warns us we could get egg on our face if Park's skirts are clean in this whole affair. Park has some very influential friends. He wants me to understand that the agency could be in for a dressing-down if Park isn't involved."

"We've had egg on our face before," Bogner reminded him. "Haven't seen it slow you down yet."

"Before we confront Park, I want to know what the situation is with Quinto Aircraft. Why was this man we're calling Mr. Pan dealing with Quinto? A couple of M16s, a .45 issue automatic still in a kerealene bag, and a couple of grenade launchers are one thing. Every paramilitary group in the country is sucking up this stuff. When they start buying aircraft, we've got a whole different beast on our hands. Bottom line, we check out Quinto first. And I've got just the man to help you."

"Who?"

"Rooster Ricozy."

"Ricozy?" Bogner repeated. "Since when is he on the payroll?"

"Rooster insisted. He says he's got a score to settle with Park. Rooster feels responsible for what happened to Shank and the other man. Unless you come up with some strong reasons why, Rooster is your backup."

"This could get a little sticky," Bogner said. "He's big, but the question is, can he handle himself in something like this?"

Packer got up and closed the door. "This is strictly off the record, T.C. I had to get clearance from Jaffe to use Rooster Ricozy. Jaffe has had him assigned to the CIA's counterinsurgency section for more than seven years now. When Rooster retired from the Redskins, he had a lot of friends, savory and unsavory. He was a celebrity, a natural. He knows his way around town, and I'm talking about the side streets and alleys. He has connections. He can get us into places that are off limits to anyone who even looks like they might be Establishment. Rooster was looking for a way to contribute, and Jaffe decided to capitalize on that. Now it's our turn."

"That puts a different spin on it," Bogner admitted. "When and where do we start?"

Packer held up his hand. "I buy your theory about Mao Quan. I think he's going for bigger game than we've seen so far. He's not going for numbers, he's going for individuals—and the bigger the individual, the better. We've been playing catch-up since this damn thing started. For the last sixty hours it's been all his show. But the pendulum may have swung back in our favor when that van overturned this morning. All of a sudden, this so-called Mr. Pan is leaving a trail, and now we've got something to work with. The first stop on that trail is Park and then Quinto Aircraft. We want to know why Pan was there and what he was doing. It'll be interesting to see if Park cooperates."

Bogner was still waiting for Packer to wrap it up when Miller barged in.

"We're on a hot streak," Miller announced with a grin. "I just got a call from a Lieutenant Jacoby.

He's with the bomb squad investigating that explosion across the street from the Crane house this morning. So far they've found five bodies in the debris. None of which appears to be Crane's killer. Two of the victims are police officers, a Lieutenant Andrews with the homicide division and a homicide detective named Henderson. There were three others, a woman they've tentatively identified as Rita Ann Stern, who works for the CIA, and an elderly couple, in all probability the ones who own the house. All five bodies have been taken to the morgue. Jacoby says their preliminary thinking is that Rita Ann Stern was rigged with a bomb, and Andrews and Henderson just happened to be in the wrong place at the wrong time.

"Another detective, who was Henderson's partner, claims they went to investigate the house where the limo driver said the shots came from. He was the lucky one. Andrews had him looking around outside. He's pretty well banged up, but he was conscious enough to let Jacoby know what happened."

Packer shook his head. "I've met this Rita Stern. She works in the same section over at the CIA as Peter Langley. Check with Peter, see if he can shed any light on this."

"That's Mao," Bogner said. "With Mao there's always a wrinkle—a gotcha. The body with the rocket launcher down in the Baja, the burning car with the Chow kid in it, stealing Worling's report even though some of us already knew what was in it, and now the Stern woman. Mao wants us to know just how close he can operate. My guess is he figures he's got us on the ropes and he likes it. Five will get you ten Andrews went in that house thinking he would find where Crane's killer fired the shots. Instead he gets himself blown to pieces by a damn bomb."

"There's more," Miller said. "Jacoby says they've got an ID on the passenger in the van. His name was Quin Lo Wan, a Chinese American. Twenty-seven years old, single, born in Compton, California, graduated from Cal Tech, was commissioned and spent four years in the USAF. He resigned his commission and went to China a couple of years back. According to State Department records, he's been in and out of the country a couple of times since then. The only address we have is bogus."

Packer leaned back in his chair. "Well, we know one thing for certain. Whoever shot him considered him expendable."

Bogner stood up, walked over to the window, and stared out at the cold rain. "Try to put yourself in Pan's place, Pack. We know he's hurting. And with this Quin character stretched out in the morgue, he's minus one resource—maybe his only resource. If that's the case, where does he go and what does he do? Who are his contacts? Where's his backup?"

"My guess is he gets out of town," Miller said, "and gets reinforcements."

"Or they may already be here," Bogner guessed. "Either way, we've got to figure out a way to run this guy Pan down."

"Let's start with Park," Packer said. "Ricozy will make the contacts."

"I'll get in touch with Ricozy," Miller volunteered.

"Good," Packer said. He reached for the telephone.

Time 1630LT:

Park Shin Ho looked past his visitor out the window, assessed the gloomy day, and scowled. "You took quite a chance in coming here. I am not at all certain that it was a wise move on your part. Suppose you were followed. If that were the case, my company could be implicated—and that would be most unfortunate."

Even now, Liu Shao's expression was no different than it had been during their previous conversations. "I do not understand your reticence nor your reluctance to—"

"On the contrary, Mr. Liu, I believe you understand completely." Park stood up, walked around the desk, and stood staring down at the man. Liu's face was swollen, and there was a patchwork of small cuts and abrasions on the left side of his face. "I am an arms dealer, Mr. Liu. As an arms dealer, what I do is legal, but I walk a very narrow line and I carefully cultivate a network of people who can insure, if need be, that I stay in business."

Liu stiffened. "I do not see—"

Park cut him off. "It is not for you to see, Mr. Liu. I now find myself in a somewhat delicate position because of your unfortunate blunder this morning.

My business is selling arms, not harboring fugitives—regardless of their value as a customer."

"Fugitive?" Liu repeated.

Park towered over the man. "Do not take me for a fool, Mr. Liu. If a man buys five gross of M16A1 rifles, or a dozen M203 grenade launchers, I think nothing of it. The world is full of would-be insurgents: high-minded, often misguided individuals who actually believe that they can run their country, any country for that matter, better than the current regime. There have been days when I sold tanks to one country and antitank weapons to their enemy. I am a businessman, a weapons dealer. But you, Mr. Liu, present me with a considerable quandary. Who traces a .45 automatic used in a shooting in Baghdad or some village in Cambodia? The answer, of course, is no one. On the other hand, if during the course of the investigation into the murder of Senator Crane this morning it is learned that the serial number on the weapon that killed him matches one sold by a DRMO depot at some base in Georgia to Park Salvage, I have an altogether different concern. In that case, Mr. Liu, I have unwittingly become an accomplice to an act that is certain to foster an intensive search for the man or men that committed the nefarious act."

Liu stared back at the man.

"I hope you will not insult my intelligence by denying that you were involved in Senator Crane's assassination," Park said.

Liu did not answer him. Tonu Hon had taught him well. Still, Park's response was a disappointment. Liu realized that he was fast running out of options. He had hoped that the salvage dealer would be more amenable. In what way, he wasn't certain.

Park walked to the door and opened it. "There is a word that has become popular with the Americans. That word is agenda. I would be less than candid if I said I do not know what your agenda is, Mr. Liu, because I too read the papers and I too view what is happening. In my business there is no right or wrong. There is no judgment. There is only the danger; the danger that I may be implicated by virtue of someone's carelessness. I feel certain you understand my position."

Liu stood up and half limped, half walked toward Park and the open door. His departing nod of the head was barely perceptible.

Chapter Eight

Time 1820LT:

Jacqueline Marceau stepped out of her car, locked it, braced herself against the weather, and walked across the parking lot to the foyer of the apartment building. It was one of the few times since eight o'clock that morning that she had been away from either a radio or television set. She had spent the day in her office listening to every word, every speculation, every news bite concerning Crane's assassination. Richard Crane, a former lieutenant in the United States Army and the man who had lied about her father's allegiance to the Khmer Rouge, and ultimately executed him for crimes he never committed, was dead. She took solace from that fact, and if she had any regrets, it was that Crane never knew that the daughter of Gerrold Marceau had been the one who'd convinced Tonu Hon to include the name of the Iowa senator on Mao's list.

Now that it was done, all that remained was an assessment of her performance. Her own brief affair with Crane had helped her get the job with the CIA. That, like everything else, had been planned. Crane, as it turned out, had proved to be an easy mark. All of this left her with both a feeling of euphoria and, at the same time, a tinge of melancholia. It was a feeling, a disturbing sense of raw-edged emotion, she had not anticipated. Crane had opened doors for her, doors that made her far more valuable to Mao's plan than originally anticipated, but there was the undeniable truth that his deceits, the same deceits that he had brought with him through his entire military and political career, had killed her father.

She put her car keys in her purse, pressed the up button on the waiting elevator, and got in. Three floors later she got off, walked to her door, unlocked it, and entered. She had not anticipated finding Liu Shao waiting for her.

"What are you doing here?" she demanded. "You were not supposed to come here."

Liu Shao turned away from the window. His face was bruised and swollen. When he turned toward her, it was obvious his movements were impaired. He said nothing.

"What happened this morning?" she hissed. "Have you been listening to the news? Are you aware that they have identified Quin Lo Wan?"

"It was necessary," Liu said. "There was no other alternative. He was dying, but he could have lived long enough to—"

"You have bungled everything; the police have a likeness of you. They are using an artist's sketch from a description supplied by the driver. It is being shown on every television station."

Liu moved wearily across the room and sat down. "Tonu Hon must be informed."

"Fool," the woman said. "By now Tonu Hon knows everything. Every major news source in the country is carrying the story, along with your picture. You have imperilled our entire mission. Because of you the entire operation may be compromised."

Liu closed his eyes. Mademoiselle Marceau had called him a fool. In his country, women did not call men a *fool*. This daughter of a French Cambodian took liberties with her rank that even Mao Quan would not approve of. It would be a simple matter to dispose of her as well—if it were not for the fact that now he needed her. When he left Park's office he'd run out of options; he had sought her out even though he knew Tonu Hon would not approve. "I will need a place to stay," he said. "Time to revise our plan."

Jacqueline took off her coat. "There will be no revisions, no changes. Mao would not approve. We will stay with our original schedule. I will send for Chen Po Lee."

She had already voiced her disapproval of the

complexities in Tonu's plan. Now she was declining to debate the matter with a mere underling. Discussing the matter further would accomplish nothing. From the beginning she had tried to convince Mao Quan that the plan of his aging strategist was too elaborate, too involved; that the theatrics and posturing leading up to the attempt on the President would accomplish little except to put the Americans on alert.

When it became apparent that Mao would not listen, she chose to wait. Now was her chance. Liu was exhausted—beyond thinking clearly—in all probability, no longer useful. The mere fact that he had sought her out, when Tonu Hon had given specific instructions that there would be no contact, was proof of the fact. If it was somehow learned that she had known or given refuge to the very man who had killed Richard Crane, her role as a 5A operative would be ended. Philosophically as well as financially, it was a role she was unwilling to relinquish. She remembered her mother reading the passage from the Bible to her the night her father had been killed. " *'Retribution is mine,' saith the Lord.* " She had embraced that passage, and Richard Crane's death was only a partial retribution. There was also the matter of the government that permitted such atrocities—and who better to pay that debt than the American President, David Colchin.

"Very well," she said. "It is apparent that you must rest. You may stay here—but only until I am able to contact Tonu Hon. In the meantime I will give you something for your pain, something to help you sleep."

Two hours later, at seventeen minutes after eight, Jacqueline Marceau had her instructions. During those two hours she had carefully coded the information and faxed it to the number at 112 High Street in Florida, where she knew the young Chinese woman Tian would relay it. Tonu Hon had wasted no time replying. His answer had been cold and concise. Liu Shao had become a liability. Dispose of him. Tonu Hon would send Chen Po Lee.

Time 2102LT:

Bogner had met Park Shin Ho on two previous occasions. The first had been at one of the Capital's seemingly unending charity affairs: date, cause, and location long forgotten. The second was more memorable, if for no other reason than that Joy had asked Bogner to escort her. That second occasion had prompted Park to make a sizable donation to a children's hospital, and he had asked Joy, one of the chairpersons of the fund drive, to dance. Bogner remembered anyone who asked his former wife to dance.

Now Park sat across the table from him, smiling affably and ordering a second round of drinks. He was dressed in a meticulously tailored silk suit and sported a fresh manicure. "So, Joseph." He smiled. "I could pretend that it is my wit and charm that is behind this sudden invitation, but I surmise that there is more to it than that. Do I detect a certain sense of urgency?"

Bogner was seeing Joseph Albert "Rooster" Ricozy in an entirely new light—and it had little to do with Packer's revelation. Ricozy, appropriately attired in a three-piece suit, looked every bit as comfortable in the Hotel Cheveron dining room as any man standing six feet seven inches tall and tipping the scales at nearly three hundred pounds could possibly look. "It's urgent, all right. Captain Bogner here thinks you have something he wants."

"And for a price you were willing to arrange it? Correct?"

Ricozy nodded. "Hey, a man's gotta make a living."

Park smiled and leaned back in his chair. "And just exactly what is it you want, Captain Bogner?"

Bogner started to speak, but Park held up his hand.

"Before you begin, Captain Bogner," Park said with a smile, "let me lay one of my own cards on the table. It may have some impact on what you have to say."

Bogner picked up the three-by-five file card. It had his name on it. It gave his rank, age, height, the date he was recruited by the ISA, the names of Joy, his wife, and his daughter, Kim. He scanned it twice and handed it back. "Tell your source it's not current. Joy and I are divorced."

"All information is subject to update," Park said, continuing to smile.

Ricozy leaned forward. "At this point, gentlemen,

I can stay or step out in the hall. It's up to you."

"Stay," Park said. "If I can be of assistance to my adopted country . . ." His voice trailed off.

Ricozy looked at Bogner. "Very well then. I stay. It's your nickel, Captain."

"I'm curious, Mr. Park. Does the name Frank Pan mean anything to you?" Bogner asked.

If it did, Park did a masterful job of concealing it. There was a barely perceptible twist to his mouth—a squint, and nothing else, as he repeated the name. "I'm afraid not," he said.

"Let me lay a card on the table then, Mr. Park. We think it does. Our records show that within the last three weeks your company has made shipments of certain supposedly demiled items to a firm in Miami—"

"Those items were purchased from authorized DRMO depots," Park interjected.

"And the firm in Miami rerouted those shipments to Cuba," Bogner continued. "We have the name of the shipping agent, the manifest numbers, detailed copies of the inventory, and POO documentation. The point-of-origin papers show Park Salvage to be the original shippers."

Park continued to smile. "All, I assure you, perfectly legal, Captain. We are a contract supply house. We have no control over subagents. What they do with what they buy is their business. Need I remind you of how the free-enterprise system works? Perhaps a more relevant question might be how you came by this information. Does the government of my adopted country make it a habit of delving into the business transactions of even small companies like mine?"

It was Bogner's turn to lean forward. "You can count on a certain vigilance where the nation's security might be jeopardized."

"Continue," Park said. He finished his drink and ordered another. "What about this man you call Pan?"

"We have reason to suspect that Mr. Pan is affiliated with a group known as the Fifth Academy. And we are reasonably certain he is the man behind not only the death of Senator Richard Crane, but the explosions aboard two different military aircraft, the death of Robert Worling, and the attempted assassination of Lattimere Spitz."

"Your Mr. Pan has been a busy man," Park said. "However ambitious his agenda, I should point out that this is not the type of individual my company deals with."

Bogner waited until the waiter put the drinks on the table and left. "Perhaps I should be a little more direct, Mr. Park. We also have reason to believe weapons sold by Park Salvage were used in these attacks."

"As I said, Captain, a small portion of Park Salvage's business is selling weapons. We are registered and licensed with the appropriate government agencies. It is all aboveboard and legal. But I hasten to add, for the second time, we are not in a position to control what our customers do with what they buy. If you have proof that we have violated some law, tell me. Or should I consult my lawyers before this conversation goes any further?"

Ricozy reached across the table. "Look, I agreed to arrange a meeting, that's all. I agreed to do it because I believe you can help each other. Nothing happens if you two start threatening each other. I think you better hear what else Captain Bogner has to say."

Bogner was a quick read. It had taken Park all of thirty seconds to regain his composure. The smile returned. "Shall we try again, Captain?"

Bogner reached in his pocket and took out a copy of the artist's sketch. It was the one that had appeared in the evening paper. "Same question, different approach. Have you been contacted by or do you know this man? It's probably an alias, but we know him now as Frank Pan."

Park took the drawing, studied it, took a sip of his drink, and handed it back. His expression hadn't changed.

"Before you answer, Mr. Park, let me warn you. We have traced Pan, from the scene of an accident this morning, to the place where he dumped a stolen car, to his motel. At his motel we learned that in the past two days he has made a number of telephone calls to Park Salvage. So . . . if you still aren't certain what posture you want to take on this matter, you should also know that we now believe we have him tied to the scene of the Crane shooting earlier today."

Park arched an eyebrow, reached for the drawing again, and lingered, trying to give the impression he was studying the drawing. It took several seconds before he finally shook his head. "I'm afraid not, Captain. However, you must understand, I have many customers who would prefer that I did not recognize them. I have steadfastly adhered to the practice of avoiding any kind of familiarity with my customers."

Bogner folded the drawing, put it back in his pocket, looked at Ricozy, then back at the arms dealer. "What the hell, maybe it's time to show you my hole card, Mr. Park?"

Park laughed. "I may find it amusing, Captain. Go right ahead."

Bogner nodded and took out a pen. He spread his napkin out on the table and began writing. "I think you're going to find this quite interesting, Mr. Park." While he talked, Bogner sketched a bridge, a road, and a river. "There was this blue panel truck—it was spotted under a bridge over the Anacosta. Two men were observed removing two rather large and ungainly parcels from the cargo area. Then a very strange thing happened, Mr. Park. After the two men had gone to all the trouble of getting these oversized bundles out of the van, they simply dumped them in the river. Can you imagine that?"

"A more pertinent question might be, why are you telling me this, Captain?"

"Well, for one thing, I thought you might be interested in what some of your employees do in their off-hours."

"My employees?"

"Wouldn't be too hard to prove. The panel truck

was a blue Chevrolet. Not only that, it carried the name of Park Salvage painted on the side. All we had to do was check the license plate, and since it wasn't then or hasn't been reported stolen, we assumed you knew all about what your employees were up to."

Park hesitated. "You are implying what, Captain?"

"There's no implying to it. We fished two bodies out of the river early the next morning—right where whoever was driving your panel truck that night made their drop."

Bogner was starting to get through. Park's smile was less evident, but the bluff was still there. "So far, Captain, your little scenario sounds somewhat circumstantial. We have a fleet of vans and trucks, many of which are sold when we no longer have use for them. Perhaps the individual who bought the van in question simply neglected to remove the name of my company."

Bogner pushed himself toward the table and braced himself. "You and I seem to be having trouble communicating, Park." This time he made certain the arms dealer knew he had taken off the gloves. The word *Mister* was gone, and so was Bogner's smile. "Maybe this will get through to you. How about accessory-to-murder charges?"

"Ah, my dear Captain, do you really think you could make those charges stick?"

Bogner shrugged. "Maybe, maybe not. But I'd damn sure tie up a lot of your time, and those lawyers of yours don't come cheap. How much money and time can you afford, Park? Not to mention the bad publicity."

Park studied the man across the table from him for several moments. "Are we negotiating, Captain, or are we arbitrarily drawing lines in the sand?"

"No guarantees, Park. What happened that night under the bridge is out of my jurisdiction. On the other hand, if the DC police put two and two together and come after you for the murder of those two men, you can color me invisible."

Park looked around the dining room to make certain no one was near enough to overhear him. His voice was reduced to slightly more than a raspy whisper. "Pan's real name is Liu Shao."

"Where is he?"

Park shrugged. "Who knows?"

"When's the last time you saw him?" Bogner asked.

"This afternoon. He was looking for a place to hide."

"And you said?"

"What I said is immaterial, Captain. The bottom line is, as you Americans like to say, I told him that in my line of work, I could not afford to become involved in the affairs of my clients, especially those with an agenda such as his."

"You're telling me you don't know where Liu went after he left Park Salvage."

"I am afraid I cannot help you," Park said. But as an afterthought, he added, "Perhaps it is nothing more than the machinations of a man who is too close to the forest, Captain, but I have a feeling that while Mr. Liu looks south for his marching orders, there is another contact here."

"You're saying Liu may have had someone else to turn to here in Washington?"

"Perhaps, perhaps not. It is just a feeling. However, you should know, Captain, that I have spent a lifetime playing my hunches. I would play this one to the hilt."

Time 2257LT:

Tonu Hon's instructions brought with them both a sense of urgency and a renewed sense of commitment. Now Jacqueline Marceau was eager to get on with her task. She had used much of the time in the past two hours to review what had previously been solely Liu's responsibility. In essence, she had less than forty-eight hours to bring Chen Po Lee abreast of Liu's plan. Tonu Hon had assured her that Chen Po Lee was prepared and equal to his assignment. Even more fortunate for both of them, Liu had meticulously documented his plan. Tonu Hon had been able to relay even the smallest detail.

To kill time, Jacqueline busied herself with the more mundane details of Chen Po's arrival: arranging for accommodations at an out-of-the-way motel, and preparing a packet of maps, photographs, and other papers. With a simple phone call from a public telephone, she would arrange a pickup point just as she had in her dealings with Liu. At Tonu Hon's insistence, there would be no contact with any of the operatives until the final phase of their plan.

Finally, it was time. It was now shortly after eleven o'clock. She went to the window and studied the street from her second-floor vantage point. The weather was in her favor. Traffic was almost non-existent, and the hospital was only three blocks away. She checked her watch for a second time, and decided there was no reason for further delay.

Liu Shao, because of the painkiller she had given him, had slipped into a deep sleep, and she had difficulty waking him. When he opened his eyes, he was groggy and disoriented. Jacqueline kept her voice low.

"We must go now," she said. "Tonu Hon has made arrangements."

Liu did not question her.

She struggled to get him to his feet, and helped him put on his coat. He was decidedly weaker. He was unsteady and stumbled twice as she led him through the apartment to the door. "Wait here," she said, "until the elevator comes, and I'll come back to get you." Jacqueline Marceau moved cautiously and quietly; she had already determined that the next five or six minutes would be extremely risky. She had to get Liu down the elevator, through the foyer to the parking garage, and finally to her car without anyone seeing her. A high percentage of the people who lived in the apartment complex where she lived worked at the nearby Washington General Hospital. From observation she knew that those who worked the night shift left for the hospital somewhere around ten-thirty. Those who were coming off duty usually made it back to the complex shortly after eleven.

She led Liu out of the elevator, into the foyer, and stopped. Two young nurses, bundled in coats that revealed they were still wearing scrubs, were crossing the parking lot. The women were talking and laughing. Jacqueline maneuvered Liu back into the shadows and waited. The two women passed without noticing them.

She waited until the women got on the elevator, then steered Liu toward the car. He was shivering and weak; twice she had to pause while he regained his equilibrium. By the time she had unlocked the car and pushed Liu into the passenger's seat, she was covered with a thin powder of snow. She smiled as she slipped behind the steering wheel. Luck was with her. She could assure Tonu Hon that no one had seen them.

Jacqueline Marceau drove directly to the hospital, circled the complex while the last stragglers from the evening shift worked their way to their cars, went up the ramp, and parked the car at the far end of the fourth-floor parking garage. When she looked at Liu, she realized that he fallen asleep again. The task would be even easier than she had anticipated.

Jacqueline got out of the car, walked around to the passenger's door, opened it, and awakened the man. "We're there," she said. "The car that picks you up will be here any minute. All you have to do is wait. They won't come up the ramp until they see I'm starting to leave."

With her help, Liu managed to work his way out of the car, wavered, and sagged back against the four-foot-high barrier. He was trembling and lethargic. Twice she saw him shake his head, trying to keep his eyes open. Finally, Jacqueline moved methodically back around to the driver's side, crawled in, started the ignition, put the car in reverse, backed up several feet, turned on the lights, shoved the car into first, and pressed the accelerator. Liu Shao never moved.

Blinded by the headlights, he was pinned against the concrete barrier. Jacqueline Marceau heard him scream. He pitched forward, the upper half of his body slamming against the hood. When she backed away, he lolled backward, hanging momentarily over the railing, and fell four stories to the concrete parking lot below.

It was over. Jacqueline got out of the car, went to the railing, and stared down into the darkness, but there was nothing to see. It was snowing harder than it had snowed all that evening.

4 Nov: Time 0517LT:

Bogner pulled into the Washington General Hospital parking lot and brought his car to a stop. Sam Churchill was waiting.

"Sorry to haul you out of bed at this hour, Captain, but I figured you'd want to know. We got the call at two-forty. One of the hospital security people was making his rounds and he saw something lying over at the base of the parking garage. He called the station and we sent a car over. The officer took one look at the body and they called me in. I got here about an hour ago. I think maybe we found your man."

Bogner, collar up against the cold and snow, followed the heavyset officer through a maze of police cars until they came to the body. The area had been cordoned off by a ribbon of yellow plastic, and the body was covered by a blanket. Churchill bent over and lifted the blanket, and Bogner bent down. The back of Liu's head had been crushed, reduced to a semi-identifiable pulp, but his eyes were open and he stared blankly back at him.

Churchill reached in his pocket and handed him a copy of the artist's rendering that had been seen on a hundred television stations. "What do ya think?" Churchill asked. "Is this your man?"

Bogner hesitated. "Hard to tell. There isn't a hell of a lot left of him."

Churchill shoved his hands in his overcoat pocket. "The coroner's people haven't been here yet, so I don't have anything official, but look at this." He pulled the blanket away to reveal the rest of Liu's body. "Take a look at those legs."

Bogner looked down. The area between Liu's hips and knees had been crushed. His coat from the waist down was soaked in a black-oily residue of crusted blood.

"How the hell . . . ?"

Churchill cupped his lighter between his hands as he lit a cigar. "Want a guess?"

Bogner nodded.

"I had a friend a number of years ago. His son has just passed his driver's test, and when they came home there was something in the way so he couldn't pull into his garage. Bill got out of the car, moved whatever it was, and told his son to drive the car on into the garage. The kid hit the accelerator too hard, the car plowed into Bill, pinned him against the wall at the back of the garage, and took both his legs off."

Bogner pulled the blanket back in place and stood up.

"You know what my friend did for a living?" Churchill continued.

Bogner shook his head.

"He sold shoes."

Bogner stood up, and Churchill pointed at the parking garage. "If I was a bettin' man, I'd say your man here fell or was knocked over the barrier of one of the levels of that garage. And from the look of his legs, someone used a car to do it. When we get some daylight, I'll have my men comb the area."

Bogner looked up into the swirling snow at the top of the building. If the body of the man lying at his feet was the man called Pan, their best lead had just come to a dead end.

Time 0615LT:

Jacqueline Marceau had returned to her apartment, changed the sheets on the bed where Liu had slept, washed, dried, folded them, and put them away. Then she'd made two trips through the apartment to make certain Liu had left nothing behind. When she was satisfied with her search, she'd showered and gone to bed. Much to her surprise, she'd had little difficulty spiraling into a deep, untroubled sleep.

Now she was awakened by the telephone. It was Julie Simon. The woman's voice was thick and slurred.

"Julie, is that you?"

"I'm sorry, Jacky, I know it's early, but I just—had to talk to someone." The words edged their way out between sobs.

"Where are you?"

"Home—I've been here since—since . . ."

Jacqueline tucked the receiver between her head and shoulder, pushed the covers back, and swung her legs over the side of the bed. "Look, Julie," she said, "let me put on some clothes, make us a pot of coffee, and you come down to my apartment. We'll talk. Okay?"

Jacqueline waited until Julie agreed and hung up. Then she got out of bed, dressed, and started the coffee. Julie Simon was weak and she despised her for that—but she still needed her. Julie Simon still had a critical role to play in her plans.

As an added precaution, she quickly conducted one last inspection of the apartment, then turned on the television and tuned into the local news station. Fifteen minutes later, when Julie Simon knocked on her door, there still had been no mention of finding a body in the Washington General parking lot.

When Jacqueline opened the door she was taken a back by Julie's appearance. Her eyes were swollen, her hair wasn't combed, she wasn't wearing makeup, and she had been drinking.

Julie Simon wavered and leaned against the door frame.

"I tried to call you when I heard. . . ." Jacqueline lied.

"Sw—sweet of you," Julie slurred. "I—I didn't answer my—phone all day. I called in sick and . . . then I lay there and cried. . . ."

Jacqueline sat her down and poured her a cup of coffee. Even now, she wasn't sure what she would say to her.

She had met Julie Simon the day she'd moved in. Julie was lonely, pretty, and most important, unattached. Then, after Jacqueline's fortuitous meeting with Crane at an agency social affair, she had capitalized both on the senator's propensity for bed-hopping and Julie's loneliness, by arranging for the two to meet. It had worked out even better than she had planned. Julie had proved to be a willing conquest, and the senator from Iowa had taken it from there.

In the end, because Julie Simon needed someone to talk to and Jacqueline Marceau was a ready listener, Jacqueline knew Crane's every move, including the fact that the Cranes were having a dinner party the night before he was killed. That information, along with a simple phone call, masquerading as the Cranes' housekeeper to confirm the fact that the senator would require a limo, was all it took. Liu Shao had taken it from there.

Now Jacqueline wondered if Julie had any idea that her parade of indiscreet conversations about her affair with the senator had directly contributed to Crane's death.

"Why—why did he have to be killed?" Julie sobbed. "Just the night before he promised me he would tell his wife about us. . . ."

Jacqueline sat down beside the woman and put her arm around her. "Drink some coffee," she said. "What's done is done. There is nothing you can do about it. You'll have to get hold of yourself."

"I—I can't even go to—to the funeral home," Julie said. "Someone might see me and recognize me— we were seen together—I know we were."

"Julie, you've got to get your bearings. Life goes on. You can't go on like this."

"Maybe—maybe I could take a couple of weeks off?" Julie ventured. "Get a grip. I could tell my supervisor I'm sick—something—anything—until I can get my bearings. Or—or maybe I should just quit and go back home."

Jacqueline stiffened. "No," she said abruptly. She had said it before she thought. "I—I mean, you can't just up and quit. Believe me, you'll get over this. Sure it hurts now, but believe me, there's another day and each day a little bit of the hurt will go away. Trust me."

Julie nodded, leaned her head back, and closed her eyes. "You're a real friend, Jacky," she muttered.

"I don't know what I would do without you." She had momentarily escaped from reality, only to plunge herself back into a world where her nightmares would haunt her.

Jacqueline nodded as the woman dozed off. "On the contrary, my foolish and gullible friend," she thought, "it is I who need you—at least for a few more days."

She got up, walked into the kitchen, and checked the time. If Chen Po Lee had caught the early morning flight out of Miami, he would be landing in Washington shortly. Even though it was Saturday, it would take him an hour or more to get to the motel. When she called the motel, she would disguise her voice as she had done in checking on Liu Shao. She would tell them she was with the embassy, and that she was merely checking to see if Mr. Yen had arrived safely. Yen. She repeated the name. She liked that. Tonu Hon had thought of everything, even a code name.

Time 0817LT:

Ricozy and Bogner pulled into the small rural airport in Creighton, Virginia, a little after eight o'clock on a Saturday morning, searching for Quinto Aircraft. They located it on a rutted road at the back of the airport. It consisted of two large hangars, a Quonset hut sadly in need of a coat of paint, and a small one-story, wooden-frame building connected to one of the hangars. The latter appeared to serve as the firm's office.

229

Behind one of the hangars was a brace of ancient DC-3s, a tired Boeing 707 minus engines, and an assortment of wing assemblies, engines, and other gear, most of it uncrated and exposed to the weather. The entire area was fenced in and patroled by a pair of mangy-looking guard dogs who obviously owed most of their heritage to a German shepherd. The dogs, preoccupied with eating what appeared to be the remains of a rabbit, were far too busy to pay any attention to Bogner and Ricozy.

Ricozy parked in front of the frame building, and Bogner got out of the car, walked up to the office, tried the door, and walked in. Yamir Quinto was sitting at a cluttered desk rummaging through a stack of papers. When he saw Bogner he leaned back in his chair and waited.

"I'm looking for Yamir Quinto," Bogner said.

"Who wants him?" the Armenian grunted.

"Tell him the name is Bogner, T. C. Bogner."

"So what do you want with him?"

"Ten minutes of conversation."

Quinto pushed his chair back up to the desk. "Come back Monday, we're closed."

Bogner leaned forward and put his hands on the desk. "Look, pal, I'm in no mood to play games. I got hustled out of bed this morning at the crack of dawn after a night that was short on sleep and long on misery. You round up Quinto and tell him he's got company."

Yamir Quinto's sneer had begun to dissipate. He had underestimated the situation. The one who called himself Bogner wasn't going to be put off as easily as he had anticipated. Not only that, Bogner was suddenly backed up by a hulking shape in the doorway. Worse yet, the shape was frowning.

"Okay," Quinto said, forcing a half smile, "so you found me. Now, what the hell do you want?"

Bogner reached in his pocket, unfolded the drawing of Liu Shao, and dropped it on his desk. "You can start by telling me what you know about this man."

Quinto glanced at the sketch and pushed it away. "Who is he? Never saw him before."

Ricozy moved across the room and settled into the first chair that looked like it had a sporting chance of supporting his weight. He took out a cigar, unwrapped it, bit off the end, lit it, and threw the match in Quinto's wastebasket. The match was still lit. "What the hell . . . ?" Quinto started to protest.

Bogner reached down, put out the fire, and looked at the fat man. "Perhaps you better look at the picture again."

Quinto picked up the sketch, studied it, and dropped it back on the desk. "Okay, whatever the hell you said your name is, I looked at your damn picture. I said I don't know him and now I got a question for you. Who the hell are you to come bargin' in here pushing your way around?"

Bogner reached in his pocket and pulled out his identification. "Internal Security Agency." He put the badge away before Quinto could get a good look at it, and started strolling around the cluttered office. "You know," he said, "I've been looking around, Mr. Quinto, and there's a few things missing."

"Like what?"

"I don't see a business license posted. I don't see an AR-47 authorization to sell aircraft parts, and I don't see a AIRIP permit. Maybe I ought to shut you down until—"

Quinto's face was flushed. He got up out of his chair, looked at Ricozy, and hesitated. "All right, all right. The little bastard was here two days ago."

"Glad to see your memory improving," Bogner said. "Now, let's see if it's improved enough for you to remember why he was here."

"Park sent him. Park has a few bucks invested in this place. The guy wanted to buy a chopper."

"And?"

"I showed him what we had. He said he was with a company that contracted emergency medical transportation for two small hospitals in Maryland. I told him we had just retrofited a couple of thirty-year-old Kaman SH-2 Seasprites for that purpose and he liked the idea. I told him the one we still had was purchased from a DRMO depot in Florida."

"What about the armament and special gear?" Bogner pressed.

"He didn't exactly say it, but most of them hospital guys want it stripped out. Most buyers want us to take out the sensor operator's seat, all the AWS and surveillance radar, and the AS torpedo linkage. We leave the nav/com and display systems in. Doesn't matter to us—we can always sell that shit to someone else."

"When did he want it?"

"He didn't say. All he said was, he'd get back to me. So far I haven't heard from him. These little gems are expensive. Maybe he choked on the price."

"Better not count on selling that little gem, as you call it, to our friend in the picture," Bogner said. "They found him lying in a parking lot early this morning. And I guarantee you, his chopper-shopping days are over."

Quinto shrugged. "No skin off my ass. It ain't sold till I got a check in my hand—and we didn't get that far."

Ricozy got up and started for the door. Bogner was right behind him.

"Hey," Quinto said, "what the hell was that permit you said I didn't have?"

Bogner stopped. "You mean the AIRIP permit?"

Quinto nodded. "Yeah, that one. Where the hell do I get it?"

Bogner shrugged. "Couldn't tell you. I just made it up."

Time 0917LT:

Originally, Mao Quan had recruited and Tonu Hon had selected Chen Po Lee primarily because he had been trained as a pilot. Since then, however, he had proved himself equally adept at other assignments. In addition, he had demonstrated his loyalty to the Fifth Academy on numerous occasions—primarily in the role of student dissident and agitator on the Chinese mainland.

He became all the more valuable to Mao when he spent time in America doing graduate work in engineering at Kansas State University, becoming familiar with America's language as well as many of its customs. He had quit school before completing his studies when he was ordered to return to Hainan by Mao Quan.

It was then, under Mao's guidance, that he received extensive training in insurgency tactics, and now he had been selected to fly the helicopter in the final and most critical phase of Tonu Hon's plan.

Tonu Hon had praised him for his handling of the Chow affair and the downing of Swelling's plane. His reward was a role in the final two stages of the plan. The loss of Liu Shao's services had also necessitated Chen's involvement in the Langley matter, a situation he relished because it gave him the opportunity to make an even more significant contribution to Mao Quan's objective of 5A domination.

Chen Po Lee had spent much of the night and most of the day up until this point reviewing his role in what would transpire. He was still unpacking his few belongings when he heard a knock on the door. When he opened it, it was the little man from the registration desk in the lobby. Chen had already decided he wanted as little to do with the man as possible. The motel operator was fat and smelled of garlic, and now his breathing was labored after doing nothing more than climbing the stairs to the second floor.

"This came for ya," the man said, and handed Chen an oversized brown envelope. "Oh, yeah, the dame at the embassy called to see if you got in all right. I told her you was in your room, but she said she was just checkin'."

Chen looked at the package, lowered his head in a polite bow, closed the door, and went to the window.

He waited until he was sure the man had walked away before he opened the package and emptied the contents on the bed. There were two folders, one with the name Langley on it, the other without a name. Chen Po opened the one with the name of the senator. It contained several photographs, two Washington street maps, newspaper clippings, and background information. More importantly, it gave Chen a time and location when he could expect the senior Langley to be most vulnerable—following the ten o'clock Mass at Saint Patrick's Church the following day. Chen read the contents of the envelope several times before putting the information back in the folder, pulling the covers back on his bed, and lying down. He would sleep now. There was no telling when there would be another opportunity.

Chapter Nine

Time 1000LT:

"Everyone is here except T.C., Chief," Millie said. "He caught the nine-thirty shuttle to Miami to check out that Bunche Park address. Hathaway is picking him up at the airport. T.C. said he'd call in around noon or as soon as he knows something."

Packer nodded, paged through his copy of Churchill's report a second time, slumped back in his chair, and glanced around the table. "Well, like T.C. said, it looks like we've run out of luck."

"We had it all yesterday," Miller observed.

Packer threw the report down on the conference table. "One of the biggest, busiest damn hospitals in the country," Packer grumbled. "You'd think someone would have seen something."

Millie continued to rummage through her own stack of papers until she located another copy of the homicide report on the man they knew as Frank Pan. "According to Churchill, he claims he couldn't find anything on Pan in their files so he faxed a copy of Pan's fingerprints to the FBI. He thinks we should know something later this morning—if they have anything on him, that is."

Packer was agitated. "Dammit, it seems like we're snakebit—we're always a couple of steps behind these clowns. According to Churchill's report, he's convinced Pan was either thrown or knocked over the barrier from the fourth floor of that parking garage."

Jude Parrish took out a piece of paper and started to sketch. "Lets go back to square one. Churchill's theory is it went something like this: Someone took Pan up to the fourth floor of that parking garage, pulled him out of the car, stood him up next to the barrier, crawled back into the car, backed up, put the car in gear, plowed into him, and over he went. He's basing most of his theory on the fact that both of Pan's legs were crushed."

"Why would Pan just stand there and let it happen?" Miller wondered.

"Churchill has two theories on that," Parrish said. "One, it was someone Pan trusted and he never expected it. Or two, the painkillers they gave Pan at the Rosewell Clinic made him so groggy and incapacitated he couldn't react when he saw what was happening. Either or both may have made it impossible for him to do anything."

"Either way," Packer said, "it confirms something we've expected from the very beginning. There's more than just the kid in the van and our friend Pan involved in this damn thing. The question is who are they and where are they?"

Millie Ploughman studied Parrish's sketch. "How fast would that car, or whatever the killer used, have to have been going to pin Pan to the wall, crush his legs, and throw him over that barrier?"

"Fast enough to cause some damage to the front end," Parrish said. "Churchill is convinced it was no accident. He is likewise convinced that if we knew the kind of vehicle Pan's killer used and where to find it, we'd find some sort of damage. There was blood on the wall—and there is probably blood plus damage to the front of that vehicle."

"All right, then, what are we looking for and where do we go to look for it?" Packer pressed.

"There's some reason why Pan's killer used the parking garage at Washington General," Parrish said. "Maybe it was convenient and the killer was familiar with the area, or . . ." Parrish frowned. When he said his theory out loud, it didn't sound as feasible as when he'd first thought it through.

"Like an employee, maybe?" Millie asked.

"Or someone who knew the fourth floor of the hospital parking garage would be pretty much deserted that time of night?" Miller tried.

"Possible," Packer replied. "But if that's the case, it wouldn't be anyone who went on duty at eleven o'clock because the car would still be there when Pan's body was found."

"By the same token, it wouldn't be anyone who went off duty at eleven because they would have cleared the area before Pan was killed," Millie said.

Packer leaned forward with his hands on the table. "It's a long shot, Millie, but I want you to talk to the personnel people at Washington General. Have them run a computer check for us. Tell them we want to know the names, hiring dates, and occupation of every Chinese employee on their payroll. It doesn't make any difference whether they're here on a student visa, or they're American nationals, or what. So far Mao has shown an inclination to stick with his own people; Pan, the body in the van, the Chow kid down in Florida, and the body in Mexico . . . were all Chinese. Maybe we'll learn something."

Time 1033LT

Chen Po Lee picked up the rented white four-door Dodge sedan at ten o'clock, and using Jacqueline Marceau's maps, drove directly to Saint Patrick's Church. He had anticipated some difficulty at the rental agency, but there had been none. A bored and preoccupied young woman behind the counter at Capital Leasing appeared to be more interested in her conversation with a fellow employee then she was in company business. She gave Chen's forged driver's license little more than a cursory look, took his money, handed him the keys, informed him of the color, make, and model of the car he had rented, and pointed him toward the parking lot where the car was located. Then she went back to her conversation.

Now Chen found himself driving around the church. The main entrance was on Delaware, located between the structure's twin spires. Chen Po counted eleven steps, and glanced at the drawing in his hand. Beyond the three doors at the entrance was the nave, and Jacqueline Marceau indicated this was where the senator and his family worshipped. He reread the note she had attached to the street map:

Senator Langly leaves by the front entrance. He is usually accompanied by his wife and two grandchildren, and is one of the first to leave. The grandchildren are a boy (10) and a girl (7). On the three occasions I have observed him, he usually stops to chat with the priest following mass. The senator's car, a black, late-model Lincoln with a Massachusetts license plate, will be parked across the street in the church parking lot. The senator and his family will cross the street at the light at the corner of Anchor and Delaware. At this point there is a steady stream of parishioners crossing the street and a clear shot will be difficult. From my observation, it appears that there are two times when you can get a clean shot, when he is talking to the priest and when he starts to pull out of the parking lot.

Chen took out his lighter, burned the note, crushed the ashes, and turned his attention to the photographs. There were three pictures of the senator, all revealing a man who was tall, gray-haired, and ramrod straight. He would be easy to recognize because of his height, and because of Jacqueline's note that he *"seldom wears a hat regardless of the weather."*

In addition, there were two pictures of Mrs. Langley, a blonde, herself quite tall. The most distinguishing feature of all was that she walked with a cane. The pictures, coupled with the fact that Langley was likely to have his two grandchildren with him, made Chen confident he would recognize him.

He slid the photographs back in the envelope and scanned the area around the church. He decided it would be too risky to attempt a shot after the senator got into his car, for the simple reason that Chen himself could get caught in the traffic leaving the parking lot. For that reason alone, he decided his best opportunity would be when Langley stopped to chat with the priest after the service. Then he decided the best vantage point would be across the street directly in front of the church. There was no traffic light and it was a one-way street.

Satisfied, Chen turned his attention to his next appointment. He remained there for several moments, studying his street map. Jacqueline Marceau had marked the route from Saint Patrick's to the place in Virginia called Creighton. He repeated the name aloud, Quinto Aircraft. He had two hours before his appointment.

Time 1131LT:

Frank Hathaway had been with the ISA for ten years, but this was the first time Bogner had worked with him. Hathaway was the prototypical Packer man. At age forty-seven, he had a resume that included thirteen years in the Marines, a degree in mathematics from Florida Southern, and service as a part-time Baptist minister. He could also claim to be a bachelor again after a tumultuous four-year marriage that had ended in a messy divorce. His fitness report indicated he worked hard as well as smart and, like Miller back in Washington, readily admitted that the ISA was his life. He picked Bogner up at the airport and drove to the 112 High Street address in Bunche Park. Along the way he filled Bogner in.

"When Millie called yesterday, I drove over here so I could get a look around. If this is their base of operations, T.C., they've got a slick one: quiet neighborhood, cozy-looking little bungalow, neat as a pin."

"We don't think this is their headquarters, Frank. What we do think this is, is a relay point. We've got a pretty good indication that the real base of operations is in Cuba. But we learned yesterday that their man in Washington was making calls to this address. Last night he bought the farm, and now we're hoping that we can learn something here that will shed some light on this mess."

Hathaway drove north on 95, turned west at Biscayne Gardens, exited on N.W. 27th, and circled back to Bunche Park. By the time he turned onto High Street, he was telling Bogner, "I talked to two neighbors. They tell me the house is a rental—some Chinese guy rents it. Hasn't been there long, maybe a month. They say they don't see much of him, and neither of them can remember seeing him in the past couple of days. They say his girlfriend or live-in pretty much stays to herself. One of the neighbors thinks she might be a student. They see her lugging what appears to be textbooks back and forth from her car. Neither one of the neighbors knew her name, and one of them said they couldn't be certain she even speaks English. Apparently she doesn't socialize much."

Bogner rolled down the window, while Hathaway edged the car over to the curb a block south of the High Street address, and looked up and down the street. The temperature had crawled into the low eighties, and he could hear children playing.

"No use beating around the bush," Bogner said. "If someone's there, we muscle our way in. If no one's at home, we go in anyway."

Hathaway moved up a block, parked at the curb, and looked around. "I don't see a car. This morning there was a Ford Probe with Mississippi license plates parked here. I checked with the Mississippi MVD. The car is leased. I checked with the rental agency, and they claim the car is leased to a Frank Pan, who gives his address as Merdian, Mississippi."

Bogner grinned. "Bingo." He had picked up the word from Packer. "That's our man." He got out of the car and started up the sidewalk with Hathaway behind him. When no one answered the doorbell, he looked at Hathaway, took out a credit card, slipped it between the door and the frame next to the lock, and turned the knob. The door opened.

"Haven't lost your touch," Hathaway noted with a smile.

"Let's hope none of the neighbors were watching," Bogner answered. "I don't want to have to explain this to the local constabulary."

Bogner started by rummaging through a pile of papers on a desk in the living room, while Hathaway worked his way through the rest of the house. When he heard Hathaway shout "Eureka," he knew his partner had found something, and he started for the rear of the house. "My, my, my," Hathaway continued, grinning. "Look at all the toys."

To Bogner's way of thinking, Frank Pan, or whatever his real name was, had done a more than adequate job of covering his tracks—up until the last twenty-four hours. Since then he had left a trail a blind man could follow.

There it was, all laid out on the top of a cheap pine desk in the middle of a housing development in Bunche Park, Florida: two telephones, an elaborate computer, a fax machine, a modem, and a list of telephone numbers. In the drawer of the desk there were credit cards and drivers' licenses, all with Chinese names just waiting for the right photo, and a drawer full of all the other accoutrements of a mission in need of several identities.

Bogner was just sitting down to begin sifting

through their prize when they heard the front door open. The young woman saw Hathaway and froze. Hathaway had taken no chances. He had his revolver out and pointed directly at her. Despite the weapon, his voice was calm and reassuring. He was doing his best to keep the young woman from all-out panic.

"Okay, now, slow and easy, miss. No screaming, no sudden movements, don't do anything foolish, and you'll be all right. Do something dumb and all bets are off. Keep your hands in front of you where I can see them and walk toward me."

Bogner watched while Hathaway moved around behind the young woman and marched her down the hall toward the rear of the house. She was a pretty girl, petite, with coal-black hair and piercing brown eyes. She wore shorts and a Dade County Junior College T-shirt. "Suppose we start with a name," Bogner said.

The girl hesitated; surprisingly her expression reflected more of an air of anger than intimidation.

"Let's try it again. Do you speak English?"

"Probably better than you do," she shot back. "You don't tackle something like this if you can't read English." She held out her textbook for Bogner's examination. The title was *Principles of Human Anatomy*. "Now what's this all about?"

"Do you speak Chinese?"

"Enough Mandarin to get by. I fake the rest."

"Back to the name."

"Tian," she replied. "Now suppose you tell me who the hell you are?"

Bogner started to smile. "He's Frank Hathaway, my name is T.C. Bogner, we're with the Internal Security Agency." Hathaway flipped open his wallet to show the woman his badge.

Tian moved closer and studied Hathaway's credentials. "ISA? Never heard of it. Who let you in?"

Bogner smiled. "Suppose you let me ask the questions. For a start, what's going on here?"

The young woman shrugged her shoulders. "Who knows? It's a job. Actually it's a sweet deal for a student: room, board, and more than half the time there's no one here but me. I pretty much come and go as I please."

"Who hired you?"

Tian shrugged again. "Who knows? A month ago I saw an ad in the paper. It said they were looking for a 'house sitter.' I applied and got the job. Now, you tell me, what's going on here? Why did you bust in?"

"Suppose you answer my questions first," Bogner said. "We'll start with all this electronic gear and a drawer full of dummy driver's licenses and credit cards."

Tian shrugged for the third time. It seemed to be her standard response. "I have no idea what's in that drawer. Mr. Pan told me to stay out of it. I do what I'm told."

Bogner heard the name he was looking for. Pan. If she was covering for the man, she had dropped the name inadvertently. On the other hand, she made no effort to recover. Either she was careless, or cool, or she really didn't know what was going on. He was inclined to believe the latter. "Tell me about this Mr. Pan?"

"You mean what he looks like?"

"We'll start there."

"Tall, slight, old. Maybe not as old as you guys, but old." She shrugged again. "What else is there to tell you?"

"Just exactly what does your job entail, Tian?"

"I keep the house straight and I stay out of the way when they're here."

"Who is 'they'?"

For the first time since their conversation started, Tian appeared reluctant to answer. "One of the first things Mr. Pan told me when he gave me the job was that I was to keep my mouth shut about what went on here."

"Didn't you think that was a bit unusual?"

"Mr. Pan said people around here were prejudiced toward foreigners and I'd get along better if I kept to myself. It didn't bother me. I've got lots of friends at school."

"In addition to playing house sitter, what other kinds of things does he have you do?"

Tian thought for a moment. "For the first couple of weeks, nothing. Then I started picking people up at the airport and bringing them back here, but I'd usually take them back to the airport again."

"Which airport?" Bogner demanded.

"They come in at the local airport here, usually in a private plane. Those are the ones I take to the airport in Miami. When they come down from Washington, I take them back to the local airport.

I've been doing so much of it that I called my father and asked him if I should get a chauffeur's license. I don't know if my insurance covers what I'm doing."

Bogner laughed. He was on the right track. "When you take them to Miami International, do they always fly out to Washington?" Hathaway asked.

The young woman nodded. "Most of the time."

"What about all of this?" Bogner asked, pointing to the electronic gear.

"The only time I use it is when I have to fax something to either Cuba or Washington. Lately there's been more of that kind of thing then there was at first."

"What kind of messages are you faxing back and forth?"

"Maybe I should be talking to a lawyer instead of you guys," Tian said. "Am I in some kind of trouble?"

"The more questions you answer, the less trouble you're in," Bogner assured her. "Now, what do the messages say?"

"Don't know. Most of the time the messages are in Chinese. I don't read Chinese. The only Chinese I can speak is what little Mandarin I picked up from my parents at the dinner table or when they didn't want me to know what they were talking about."

"Back to the airport. When's the last time you picked someone up?"

"Last night. I was told to pick up a Mr. Yen at the local airport, bring him back to the house to pick up a few things, and then take him early this morning to catch a flight to Washington."

"Describe Mr. Yen."

"Average height, a bit on the homely side for my taste, seemed to be uptight. The difference between him and the others, he's more friendly—he at least tried to talk to me. I picked him up once before and drove him down to a place on Toll Reef at Biscayne Bay."

"When?"

Tian thought for a minute. "Three days ago."

Bogner looked at Hathaway and smiled. Then he took the sketch of Liu Shao out of his pocket. "You're almost off the hook, Tian. Do you recognize this man?"

Tian took the sketch and studied it. "It sorta looks like Mr. Pan."

"When's the last time you saw this Mr. Pan?"

"Two days ago."

"When's the last time you heard from him?"

"Same answer, two days ago."

"One final question. Who have you had contact with either by picking them up at the airport or by fax or telephone other than Pan and the man you took to the airport earlier today?"

Tian thought for a minute. "I receive lots of fax messages from some woman in Washington."

"How do you know it's a woman?"

"Just a feeling. She uses good English, and the way she structures her sentences. She seems to flip back and forth from English to Chinese without much difficulty. She gives instructions in both English and Chinese, but the content of the message is always in Chinese. None of the others do that. She ends all her transmissions with a lower-case m."

Bogner was convinced they had made progress. "Tian," he said, "you've been most helpful. Now we have a favor to ask. Agent Hathaway is going to stay with you and we're going to tap your phone lines to monitor all incoming calls and fax transmissions. All we ask of you is that you don't reveal the fact that the lines are being tapped. Deal?"

"Am I going to lose my job over this?"

"In all probability. We don't want to scare you, but the fact is, we think your employer, Mr. Pan, and the man you helped put on a plane early this morning are part of terrorist group that has already killed a number of people. Agent Hathaway and I are trying to stop them before the situation gets worse."

Tian stepped back. She looked at both Hathaway and Bogner with an expression of disbelief. "Killing people? You know what I thought this was all about? I knew there was something coming down, but I figured it was drugs."

"That should have been your signal to bail out," Hathaway said.

"Get real. What's a toke or a little speed gonna hurt? Do you have any idea how much it costs to go to college these days? I may not agree with what they're doing, but I've got a sweet deal here. Not only that, they pay me."

"It looks like the ride is over," Bogner said, "but

for the time being we need to keep these lines open. Sooner or later, someone is going to say something we can use to shut them down."

Tian dropped into a chair. She looked disappointed. "If that's the case, do either one of you guys want to float a poor premed student a loan?"

When Tian had gone to her room, which had already been searched, Hathaway and Bogner discussed what they had learned. "So what do we tell Packer?" the Miami-based agent wondered.

"First we tell him to keep his guard up; if Tian took someone to the airport to catch a flight to Washington, that could mean Tonu Hon has already hustled in Pan's replacement. The fact that he looks like your 'average Chinese' and goes by the name of Yen sure as hell doesn't give us much to go on.

"Then we tell Packer we may have learned something about Mao's mole in the Capital. I'm inclined to think this girl may know what she's talking about. Women often have a sixth sense on this kind of thing. If she thinks it's a woman, it may well be one. Again, it's not much to go on, but it's more than we had. The initial m on those fax transmissions is probably a code sig. On the other hand it might just be a crack in the veneer—one of those habits a person gets into.

"The main thing is, with you here, we've shut down their link to Cuba. Now we wait and see what happens when they can't get through to each other."

Time 1151LT:

It was shortly before noon when Jacqueline Marceau returned to her apartment. It had taken her most of the morning to obtain the required two insurance estimates for repairs to her car. Even though the damage was minimal, a mere 470 dollars worth, she made arrangements to have it repaired.

Always cautious, Jacqueline had examined the grille and bumper following her episode with Liu Shao, and discovered the damage as well as traces of what she was convinced was blood. She ran her car through an automatic car wash, and told the man at the repair shop that the damage to her unattended car had occurred in a mall parking lot. To further cover her tracks, she called her insurance company and told them the same story.

Now that she was back in her apartment and had some time to herself, she pulled out the sketches of Washington General Hospital to study the layout of the sixth floor. The drawings were copies, obtained from classified files in the CIA records room just down the hall from her office. The drawings were important because they indicated the location of the sixth-floor suite of rooms used by prior Presidents when they went in for their annual physical. Indications were, David Colchin would use the same rooms.

With the drawings laid out on the table in her kitchen, Jacqueline next traced the projected flight path of the helicopter from Creighton to the hospital and estimated the flying time, all based on information supplied by Tonu Hon and Liu Shao.

The original plan had called for Liu Shao to fly the aircraft. Like Chen, Liu had been trained in a similar Kaman SH-2 Seasprite purchased from the South Koreans at Mao Quan's base of operations in Hainan. In the initial plan, Chen would have been the one to operate the shoulder-mounted M136 launcher. Now, with Liu Shao out of the picture, Chen would move into the pilot's seat and manning the launcher would be her job. She was trained and ready.

At the same time, Jacqueline was pleased that Tonu Hon trusted her with what had to be considered the most critical component of their campaign.

Now that she knew what her role would be, Jacqueline Marceau closed her eyes and reflected back on the grueling days of training before Mao Quan had selected her for the campaign. The training had been intensive, comprehensive, and brutal. Like all of Mao's recruits she had spent time learning to operate an M16A, an M249 machine gun, an M203 grenade launcher, and, of course, the *piece de resistance*, the M136 launcher. It was understood that each of them was training with weapons Mao knew were readily available and easily obtainable through DRMOs in America. It was Tonu Hon who'd said the American military's penchant for excess made the task of outfitting his people incomprehensibly easy.

The rest had not been so easy. She had spent days

trudging through swamps and nights sleeping in flea-infested foxholes. She had been forced to go without food for days on end, and had relished the taste of a small dog when she was finally able to lure one into her snare. When she wasn't in the field, she was in the classroom. There were the predictable courses in American history, in the American system of government, in English, in Mandarin—and when she felt as though she was too exhausted to go on, there was always the *Little Red Book*. She had religiously studied the writings of Mao Zedong, Zhou Enlai, and Jiang Qing, and could recite extensive passages from the works of all three.

While all that she had accomplished had weighed heavily in her favor, in the end, Jacqueline suspected that Mao knew that her hatred for her father's killer and the desire to revenge his untimely death motivated her more than any Party ideology. She had vowed on the day of her father's death that someday, somehow, she would have her revenge—and that the obscure American army lieutenant, destined to become the senior senator from Iowa, would pay with his life. In return for that satisfaction, she was eager to accept the final challenge.

Slowly, Jacqueline Marceau's thoughts returned to the present. She had insured Chen Po Lee's arrival with a telephone call, delivered the packet via a local parcel service, and taken care of a variety of lesser matters.

Now it was time for Julie Simon.

*　　*　　*

In the two days since the Crane shooting, Julie Simon was aware that she had spiraled completely out of control. For the second day in a row, she had found it impossible to even leave her apartment. She refused to answer the telephone and continued to drink heavily. When she heard the knock on her door, she considered ignoring it until she heard Jacqueline Marceau's voice.

"Come on, Julie, I know you're in there. Open up, I made a pot of tea for us."

When Julie opened the door, Jacqueline realized the woman looked even worse than she had the day before. Her eyes were still swollen, her complexion appeared to be drained of all color, and she was shaking even harder.

"For God's sake, woman," Jacqueline said, "how long has it been since you've had anything to eat?"

Julie shook her head. "Not hungry. Besides, who needs food," she slurred. "I've—I've got my old friend here." She held the half-empty fifth of scotch up to the light. "Still—still plenty left."

Jacqueline took Julie by the arm and steered her to the couch. "Sit down and give me that," she said. She took the bottle out of the woman's hand and headed for the kitchen. When she returned moments later, she had poured Julie a cup of tea and made her some toast. "Here," she said, "work on this."

Despite the hour, Julie was still dressed in her robe and nightgown. She had trouble focusing her thoughts, sobbed intermittently, and tortured her handkerchief; twisting, jabbing at tears, and blowing her nose. When she finally looked up at Jacqueline, the tears erupted again.

"What the hell did you expect, Julie? Sure it hurts. But you're playing with dynamite. How much longer do you think you can go on like this?"

Julie couldn't find the strength to answer.

"Keep going like you're going and even though you don't think it's possible, your life is guaranteed to get a whole lot worse."

Julie studied the woman who had introduced her to Richard Crane, reached for her tea, took a sip, and set the cup down.

"Did you hear what happened last night?" Jacqueline asked.

"I haven't—haven't even turned the television on since . . . that day," Julie admitted. "I was afraid they might say something about Richard. I—I couldn't take that."

Jacqueline cocked her head to one side. "Some man either fell over or was knocked over one of those cement barriers in the hospital parking garage last night. They found him sometime early this morning. The police think he fell from the fourth level."

If Julie heard what Jacqueline told her, she gave no indication. She stared past her friend into the abstract emptiness and started to cry again. "I don't know what to do, Jacky. I've cried until I'm cried out. I can't sleep. I can't eat. All I want now is to crawl into a hole somewhere and pull the world in on top of me."

It had taken less than two days for Jacqueline

Marceau to grow impatient with Julie Simon's weakness. During her training in Hainan, Tonu Hon had cautioned her against that impatience; now she had to guard against alienating the woman she still needed. Still, she was beginning to feel the pressure; she was keenly aware that the President's admission to Washington General was now less than two days away. The information she still needed about Colchin's schedule could come from no other source, it was too well guarded.

To insure uncompromised success in the final phase of their mission, Jacqueline was dependent now upon only one person, Julie Simon. She was the one person who would regard Jacqueline's questions about the President's stay in Washington General without suspicion.

Jacqueline sat down beside the sobbing woman again and put her arm around her. "Suppose I send out for something to eat. How about something from the deli down the street?"

Julie closed her eyes and leaned her head back.

Time 1313LT:

"When he was here the other day, I told your friend we need much more than a day or two to get her ready," Quinto wheezed.

Chen Po Lee moved around the craft. He was familiar with the model except for the few modifications added by the last operator. He ignored the superficial dents and dings, and carefully inspected the main rotor engines, two General Electric T58-

8Fs with turboshafts. He lifted the tarpaulin to gain access to the cockpit, got in, situated himself in the pilot's seat, and studied the configuration of the flight panel. The retrofit was recent. The last engine overhaul had been accomplished less than three months earlier, and a complete safety check, as Quinto had promised, had taken place within the last twenty-four hours. Based on Liu Shao's detailed last report to Tonu Hon two days ago, Chen had expected worse.

Quinto lit a cigar and lowered his bulk onto a nearby shipping crate. He watched Chen with a veiled curiosity. There was little doubt in his mind that this man who called himself Yen was one of the men the two ISA agents had warned him about. He glanced down at the card Chen had given him. The company name was Weitock Hospital Support Services, and the name of the man was Harry Yen, with the vague title of "Administrator."

After several minutes, Chen stepped out of the craft. "I am told you assured my associate that it is flight-worthy."

Quinto laughed. It was a wheezy sound, half choked by an intermittent cough. "Hey, I told your Mr. Key, she's ready to go. You show me the necessary papers and hand over a check—that's all there is to it."

"My associates will conclude negotiations with Mr. Park within the hour, and I will have the check when we accept delivery tomorrow evening," Chen said.

Yamir Quinto's usually flacid face warmed at the

news. "As soon as I get confirmation from Park, we're in business."

"You will call Mr. Park to confirm?"

Quinto nodded.

"It will be possible to arrange a brief check flight tomorrow afternoon?" Chen pressed.

"Tomorrow is Sunday," Quinto reminded him. "None of my people will be in. How about Monday afternoon?"

Chen's expression remained unchanged. "Unfortunately we must demonstrate our readiness to our new client on Monday. If we cannot do so, our service contract is in jeopardy."

Quinto looked at his watch. "Tomorrow it is. What time tomorrow?"

"Late afternoon, early evening," Chen said, "I have other commitments during the day."

"Don't be too late," Quinto grumbled. "I'm already spendin' six days a week around this damn place, and I sure as hell ain't anxious to spend another."

As Chen Po Lee turned to walk away, Quinto started after him.

"I'm curious. Your friend Key, what happened to him?"

Chen stiffened. "Mr. Key's duty was to locate a suitable aircraft. He has fulfilled that responsibility. Now, I am in charge."

Quinto followed Chen to the door, and watched as the little man walked to his car, got in, and drove away. Then he went back into his office, and picked up Bogner's card and the telephone. Halfway through the number he quit dialing and nestled the receiver back in its cradle. "Fuck the feds," he grunted. "What they don't know won't hurt 'em."

Time 1741LT:

For Chen Po Lee it had been a tiring twenty-four hours. There had been little opportunity for sleep during his flight from Miami to Washington, and there had been little time to relax since his arrival. At the airport he had made arrangements for a car to be picked up later that morning, caught the transit into the city, checked into his motel, reviewed the first packet containing documents supplied by Jacqueline Marceau, and observed the layout at the church. Finally, he had driven to the small airfield in Virginia to make certain he was familiar with the aircraft they would use in the assault on the hospital.

By the time he returned to the motel, the weather had taken a turn for the worse again. Despite a forecast of little more than intermittent snow showers, the snow had started to accumulate, and Chen Po Lee was beginning to be concerned. If the snow continued, it could become a factor in his escape from the scene at the church the following morning.

After parking his car, he stopped in the motel's lobby to check on the arrival of the second courier package. The preoccupied young woman behind the desk pulled it out from under the counter and handed it over without diverting her eyes from the television. When he asked for seven-thirty wake-up call, she acknowledged his request with a disinterested "You got it" and went back to her program.

Chen climbed the stairs to his second-floor room, went into the bathroom, grabbed a towel, placed it on the bed, opened the package, and carefully arranged the contents on the towel. The package contained an M9 automatic and three loaded clips. Chen, like Jacqueline Marceau, had been thoroughly schooled in a variety of American weapons. Now he hefted the automatic, shoved the safety lever into the locked position, removed the clip, inspected the chamber and bore, reinserted the clip, and released the slide. When the slide engaged, he heard the reassuring metallic sound that indicated he was ready.

For the rest of the day after leaving Julie Simon, Jacqueline spent much of her time listening to newscasts on both television and radio. The news was always the same. The police had found Liu's body, but as yet they gave no indication he had been tied to the recent terrorist attacks. They were still referring to the dead man as Frank Pan. Despite the delay, she knew it was only a matter of time until the authorities knew Pan's true identity. It would be a simple matter to check Liu's fingerprints, fingerprints that even Tonu Hon knew were on file with the FBI. Liu Shao's brief stint as an interpreter with the State Department insured that.

Since her session with Julie earlier in the day, Jacqueline had left the house only once, to drop a package off at the courier station. It had taken longer than she anticipated because she had driven across town to insure that she was not recognized. Two different messenger services, two different disguises, different times of day; Jacqueline was convinced she had not been detected. Now it was time to check on Julie again. She had promised to look in on her later in the evening and bring her something to eat. She fixed a pot of soup, prepared a tray, and took the elevator to Julie's floor. When Julie did not answer, Jacqueline tried the door. It opened and she went in. She found Julie sprawled across her bed, crying.

At the ISA offices on Delaware, Robert Miller and Millie Ploughman went over the employment printouts supplied by Washington General. The computer search had come up with the names of 137 Asian employees. They had segmented the list by occupation and shift. Of the 137, the majority were on the day shift. Thirty-one were either doctors, nurses, or technicians. The rest were service personnel. Most of the service personnel were assigned to the swing and midnight shifts.

After three hours of poring over the records, they had identified seven that had returned to China during the last three years.

Packer came out of his office, scanned the list, and instructed Miller to get into the personnel files of the seven. "Tear those damn files apart if you have to. If you see anything that looks the least bit suspicious, check it out."

Millie Ploughman leaned back in her chair and took off her glasses. "Chief," she said, "I've been thinking. Suppose Pan's killer isn't Asian. Then what?"

"Then we're damn near back to square one."

(copy) WNBS . . . 2300LT broadcast
Newsbreak—Dateline: Washington: NEWS ON
THE HOUR

This is WNBS news on the hour. I'm Joy
Carpenter.

Police still have not released the name of a
man whose body was found in the parking
lot at Washington General Hospital early
this morning.

However, sources close to the investigation
indicate the dead man may have ties to a
terrorist group believed to be responsible
for bombings aboard the planes of Secretary of the Air Force James Dunning, and
Undersecretary of State William Swelling. . . .

RED WIND

The weather . . . continued cold with snow flurries likely . . .

Stay tuned to WNBS for late-breaking news . . . twenty-four hours a day.
This is Joy Carpenter reporting.

Chapter Ten

5 Nov: Time 0247LT:

For most of the three hours since she had retired for the evening, Jacqueline Marceau tossed and turned, finding it difficult to sleep, experiencing instead a nettling kind of semiconsciousness, troubled and fretful.

Twice, she had given in to those concerns and gone back to the rear bedroom where she kept the fax machine. Each time she failed to find what she was looking for, some kind of acknowledgment of her report. Now she was checking for the third time. Four hours after her transmission, there was no indication that her report to Tonu Hon had been received and relayed. Nor, as there usually was, was there a return message from Tonu Hon.

Two hours after her original transmission, she had faxed her message, in Chinese, for a second time, in the belief that the young woman at Bunche Park had simply not received the first one. But there had been no acknowledgment or any kind of response to the second transmission either. That was when Jacqueline became concerned. She had checked her log, the fax number in Bunche Park, and even reread the instructions on her machine; in the end there was nothing that would indicate an equipment malfunction or that she had done anything wrong.

Worried that Tonu Hon might think her in some way derelict, she had even switched over to the Weather Channel on two different occasions to see if there was a possibility of storms in the Miami area; downed phone lines, power failures—anything that might have interfered with her transmissions.

It was almost three o'clock in the morning when she finally returned to her bedroom and tried to sleep again. Then it was more of the same: a deteriorating, eroding confidence, and the singular conviction that something had gone wrong.

After sending Bogner back to the airport, Frank Hathaway had spent most of the afternoon waiting at the Bunche Park address. The young woman talked to him on two separate occasions. Finally, with darkness settling in, she offered him a glass of ice tea.

To Hathaway's surprise, the invitation was accompanied by a series of questions. What was the ISA, what was their mission, where did he live, and more. Later, after Hathaway had confirmed that there had been no calls or transmissions, and that he would be on duty throughout the night, the young woman warmed even more, and informed him it would be all right with her if he slept on the couch in the front room.

"Mr. Pan arranged it so that a bell rings on an incoming transmission," she informed him. "If I happen to be asleep, the bell alerts me and I forward the transmission. After I receive and relay a message, he told me to destroy the document." Then she added, "If you sleep on the couch, you'll be able to hear the chime."

Hathaway accepted, and now, a few minutes before midnight, he heard the chime. As Tian indicated it would be, the message was in Chinese and the signature was a lower-case m. It took less than four minutes for him to reroute the message back to the ISA night crew in Washington.

"The one in Cuba will be suspicious when he doesn't get his report," Tian reminded him.

"Then relay it," Hathaway said. "Let's not do anything to arouse suspicion." Then he added, "You called it a report. How do you know it's a report?"

"It's the only thing that makes sense," Tian said, "What would you think if every night around midnight you received a fax from Washington and you were told you were supposed to relay it? Sometimes there's a reply, which I relay, sometimes there isn't. So I figure it's a report."

Hathaway stood up and began walking around the room. "Like T.C. said, faxes are sent to a number. You don't happened to recall the number in Washington, do you?"

Tian shook her head. "As soon as the transmission ends, I destroy the original. Besides, they've changed the number several times."

"Changed the number?"

"Yeah—changed. And even if they didn't, I wouldn't remember; numbers aren't my thing. I'm too busy trying to remember my human anatomy. Do you have any idea what the left common carotid or the right common iliac is?"

Hathaway shook his head.

"Well, that's why I don't remember fax numbers, because I'm too damn busy trying to remember what the aorta and its principal branches are to remember something that isn't going to help me pass my human anatomy course."

The rerouted copy of Jacqueline Marceau's fax had been logged in at ISA operations shortly after midnight, and Hatton had called in one of the agency's interpreters. Her name was Nancy Ming, American-born, a recent graduate of Georgetown who had been with the ISA less than a year. Hatton had used Ming on several occasions, not only because she was good, but because she was quick and had a working knowledge of cryptography as well. Less than ten minutes after her arrival, she had translated the message and put a copy in front of Hatton.

"There is a series of numbers at the beginning of the message," she said, "probably a code of some sort. If I was guessing, I'd say those numbers have something to do with time and date of the fax. If it is a code, it's inverted or arranged in some kind of sequence known only to the sender and receiver. Those are the hardest kinds of code to break because there is no logic or key."

Hatton picked up the piece of paper and read it.

0278-08976-44tt45te-f(pt)
Yen in place. Pan resolved.
L.L. Sunday. Monday go. m

"Yen arrived?" Hatton repeated, "Pan resolved? What the hell does that mean?"

The young woman looked over his shoulder and shrugged. "In English, a yen is a longing of some sort. In Japanese it's a unit of currency." She was smiling.

"Hell, I know that," Hatton said with a sigh, "but what does it mean?"

Time 0731LT:

The wake-up call had come at precisely seven-thirty, and Chen Po Lee sat on the edge of his bed waiting for the last vestiges of sleep to fade. A gray early Sunday morning light filtered between the separations in the folds of the dingy drapes, creating haphazard patterns on a worn and faded green-gray carpet whose color was further camouflaged by stains and cigarette burns.

He sat that way for several moments reflecting on the day, preoccupied with the discipline of schedules and the magnitude of his undertaking. His concerns were procedural: timing and location, accuracy and efficiency. There was not now, nor would there be, any thought given to the man he intended to kill. His thinking revolved around the result. From his perspective, the one called Langley was not a man. He was an objective, a target, a duty.

Finally, Chen stood up, stretched, found his way through the semishadows into the bathroom, and turned on the light. In that harsh light he examined his face in the mirror. The copperish-yellow reflection staring back at him revealed the vacuum in his eyes and the disenchantment he felt when he allowed himself to contemplate his life. He had always been a soldier, a server, a vehicle for someone else's ambitions. If he entertained his own wants, they were of little consequence, and it never seemed to matter if he went on without them.

There was no need to shave or shower. He had accomplished both the previous day. He pulled on his trousers and a heavy sweater, both black, and went back into the room to finish dressing. From time to time, he went to the window and assessed the weather. It was day without color, overcast, blustery, decidedly unappealing, a funeral kind of day. He wondered if it was a portent of the next few hours.

Finally, when he was ready and there was nothing left to do, he took out the M9 and went through the ritual of checking it out one more time.

He had two hours to wait.

Sara Packer enjoyed rituals, and the Sunday morning ritual had become one of her favorites. On a Sunday, she would get up before her husband, make a pot of coffee, take a long, luxurious shower, read the *Post*, plan the day, and wake her husband ninety minutes before church. On those days that she felt like cooking after church, she often called Robert Miller and invited him to dine with Clancy and her on one of her famous crabmeat and sour cream three-egg omelettes. Robert never declined.

On this Sunday, though, it was different. She had turned on the television in the kitchen and caught the tail end of the latest update on Lattimere Spitz. Spitz had been moved to a private room—he was out of the intensive-care unit. Sara Packer sipped her coffee and wondered if she should call Lucy Spitz to see if she needed anything.

Moments later, as she was preparing to go in into the bedroom to wake her husband, the phone rang. It was Robert Miller.

"Sara, is the chief up?" When Sara Packer heard the familiar voice, she was reminded why Robert Miller was still a bachelor. Her husband's longtime aide had failed to master even the most rudimentary of the social graces.

"Well, gee, I'm fine, Bob. How nice of you to ask," she said. "And how are *you* this morning?"

The embarrassment on the other end of the line

was short-lived. "Sorry," he said, "but I need to talk to Clancy."

"I'll get him for you."

Moments later Packer was on the line. "Go slow," he cautioned. "The brain isn't in gear yet."

"First, we just got a call from Helmsing at the FBI labs. They matched prints on our Mr. Pan. His real name is Liu Shao. Born in San Francisco, graduated from the University of California, hired on with the State Department as an interpreter, and was stationed here in Washington for a while. According to Helmsing he disappeared about ten years ago—just dropped out. No one remembers seeing hide nor hair of him until we found him sprawled out on the cement at Washington General yesterday."

Sara Packer had left the room, and returned now with a cup of coffee for her husband. "What else?" Packer asked.

"Hathaway intercepted a fax into that Florida address in Bunche Park last night. It was transmitted in Chinese. Hatton had it translated. Don't know as it tells us much. But the text of the message is short and sweet. It says, *'Yen in place. Pan resolved. L.L. Sunday. Monday go.'* That's it."

Packer took a sip of his coffee and repeated the message to himself. "Any idea what it means?"

"Try this one on, Pack. It's a stretch, but take the words *'Pan resolved.'* Nancy Ming did the translation, and she says the word 'resolved' in Chinese can be used in several ways; like settled, removed, even disposed—as in disposed of. Ming says it sounds like textbook Chinese, as though it's someone who knows Chinese as a second language."

"In other words, like Pan has been taken care of," Packer said, ". . . as in gotten rid of."

"Could be," Miller said. "But what about the 'Yen in place' part?"

"Beats me," Packer said. "Code name?"

"For what? Pan's replacement?"

Packer paused. "Why not? Look, we've been taking long shots since this whole damn thing began. Let's take another one. Our mole may be using the same MO. Call Millie, tell her we need her. Find Bogner. Tell Hatton to stick around. Get anyone you can locate, work the phones. Tell them to start calling every off-beat out-of-the-way motel in the area. Start with the city first. We're looking for someone who may have registered with the name of Yen. Find out when he checked in—and if they locate him, tell the motel we don't want this Mr. Yen to know we've been making inquiries."

"That's a lot of motels, Chief."

"And I'm sure there's more than one Mr. Yen, but it's worth checking out. I'll be in the office in forty-five minutes."

Sara Packer watched her husband hang up the telephone and start down the hall. "Don't tell me," she said. "We aren't going to church, right?"

"Damn," he said, "it's Sunday. I forgot all about it."

"I wish you wouldn't use the words 'damn' and 'Sunday' in the same sentence," she said. Sara

Packer was smiling, but Clancy Packer knew he had just been reprimanded.

Time 0913LT:

Despite the hour, Joseph Albert "Rooster" Ricozy was already on his second cigar when they pulled into the parking lot of the Lincoln Port Motel. "You said your people located three people registered under the name of Yen?"

Bogner nodded, took the keys out of the ignition, and opened the car door. "This one and two others," Bogner said. "Churchill and his men are checking the others out. Two of them checked in yesterday, one of them the day before."

By the time Ricozy opened the door to the motel office, he was several steps ahead of Bogner. A slight, baldheaded man, easily in his early sixties, popped out of a room adjacent to the lobby with a half-eaten piece of toast. He was apologizing for his appearance by the time he had worked his way around the reception desk.

"Sorry," he said, trying to hide what was left of his breakfast on a shelf below the counter. "What can I do for you gentlemen?"

"Do you have a Mr. Yen registered here?" Bogner began.

"You must be the people who called earlier?"

"When did he register?"

"Yesterday. Yesterday morning, in fact."

"What kind of car is he driving?"

The little man looked at Yen's registration card.

"According to this, he's driving a Dodge, with a Maryland license plate."

"He's still registered?" Bogner asked.

"As far as I know," the man said. "I didn't check because your office said not to let him know someone was making inquiries about him."

"What room?" Ricozy grunted.

The little man hesitated. "I'm sure this is all perfectly legal, but I'm going to have to ask you for some identification. This is rather unusual. . . ."

Bogner had to give the little man credit. Ricozy towered over him by a least a foot. When Ricozy hesitated, Bogner flashed his ISA badge.

"Haven't I seen you somewhere before?" the little man asked, looking at Ricozy.

"Yeah, on the wanted posters down at the post office," Rooster answered with a smile. "Now, which one is Yen's room?"

"This is most unusual," the man repeated.

"Let the record show the inkeeper refused to cooperate," Ricozy said, winking at Bogner. Then he looked back at the little man. "Now suppose you forget what's usual and unusual and see that we get a key to Mr. Yen's room."

The hesitancy was short-lived. The man handed Ricozy a key. "He's in 242, second floor—toward the back. Try not to disturb our other guests."

Ricozy looked around the empty room and sagged down on the edge of the bed. "What do you think? Is this our man?"

Bogner was going through the man's personal effects. "Can't say, but whoever this guy is, he's traveling light."

"If it is Yen, I mean the one we're looking for, how the hell did he know we were on his tail if that little weasel downstairs didn't warn him?"

Bogner frowned. "Maybe he didn't. Maybe our man Yen had something to take care of."

"Like what? It's Sunday morning, for Christ sake. On Sundays this town is boarded up like a bordello during a Baptist convention."

"Whoever he is and wherever he went, he figured on coming back," Bogner said. "His personal effects are still here; he left clothes, shaving equipment, and a pair of shoes—not to mention this." Bogner handed Ricozy an envelope. "Someone sent him something."

Ricozy took the envelope and looked at it. The name "Capital Courier" was printed in the upper left-hand corner. "It should be easy enough to check out," he said.

"Take a wiff of it," Bogner said. "What's that smell like to you?"

Ricozy buried his nose in the packing envelope and inhaled. "Oil?"

"More specifically," Bogner said, "a light oil of some kind, maybe even a gun oil?"

Ricozy's oversized face unfolded in a smile. "Looks like maybe we found our man, huh?"

Bogner shrugged. "No way of telling until we can press him. In the meantime, I'll get in touch with Churchill and find out what his other people found.

If they haven't found anything, I'll have him put a stakeout on this place."

Time 1030LT:

It had stopped snowing by the time Chen Po Lee eased his car over to the curb half a block down the street from the front of the cathedral. He was waiting until a convenient parking place opened up directly across the street from the entrance. Finally he saw a man scurry out of the church, cross the street, jump in his car, and pull away. The parking space was the only one between Chen and the corner. It had taken him more than thirty minutes, but at last he had what he needed.

He rolled the window down, turned off the ignition, and located the precise spot where Jacqueline Marceau indicated the priest would be standing to greet parishioners following the Mass. He estimated the street to be no more than fifty feet wide from curb to curb. In front of the massive structure there was a wide sidewalk, which added perhaps another fifteen feet to the distance. To that it was necessary to add the cement steps that traversed the entire front of the church. He counted the steps. Seven. At most they added another eight to ten feet to the distance. Finally, there was the distance from the top of the steps to the huge doors at the entrance—perhaps another fifteen feet, well within range.

Chen calculated the distance a second time, and then he closed his eyes. He was envisioning the route that led him away from the scene—a route he had driven twice. The street directly in front of him was Grant; he would turn right on Grant, drive three blocks to New Jersey Avenue south of the Capitol, and take another right, following it until it intersected with the Southeast Freeway. Then, if all had gone well, he would proceed to his meeting with the Marceau woman.

Chen checked the time, and turned his attention from the route he would take to the inexpensive plastic valise on the seat beside him. Before he opened it, he checked up and down the sidewalk to make certain no one was watching. Convinced no one could see him, he slipped the .45-caliber M9 out of the side pocket and hefted it. Partially out of habit, but more out of training and discipline, he released the clip, checked it, reinserted the clip, attached the gas silencer, and released the safety. It was exactly ten-forty-five.

Jacqueline Marceau had everything arranged. Since awakening shortly after seven, she had busied herself making final preparations. Everything was checked and rechecked. For the past three days she had spent much of her time systematically destroying personal papers and her multiple disguises, and wrapping up her private affairs. By the time anyone got around to checking, and she was certain someone from the agency would, it would look as though she had just disappeared. Tonu Hon had insisted that the apartment be left with clothing intact, food still in the refrigerator, lights on, to make it look as though she had just stepped out for a few minutes—and for some reason, never returned. Tonu Hon had even instructed her to leave behind small balances in both her checking and saving accounts. "Nothing," he said, "must give them cause to suspect anything except that you have been the unfortunate victim of foul play."

As she moved from the bedroom to the living room, she heard a knock on the door. When she opened it, she found Julie Simon holding a small gift-wrapped parcel. The woman still looked wan and weak, but she had made a valiant attempt to conceal the ravages of the past days with makeup.

"Jackie," she said, holding out the gift, "I don't know what I would have done without you. It isn't much, but it's a small thank-you."

Jacqueline took the package and invited the woman in.

"Can't stay long," Julie said. "I'm going into the office for a little while. The administrator called last night and pleaded with me. He says the Secret Service people are crawling all over the place. You'd think by now we would be used to it. They always do before the President checks in."

"That's right, I almost forgot," Jacqueline Marceau lied. Then she added, "How are you feeling?"

"Weak. Confused. A little lost. I guess you were right, it will take a while."

"These things do, but you know what they say about time."

Julie nodded and turned to leave, and Jacqueline put her hand on her arm. "Look, I just had an idea.

What time do you think you'll be through over there?"

"I should be back by late afternoon. I'm still pretty wobbly."

"Why don't you stop in then. I'll fix you a toddy. I've got some brandy."

Julie pulled Jacqueline to her and hugged her. "You're an angel," she said, "and a real godsend."

Loren Langley bowed his head during the final blessing, squeezed his grandson's hand, and winked at him. It was part of their ongoing bonding ritual, a ritual he had missed out on with his other grandson.

His wife, Delores, a striking woman in her late sixties, was kneeling with her eyes closed, buttoning her coat with one hand and making the sign of the cross with the other as Monsignor Raferty concluded the blessing. Brenda Langley, their seven-year-old granddaughter, had already slipped out of their pew and was standing in the aisle when Delores Langley pulled her back. "Wait until the monsignor passes," she admonished her.

Even though some of the people had already begun to file out behind Monsignor Raferty, Loren Langley waited for the right opportunity to herd his small entourage out into the flow of parishioners.

Brenda Langly tugged at his coat, and the Senator looked down at her. "Are we going to stop at the Raddison for breakfast, Grandpa?"

Loren Langley looked at his wife. "You'll have to ask the boss," he said.

* * *

Chen Po Lee watched the flow of people pass through the front doors of the church, waiting for the appearance of the man Jacqueline Marceau had assured him would be there. Finally, he appeared. He was tall, well over six feet, with gray hair, dressed in the vestments he'd worn while celebrating the Mass.

Chen took a deep breath, rolled the car window down halfway, cocked his left arm, propped his elbow on the sill, laid the .45 in the crook of his arm, and sighted. As he did, a dark blue Oldsmobile pulled abreast of him and double-parked. The car was directly in his line of fire. The driver, a man dressed in a leather jacket, honked his horn, and waved to a young woman and child standing on the curb. The woman saw him, waved back, and began weaving her way through the slow-moving traffic. Chen pulled the .45 back and waited.

When the Oldsmobile pulled away, there was a second car. The second driver waited for several moments before pulling around the corner onto Grant Street.

Finally, Chen saw him. It was the man the Marceau woman had described. Loren Langley had lifted his grandson up for the man in the vestments. The wait was over.

Chen nestled the M9 in the crook of his arm, sighted, pulled his head back just far enough to avoid the recoil, and squeezed off five rounds. There was the familiar and repeated *phhht* sound as the gas silencer muffled each of the five explosions.

In micro-seconds, the scene just outside the vestibule of the cathedral became a kaleidoscope of panic and frenzy. Chen saw the senator drop the child and slump back against the door of the church. The tall man in vestments recoiled, clutching his throat, and sank to his knees. Chen heard women screaming, and saw a child plunge headfirst down the cement steps. In less than five seconds, he had created a scene of terror.

Chen had already prepared himself for the fact that there would be no time to assess his effectiveness. He dropped the .45 on the seat beside him, jammed the car into gear, and peeled around the corner. As he swung onto Grant heading for New Jersey Avenue, he was certain no one was following him.

Time 1124LT:

Bogner had just poured himself a second cup of coffee in the ISA cafeteria when Robert Miller sprinted into the room. "Dump it, T.C. Millie just heard a news bulletin on the radio. There's been a shooting at Saint Patrick's Church. Somebody opened fire on the people coming out of church after Mass and one of the victims is Senator Langley."

Bogner leaped to his feet and sprinted after Packer's assistant. Within moments they had crossed the ISA parking lot and jumped into Miller's car. By the time they pulled onto Howard

Street, Miller was giving him what few details he had.

"All we know so far is that Senator Langley was one of the people shot. The first report said three people were dead and several injured. Millie switched over to the police channel, and they were still trying to get a handle on what happened."

"Think this is more of Mao's shit?" Bogner said.

Miller shrugged. "Sure as hell sounds like it."

By the time Bogner and Miller reached Saint Patrick's, Sam Churchill had managed to establish a beachhead for his homicide unit amidst the chaos. The crime scene in front of the church had been cordoned off, two TV stations had already set up their on-site units, and the police forensics squad was combing the scene.

The two men were still threading their way through the labyrinth of police cruisers and onlookers, looking for Churchill, when they spotted Peter Langley. He was standing just outside the massive doors of the church at the top of the steps. The man Bogner had once referred to as "the coolest damned head in the Navy" was clearly shaken.

"We got here as quick as we could," Bogner said. "What the hell happened?"

Langley shook his head. "No one seems to know for certain, T.C. There must have been a good seven or eight hundred people coming out of church after the ten o'clock Mass when someone opened fire from a car parked across the street. About the only thing we can get agreement on is that it was a white car. So far I've heard it described as everything from 'some kind of little white car' to a damned Thunderbird."

"The radio said the senator had been hit. How bad is it?"

"It could have been a lot worse. He took a slug in the shoulder. He lost some blood, but he's a tough old bird. He should be all right—the slug went clean through. They took him to Washington General. At the moment, though, I'm a helluva lot more worried about my son, Lyle. One of the shots grazed him in the temple; he's still unconscious. They took him to Washington General too. Arlene rode in the ambulance with him. We lucked out. There were several doctors in the congregation. One of them checked Lyle over and said he thought he would be okay."

"We heard one report that said there were fatalities," Miller said. "Do you think they gunning for someone in particular?"

Langley shrugged. "Monsignor Raferty was one of the fatalities. He took a bullet in the throat. The doctor said he was dead by the time he hit the ground."

"The other two?"

"Two women. I'm told one of them was a nun. The other was the mother of two children."

Bogner left Miller to the business of consoling Peter Langley and headed for Churchill. The homicide officer was fending off questions from a bevy of TV reporters. When he saw Bogner, he excused himself. "Looks like we were a day late and a dollar short, Captain. We've had a man staked outside of Yen's hotel since you were there early this morning, but it doesn't look like it did a hell of a lot of good."

"Then you think this is the work of 5A?" Bogner asked.

Churchill nodded. "I'd be willing to bet next month's mortgage payment on it. This guy wasn't pussyfooting around—he knew exactly what he was doing. He put five slugs from an M9 in a twenty-five-inch cluster. Nobody heard a thing. We're talking a silencer." He reached in his pocket and held up a small plastic bag. "Here, one of my people dug this out of the of the door right behind where the monsignor was standing. A slug just like this is the one that killed him."

"Did anyone get a look at the gunman?"

"Everyone claims they did," Churchill said, "but none of 'em can agree on what he looks like. So far I've heard everything from a black kid to a bald-headed guy with thick glasses. The only thing they all swear to is that as soon as the people started screaming, he peeled around the corner and headed west on Grant."

"In a white car . . ."

"Late-model white car we got agreement on, but not the make."

Bogner walked along the top of the steps, studying the scene where Chen Po Lee had unleashed his unexpected attack. There was a dried pool of what appeared to be red-black blood where the priest had fallen, and more of the same on the steps immediately below. The police had chalked telltale outlines where the bodies of the monsignor and the two women had lain. When he looked up at Churchill, he knew the homicide officer was thinking right along with him.

"Different modus operandi this time," Bogner offered.

"Different man pulling the trigger," Churchill observed. "If that body we found in the parking lot at WG yesterday was responsible for the others, the new guy showed us they've got a few more tricks up their sleeves."

"Think he'll head back to his motel?"

"If we get lucky. I've got a man staked out at the back of the motel, and I'm sending in a backup unit just in case. They know how to keep a low profile. If this guy Yen isn't on his toes, he could stumble right into our little trap and we could nail his ass cold."

Chen Po Lee, like all of Tonu Hon's agents, followed his instructions to the letter. He pulled off of the Southeast Freeway, onto Lomabard, and headed east through the park until he intersected with Fairmount. Seven blocks later, still on Fairmount, he drove to the back of a new shopping mall and parked behind a cluster of trailers and Quonset buildings being used by a construction company. From his vantage point, he could see the motel—and the two police cars. One had parked a block down the street from the entrance. The other was parked at the back of the motel parking lot where the police could see everyone who came or left.

They were waiting for him. Once again he was thankful for Tonu Hon's wisdom; he had advised Chen to make certain he was not being watched before he tried to return to his motel.

As always with 5A, there was an alternate plan. The directions were clear; if he was unable to return to his motel, he was ordered to wait at the theater in the mall directly behind the motel. He would be contacted by telephone in the theater lobby. Jacqueline Marceau would call him at precisely sixteen hundred hours. It was now a few minutes after noon, and their rendezvous was not scheduled for another four hours.

Chen Po Lee edged his car into a parking space, turned off the ignition, locked his car, bundled himself against the blustery weather, and went into the theater. He had four hours to kill.

Chapter Eleven

Time 1447LT:

It had been more than twelve hours since Jacqueline had been able to establish contact with the number in Bunche Park. Thus far there had been nothing to indicate any of her last three transmissions had been received or relayed. Nor had she received anything in the way of return information from the Florida address.

At first her inability to establish contact with the relay point in Bunche Park had generated little more than concern. But as the hours wore on, concern had evolved into worry, and now there was a distressing awareness that she had been out of contact with Tonu Hon for over thirty-six hours.

In the past hour she had risked two calls to Yen's

motel to see if he had safely returned. He had not. During the second call, the motel operator told her he would check and she was put on hold. Fearing that the police had discovered Yen's whereabouts and were trying to trace the call, she hung up.

Unable to establish contact with either the number in Bunche Park or Yen, she had become even more concerned. There was now, for the first time since they had launched their campaign, a disturbing feeling that the authorities were beginning to close in.

It was that gnawing sensation of being discovered before they completed their mission that caused her to hurry through her final preparations. She sorted through her keys. Two to the apartment, the spare key to the ignition of her car, the key to her lockbox at the bank, and the key to her personal storage shed behind the apartment building were put on a key ring and left in such a place that they would be easily discovered if and when someone finally checked her apartment.

From time to time, she went to the window and looked down at the parking lot behind the complex to see if Julie had returned. Each time she carefully scanned the area, but there was no sign of Julie's silver Ford Escort. Finally, when she was convinced she could afford to wait no longer, she went into her bedroom and changed clothes, donning a pair of slacks, a heavy turtleneck sweater, and boots. She laid a jacket, a wool pullover cap, gloves, and a scarf across the foot of the bed, and left the closet door open, hoping to add to the impression that she had just stepped out.

It was now less than thirty minutes until she was scheduled to call Yen. She went over the instructions to make certain everything was in order. The call would be placed at exactly four o'clock. If someone other than Yen answered, she would try again five minutes later. If Yen failed to answer the second time, she would make one pass through the parking lot in front of the theater. In the event he was unable to intercept her call, Yen had been instructed to make himself conspicuous by standing close to the ticket office in front of the theater. If they were unable to connect at that point, there was one final and, as Jacqueline knew all to well, highly undesirable alternative—a rendezvous at Quinto Aircraft. The risk was of course that Yen's car had been identified and the authorities were waiting for him to return.

Jacqueline checked her watch. It was exactly ten minutes until four when she heard the knock on her door. When she opened it, Julie Simon was leaning against the door frame. She had been drinking. Richard Crane's former mistress managed an unconvincing smile, and had a slight slur to her speech.

"I did it, Jackie," she said. "I made it through the day without breaking down. Not one word about Richard . . . not even when we stopped in at Berkley's for a quick drink."

"Good for you," Jacqueline said, but she was more concerned whether Crane's former mistress had learned anything about the President's schedule. "You'll be glad you went in. Big day, huh?"

Julie nodded. "Like they said, the damn Secret Service is crawling all over the place."

"Will you have to go back in tonight?" Under the circumstances, Jacqueline doubted that her questions would arouse suspicion. Nevertheless, she was careful not to be too direct—too obvious.

Julie slouched against the door. "For a while there they were saying he might not come in tonight, that maybe he would wait until tomorrow."

"What do you mean?"

"I guess everyone is nervous about these terrorist attacks, so they're going to fly him in from Camp David tonight instead of driving him over in the morning from the White House."

Jacqueline suddenly had the feeling their fortunes had changed. After being unable to contact Tonu Hon for a day and a half, now came the news that there would be not one, but two opportunities to carry through their plans. "What time tonight?" she pressed.

Julie shrugged. "No one seems to know for certain, but everyone is guessing it will be late. I had to inform the hospital's security force that they would be working overtime tonight." Julie paused for several seconds as though she was trying to get her thoughts ordered.

Jacqueline Marceau's awareness of time was making her edgy. She looked at her watch; it was three minutes past four. "Look," she said, "why don't you go to your place and get changed. I said

I'd fix us something to eat when you got back. I'll do that while you're getting dressed. I'll run down to the deli on Baker Street and be back by the time—"

Julie waved her hand; she was smiling. "Sounds good to me," she said.

"It's for you, Robert," Millie said. She waited until Miller slid into his chair at the desk across from her and picked up the receiver before she hung up.

"Miller," Robert barked.

"Dave Hornsby with OTT. Are you the one that was trying to trace those five fax numbers?"

"You got 'em?" Miller said.

"It's the weekend," Hornsby reminded him. "It took a while to get authorization."

Miller picked up a pen and waited. "I'm ready when you are."

"Haven't run into one like this before," Hornsby admitted, "but all five fax numbers are issued to an executive recruiting service that goes by the name of Careers Incorporated."

"And?"

"That's it. Must be a busy place, huh?"

"Why five lines? Several locations?"

"Not according to the installation and service sheet. According to the information I have, they were all installed in Apartment 3C in the Webster Apartment complex on Fairfax Street."

"When?"

"Two months ago."

Miller scribbled down the address, muttered

something that sounded like "thanks," hung up, and headed for Packer's office.

"Chief," he said, "Looks like we hit pay dirt. Just got a call from OTT. We're in luck. We've got an address on those five fax numbers."

Time 1627LT

Jacqueline Marceau pulled into the Fairmont Shopping Center and threaded her way toward the theater complex at the back of the center. She had made one hurried call to the public telephone in the theater after Julie left, only to have one of the theater employees answer. Because it was already thirteen minutes past the hour when she got through, she'd decided not to have Yen paged. She would have to depend on Yen being somewhere in the vicinity of the theater's box office.

Julie's timely return had played directly into her hand. Not only had Julie given her the information she needed, but when the authorities started asking questions, Julie would be the last one who not only saw but talked to her. It would be only one more confusing fragment of information for the authorities to digest. Tonu Hon had indicated his willingness, if necessary, to sacrifice her cover, but if at all possible he wanted it protected. She had proved to be highly valuable as a conduit of information from her office in the CIA, as well as the one who handled the logistics for 5A's activities in Washington. Both Mao and Tonu Hon realized that she could not be easily replaced.

The traffic in front of the theater complex was still congested when she passed the box office the first time, so she circled and made a second pass. That was when she saw him. He was standing with his valise in front of him as instructed—and when she pulled over to the curb, she caught his eye. Jacqueline breathed a sigh of relief; contact had been established.

Bogner watched the elevator doors open, and stepped into the hall. It had taken him all of thirty seconds to determine that the Webster Apartments were a compromise, an upscale address with downscale appointments. An attempt had been made to make the place look expensive, but the effect was more tawdry than anything else. The carpet was a little too worn, the paint a little too old, and the odors indicated a nodding acquaintance with the seedier side of life in the city. Someone was collecting the rent, but they weren't spending a lot on upkeep.

He located Apartment 3C, knocked, and waited. On the second try, a brunette standing no more than five feet six, with a tired face and watery eyes, opened the door. She looked like she had been drinking, and her breath, speech, and the glass in her hand confirmed it. Even though she didn't say it, she gave Bogner the impression she would just as soon he had been someone else.

Bogner glanced down at the name Miller had scribbled on the piece of paper when he was talking to Hornsby. "I'm looking for Careers Incorporated," he said. The spiel he had rehearsed about his resume on the way over had been a waste of time.

Julie Simon rolled the name over on her tongue and lost it. "Careers what?" she asked.

"Careers Incorporated, Apartment 3C," Bogner repeated. "I was told to deliver my—"

"Never heard of it. Someone gave you bad information," Julie said. "This apartment belongs to a friend of mine."

"Your friend has a name?"

Julie eyed Bogner from his head to his feet, trying to decide whether or not to answer his question. It was the first learned caution of a single woman in the eighties and nineties—a telephone number maybe, and in some cases, a first name; never a complete name or an address.

Bogner took out his wallet and showed the woman his badge.

"Is it real?" Julie asked, squinting. The contacts had long since been discarded during her three-day crying jag.

"It's real," Bogner assured her. "Now, about the name of your friend," Bogner repeated.

"Jackie."

"I assume Jackie has a last name?"

Julie hesitated before she answered. "Jacqueline Marceau."

Bogner stiffened. "Tall, dark hair, dark eyes, works for the CIA?" The image of the woman that sat next to him in the briefing wasn't all that complete, but it was enough. Words started coming to mind: strong, intense, serious, impassioned, even resolute. The picture of Jacqueline Marceau was starting to take shape.

Bogner brushed his way past the Simon woman. "Hey," she protested, "you can't—"

"You'd be surprised what I can do," Bogner told her. "Now, suppose you just relax while I have a look around."

Julie's willingness to defend her friend's territory was short-lived. She eyed Bogner and retreated. "What if I started yelling for help?" she said.

Bogner ignored the question and started through the apartment. In the smaller of the two bedrooms, he found a second telephone and a fax machine. There were two small two-drawer file cabinets containing stationery, business cards, and files containing a number of resumes with the words "Careers Incorporated" stamped across the front page of the documents.

By the time he had worked his way back to the front of the apartment, Julie had assumed a less strident position on the couch. Her hands were shaking and there was a bottle of off-brand bourbon sitting on the coffee table in front of her. Bogner didn't feel it was necessary to point out that the bottled courage wasn't doing the job.

Julie looked at him a long time before she summoned up enough courage to say, "I hope you found what the hell you were looking for—because if you did, then you don't have any reason to hang around."

"I found what I was looking for," he admitted, "but I still have a couple of questions."

"If you have questions, I suggest you talk to Jackie."

"Your friend is in a heap of trouble," Bogner countered.

"No way."

"Big trouble," Bogner insisted, "and a little co-operation on your part just may save you from being dragged down with her."

Julie stared back at him in disbelief. Bogner's threat had caught her off guard. "What—what are you talking about, dragged down?"

"Suppose I told you we have every reason to believe your friend Jacqueline Marceau is involved in the terrorist ring that killed Senator Richard Crane and tried to kill Senator Loren Langley this morning?"

Julie was stunned. It took her several seconds to regain some semblance of composure. Finally, it was the way she uttered the word "impossible" that make Bogner realize he had hit a nerve. Despite her unwillingness to accept what Bogner had told her, she could not help but recall how her newfound friend had consistently questioned her about Crane's schedule, about where he lived, even about the dinner party the night before he was killed.

"How long have you known Jacqueline Marceau?" Bogner probed.

Julie Simon had to think. "Two, maybe three months, I don't remember."

"What did you talk about?"

"Work, girl stuff mostly."

"Did she ever talk about her job?"

Julie shook her head. "Not that I can remember. She seemed more interested in what I do."

"Suppose you tell me your name and just exactly what it is you do."

"Julie Simon. I work at Washington General. It's my job to see that VIPs get in and out of there with a minimum of hassle."

Bogner waited for her to continue, but the woman's eyes welled with tears and she broke down in sobs. "Dammit, dammit," she repeated, "I thought I could get through this. I was counting on Jackie. . . ."

"Do you know where she is?"

Julie shook her head. "I don't know," she sobbed. "She's supposed to be here. I need her, dammit! Why isn't she here?"

Bogner walked back through the apartment to the rear bedroom, took out his handkerchief, and being careful not to smear any fingerprints, picked up the telephone. Packer answered on the second ring. "Get a hold of Jaffe," he said. "Have someone meet me at Jacqueline Marceau's office over at CIA. I think we've dug out our mole."

Time 1741LT:

It had taken the better part of an hour for Jacqueline Marceau to convince herself they were not being followed. She had circled back over the same twisting route twice before she headed for the rental storage units on C Street near the Fifth Street Armory. She used the plastic ID card to open the main gate, and drove directly to the small storage units at the rear of the sprawling complex.

Up until now she had made no effort to communicate with Chen Po Lee. She had been too busy making certain they weren't being followed. Now, as she shut off the ignition and turned to face him, she took her first real look at the man. He was slight of build, shorter and somewhat older than Liu Shao, with a habit of grinding his teeth. His hands were small and his facial features were slightly crooked, as though they been arranged in a hurry, perhaps even as an afterthought. All in all, he gave Jacqueline the impression of a man who did not know how to smile, who presented the world with a perpetual frown.

"We dare not fail this time," she warned him.

Chen Po Lee's expression changed little, but enough to indicate he did not understand.

"Senator Loren Langley suffered only superficial wounds," she explained. "He was taken to the hospital and released earlier this afternoon."

Chen's mien was one of stoic acceptance. What this woman said meant nothing; the reprimand would come from Tonu Hon. Tonu Hon did not tolerate failure. When he said nothing, Jacqueline got out of the car, went around to the trunk, opened it, and removed a large canvas bag. Then she unlocked the door to the storage shed and motioned for him to follow.

Inside, Chen was confronted with a wooden crate nearly five feet long. The stenciled lettering on the side indicated that the crate contained both an

M203 grenade launcher and the AN/PVS-4 night-vision device that would be required for their mission.

"Open the crate," she ordered. "In our briefing, Tonu Hon indicated that you are familiar with the device. Is that correct?"

Chen nodded.

"Good. If anything happens to me, it will be your responsibility to see that the mission is completed. Now, open the container. There are tools in the bag."

Chen pried open the crate and lifted out the disassembled grenade launcher. At the bottom of the crate there were five rounds of 40mm ammunition. Then he examined the night-vision device. The sight reticle consisted of two scales; the upper determined the range, the lower was his aiming points. Finally, when he was satisfied, he handed the weapon to the woman. He was surprised at how easily she handled it.

"You have seen the helicopter?" she asked him.

Chen nodded.

"You can get me close enough, within one hundred meters? At the most we should anticipate having time to fire no more than three rounds."

Chen stood by, waiting as the woman focused the launcher, adjusted the BRT and CTR viewing controls, and cleared the range-focus lever. He had no way of knowing it was identical to the weapon she had trained with in Hainan.

With the unit fully assembled, she instructed Chen to put the launcher in the trunk of the car.

"Now, comrade," she said, "we are ready. Let us see if our friend Mr. Quinto has kept his part of the bargain."

Clancy Packer had managed to pull it off with a minimum of fanfare. Other than a ponderously slow examination of his credentials, and a personal escort by a lantern-jawed six-footer, Bogner quickly found himself in a third-floor set of cubicles.

"The third one on the right belongs to Ms. Marceau," his escort said.

Bogner entered the cubicle. Jaffe was waiting. The CIA bureau chief was slouched in the corner with the predictable cup of coffee and a cigarette. In the twenty years Bogner had known Oscar Jaffe, he could not recall seeing him without his props. He greeted Bogner with the same disdain he showed anyone outside the bureau. "Hope to hell this isn't another wild-goose chase, Toby," he groused. "I'm getting sick and tired of—"

Bogner ignored Jaffe's typical acerbity, slipped into the chair behind the woman's desk, and started going through the drawers.

"Mind telling me what the hell this is all about?"

"How long has Marceau been with the agency?" Bogner countered. He wasn't surprised when Jaffe came up with the woman's personnel file and casually threw it on the desk.

"Apparently long enough to cause us all a helluva lot of grief and embarrassment," Jaffe admitted.

"I'm sure you've been kept informed, but less than thirty-six hours ago we discovered Ms. Marceau was filing daily reports to a sing-through in Bunche Park, Florida. The messages were being relayed to a location on the southwest coast of Cuba, and the responses were coming back through Bunche Park to any one of a series of fax numbers here in Washington. We did some backtracking on those numbers and discovered Marceau had no less than five of them listed under the name Careers Incorporated. At this juncture, everything points to your language specialist being the one who is feeding info to 5A."

Jaffe scowled. "Where is she?"

Bogner shrugged. "I wish we knew."

"Just what the hell do you expect to find here?" Jaffe pressed. "If this woman is who you think she is and she was clever enough to get this far, she'd damn certain be clever enough not to leave anything lying around that would tip her hand."

Bogner continued rifling through the files. "Not necessarily, Oscar. Five will get you ten that she's slipped up somewhere. Old habits have a knack of getting in the way."

Jaffe put out one cigarette, lit another, and began sorting through the woman's personnel file. When he finished, he laid it aside and started on another file. Bogner had forgotten about the man's annoying habit of reading aloud and mumbling. "Here's a whole damn file of newspaper clippings," he said. "Obviously we didn't keep her busy enough if she had time—"

"Newspaper clippings?" Bogner repeated. "About what?"

"Odds and ends. Gossip column stuff mostly. Here's one about the Cranes' dinner party . . . and another about how Lattimere Spitz is progressing."

Bogner looked up. "What else?"

Jaffe began counting. "Let's see—one, two, three different references to the fact that Colchin is going in for his annual physical at Washington General."

"When?" Bogner said.

"When what?"

"When is Colchin going in for his physical?"

Jaffe shook his head, thumbed his way back through the stack of clippings, and glanced over them a second time. "I think you're barking up the wrong tree this time, T.C. She's so damned sinister that she's got clippings of recipes in here too."

"To throw us off maybe?"

"Come on," Jaffe sniffed. "Like she knew we were going to go through her personal files. You're a suspicious bastard, Bogner. You've been hanging around Clancy Packer too long."

Bogner reached for the file. Jaffe was right, he was suspicious. At the same time he had the advantage of knowing more about the Marceau woman than Jaffe did—he had been there and he had seen the five fax lines. Plus, Jaffe was probably skittish; twice within the past three years, the CIA had been caught with their pants down. There were embarrassing covers on both *Time* and *Newsweek* to prove it.

"All right," Jaffe wheezed, "suppose this Jacqueline Marceau is your link. What next?"

"Yesterday morning we found the body of the

man that engineered Crane's assassination in the parking lot at Washington General. This morning we intercepted a fax which would indicate his replacement hit town. We verified that—even located his motel. So what happens then? They shoot up some poor bastards coming out of Saint Patrick's this morning. I'm convinced these people are behind the death of your man Worling. And I'm equally convinced they were gunning for Senator Loren Langley this morning. Why Langley? I haven't figured that out. I'm admitting I don't know, but I'll bet *they* do. It looks random to us because Langley doesn't make any more sense than Crane or Dunning or Swelling or anyone else they've gone after in the past two weeks—except when you stand back and look at it from a different angle."

Jaffe waited for him to continue. "I'm listening."

"I know this man. Mao Quan is a frustrated showman. He is strong and getting stronger. He loves his theatrics—and he'd like nothing more than to demonstrate to the powers in Beijing that he is a force to be reckoned with. I think what we've seen so far is nothing more than Mao's idea of a prologue. He's setting us up for the main event, the big finale."

Jaffe scoffed. "Typical Bogner bullshit. T.C., you can find more damned ghosts in a bucket of oats than a two-year-old gelding. So far you've given me nothing but a helluva lot of conjecture and theory. I'd like to see some proof."

Bogner looked around Jacqueline Marceau's office. "It's here, Oscar, here, right in front of us. We just don't see it."

Jaffe sighed. "So what do you expect from me?"

"Get some of your people in here and start tearing these files apart. Somewhere in here this Marceau dame has left a trail. It's our job to find it."

Time 1937LT:

Jacqueline Marceau drove from the storage units directly to the small airport in Creighton, stopping just long enough to call her apartment. When Julie Simon answered, she informed Crane's former mistress that she was running an errand. "I'm sorry, Julie," she said, "I had an errand to run. I forgot all about it."

That was when Julie informed her that a man who identified himself as being with some government agency had been there asking questions.

To Julie's surprise, her friend's only comment was, "Tell them I'll be there in thirty minutes." Then she hung up.

For Jacqueline the timing of the call had been another stroke of good fortune. She now knew that, even if the opportunity presented itself, it would be both unsafe and unwise to return to her apartment. And while she wondered if there was anything she had overlooked, at the same time she marveled at Tonu Hon's sense of how time and events would unfold. She began to smile, and for the first time since she had picked him up at the theater complex, Chen Po Lee appeared to relax.

* * *

Bogner, Jaffe, and two of the agency people from the CIA night crew had been sorting through Jacqueline Marceau's files for over an hour when one of them handed Bogner a file. "I don't know what you're looking for, Captain," the woman said, "but this is the third time I've come across a reference to this. Take a look."

The woman had focused on a column by David Bennet, a columnist for the *Post* who was speculating on the President's health. A portion of the column had been highlighted in yellow.

Rumors persist that President Colchin continues to suffer from a discomforting stomach malady. One source tells me that a specialist, not on the staff at Washington General, has been instructed to make himself available when the President enters the hospital for his annual physical next month. . . .

"Thought you might find it interesting too," the woman said. "It strikes me that she seems more than passingly interested in the President's health."

Bogner reached for the telephone and dialed the special NBS number Joy had given him. The young woman working the NBS switchboard had the routine down to a science. She had already begun reciting a list of special programs for "the viewer" before Bogner managed to turn her off.

"Put me through to Joy Carpenter," he said.

Fred Napper, the NBS News Director, came on the line after four rings. He recognized Bogner's voice. "Sorry, Toby, old buddy. Joy isn't here."

"Where can I get in touch with her?"

"Don't know as you can," Napper said. "She left here about an hour ago with a camera crew. She's headed for Washington General—gotta cover the head shed, you know."

"Colchin?"

"Is there another head shed in town? You and I get the silver stallion treatment and no one knows but our proctologist. If Colchin so much as gets a stomach ache, the economy gets the damn flu."

"Colchin is checking in tonight?" Bogner said.

Time 2008LT:

Jacqueline Marceau had used the access road around the perimeter of the airport to survey her surroundings on her first pass. With the exception of a few cars and some lights in a small transit hangar near the entrance to the airport, the field on the outskirts of Creighton was deserted.

On her second pass she drove by Quinto's hangars. There was one car in the parking lot, a maroon Lincoln, and the Kaman SH-2 Seasprite was parked on the tarmac under the floodlights next to the hangar. Quinto, it appeared, had kept his part of the bargain. The aircraft appeared to be ready for Chen's flight check.

Jacqueline pulled into the parking lot. Through the window to Quinto's office, she could see a heavyset man watching a flickering black-and-white television. They were in luck; Quinto appeared to be alone.

The Armenian looked up when Jacqueline and Chen walked in. His expression betrayed the fact that he was surprised to see the Asian accompanied by a woman. "About gave up on ya," he groused. "Another thirty minutes and I would have been outta here."

"I'm afraid Mr. Yen is not to blame for the late hour, Mr. Quinto. I am the reason for the delay." Jacqueline had graced her apology with a smile, and Quinto seemed suddenly less bellicose.

"All I meant was I wanted to get home in time for the second half of the Redskins game," he muttered.

"The aircraft is ready?" Jacqueline asked.

Quinto looked at Chen and then at the woman. "Ready to roll, except for one small matter—a matter of money."

Jacqueline opened her purse and handed Quinto a business card. She was shaking her head. "Again, my apology Mr. Quinto, it was thoughtless of me. I'm afraid that in our haste to get here before you left, I neglected the courtesy of a phone call that would have advised you we were running late. However, my name is Geneva Harding with Aero Associates. By way of explanation, we are the financing agent for Weitock Hospital Support Services, who will be purchasing this aircraft. My roll here is simply one of verification. We are required to verify the documentation and get a few numbers off the aircraft prior to Mr. Yen accepting delivery."

"Hey, all I need is a couple of signatures and a check," Quinto said. He was forcing a smile that was slightly lopsided and more menacing than re-assuring.

Jacqueline nodded. "If you will show us to the aircraft, Mr. Yen will help me obtain the necessary information."

Quinto lumbered out from behind his desk and guided them through a door at the rear of the office. "She's sitting out back on the tarmac," he informed them. "My mechanic used to be a chopper pilot in Nam. He took it up this afternoon to check it out. He says she's ready to go to work."

Quinto led them out into the chill night air under the floodlights, and Chen began circling the chopper. As instructed, he began pointing out features of the Kaman to demonstrate his familiarity. Jacqueline had produced a clipboard and was making notes. Chen explained the features at the rear of the craft, testing the upper fin and the anti-torque tail rotor, and pointing out the function of the horizontal stabilizer mounted forward of the tail rotor on the tail boom.

When he moved to the front of the craft, Jacqueline Marceau followed him. He opened the forward door to the cabin, read off several numbers, and climbed into the cockpit. He continued the charade by pointing out features like the location of the VHF antenna, the magnetic compass, the cyclic pitch lever, the air-temperature probe, and the location of the transponder. When Quinto stepped forward, Jacqueline was still taking notes.

"How about it?" Quinto asked. "Seen enough?"

"I believe so," she said. "As soon as Mr. Yen gives

it a brief test flight and assures me that everything is as your firm represents it, we can conclude our arrangements."

Quinto eyed Chen and lowered his voice. The visit by the two men who'd represented themselves as ISA agents was playing in the back of his mind. "You sure your man knows what he's doin'?"

Jacqueline intensified her smile. "We have been doing business with Weitock for quite some time now, Mr. Quinto. I assure you that during that time they have demonstrated a high degree of proficiency with their aircraft purchases as well as maintaining an excellent safety record."

While Quinto and Jacqueline watched, Chen slipped into the pilot's seat and threw the toggle switch on the pre-ignition. His preflight routine was systematic and polished, his fingers dancing over and tweaking the myriad of knobs and switches on the instrument panel, then moving quickly to the battery check, then to the radio, and finally to the controls themselves. He waited for the oil pressure to build and the fuel cell indicators to glide into the green zone. Finally he cranked the ignition, cautiously coaxing the two 1,350-shp General Electric T58-8F turboshaft engines to half power. At last the main rotor of the Kaman coughed to life, turning over at first with a kind of reluctance and coughing out several protests, before settling into a series of semistaccato revolutions and gathering power.

Jacqueline stepped away into the safety of the hangar as the rotor gained momentum. When the navigation lights came on, the Kaman began to lift, hovering momentarily thirty or so feet in the air. Then Chen spiraled up into the blackness with the thumping sound of the rotor following him into the night.

Time 2031LT:

Even though it was a Sunday evening, it was the kind of assignment Joy Carpenter relished. Since her transfer from New York, she had filled in on three separate occasions for Harvey Major, NBS's regular White House correspondent: twice when Major was on assignment during the CIA scandals, and now again, while the senior journalist was hospitalized with what had been diagnosed as a mitral-valve problem with his heart.

It was well known at NBS that Joy had advantages others on the White House beat didn't have. Bogner had long been one of the President's favorites, and the relationship went all the way back to the early days when both Joy and T.C. were guests of the then-governor of Texas at his ranch in Big Springs. So when others were being denied access, David Colchin saw to it that Joy Carpenter enjoyed the privileges of being a one-time member of what the press still referred to as Colchin's Mafia.

Now, on her second cup of coffee and waiting along with her cameraman for news that the President's helicopter had finally left Camp David, she saw one of the hospital's security people motion to her.

"You have a phone call, Ms. Carpenter," the

young woman said. "The man said to tell you it was urgent."

Joy reached across the desk and picked up the courtesy phone. "Joy Carpenter," she said. "May I help you?"

"Only if you'll fly away to Jamaica with me tonight."

"Tobias, where are you?"

"Where I am doesn't matter. Where you are does."

"What are you talking about?"

"Have they doubled the security yet?" Bogner pressed.

"Twice as many as usual, but no one is saying why. Why? What's happening?"

"Has the President's helicopter left Camp David yet?"

"Not yet."

"Good, then we've still have some time."

"Dammit, Tobias, what's happening?"

"Can anyone hear you?"

"I'm standing in the middle of the damn VIP lounge on the sixth floor at Washington General. The place is a madhouse, just like it always is when the President is coming in. Why?"

"Look, Joy, I'm on my way over there now. I'll explain when I get there. With any luck at all I should be there within thirty minutes."

"Damn it, Tobias, I've got a camera crew on standby waiting for the President. If something big is about to pop, for Christ's sake, let me know so I can get my crew in position to—"

Joy Carpenter heard the receiver click, and she was shouting at her crew before she hung up.

Quinto accompanied Jacqueline Marceau back into his office, explaining as he went the forms and releases that had to be signed. "The FAA requires the lien holder, in this case that would be Aero Associates, to file a number of forms with the agency. There's a Form 2D56 and a Form WW-1-52 that verifies that Aero Associates will conform to all regulations relating to the operation of the aircraft in accordance with—"

"I am curious, Mr. Quinto, can you establish radio contact with Mr. Yen?" Jacqueline asked.

Quinto was surprised by the question. "Yeah, I guess so," he said. "Is there a problem?"

"No problem, no problem at all, Mr. Quinto. It simply occurred to me that we could save some time if everything was going to Mr. Yen's satisfaction. If everything meets with his approval, I would be at liberty to sign the documents and we could have this matter wrapped up by the time he returns."

Quinto lumbered around his desk, dropped into his chair, maneuvered it over to the table, picked up the mike, and opened it to the ATC frequency. "HN-477, do you read?"

There was static but no repsonse.

Quinto repeated the call letters. "This is Quinto Aircraft. Ms. Harding wants to know how it's going. Over."

"HN-477, Weitock Hospital Support Services,"

Chen replied. The signal was weak, but he had acknowledged.

"Your banker wants to know if you're satisfied," Quinto repeated. "How's it going?"

"Tien shu wan, kuan-hua."

"Say again," Quinto said.

"That won't be necessary, Mr. Quinto," Jacqueline declared. "Mr. Yen has just assured me that everything is quite satisfactory. Now if you'll just show me where to sign, we can conclude this matter and we can all be on our way."

Quinto rolled his chair back to his desk, reached for a thick manila file folder, and slapped it on the counter. "Everything is there," Quinto said. "All the Navy maintenance records, a list of the upgrades and the dates installed, certifications, compliance checks, and a list of the armament that was on this little jewel when we purchased it from the DRMO. It's been stripped out, of course, because it wasn't a condition of sale."

Jacqueline thumbed through the stack of papers while Quinto explained what was in the file.

"Then," the Armenian continued, "somewhere in there you'll find a copy of Form 82-675-2D, which lists the MSD equipment you'll be expected to install in order to be in compliance with the HSP-Bulletin-76, and the updated code for Maryland emergency airlift manuals. If, after you've waded through that mess, you find something missing, give me a call. We probably got one or two of everythin' you'll ever need lyin' around here somewhere."

Jacqueline was still trying to give the fat man the

315

impression she was studying the file, when she heard the thumping sound of the rotor.

"Now there's the little matter of money," Quinto said.

"I presume that a certified check will be satisfactory," Jacqueline said, reaching in her purse.

"Certified is the way we like 'em," Quinto said, looking up. When he did, he was staring straight into the barrel of a small Beretta. "What the—"

"I'm afraid I've made an error, Mr. Quinto." Jacqueline smiled. "I seem to have forgotten the small matter of the check. Since that is the case, I'm afraid this will have to do."

Quinto started to get up, thought better of it, and sagged back in his chair. He was sweating and his face was drained of color. Jacqueline Marceau slid her arm forward on the scarred counter until the Beretta was less than six inches from his face.

"You have no way of knowing this, Mr. Quinto, but in your own small way you are playing an important role in what will soon be regarded as one of the darkest days in American history."

Quinto's gamble, an ill-fated attempt to wrestle the small automatic away from the woman, was not well thought out. In the end, the gesture was ill-conceived and poorly executed; it came too little and too late. He lunged forward, giving Jacqueline the only provocation she needed.

The first bullet penetrated and shattered the zygomatic bone just below his left eye. The second shot found its mark only an inch or so below the first. Quinto's body rocketed backward and finally tumbled to the floor. The first bullet had served the mission's purpose; the second gave partial vent to a fevered hostility that had begun the day her father was executed by the young American lieutenant in a grove of trees behind their Kampot Som home.

Quinto's head had erupted in an explosion of tissue fragments and bone shards. There had been no plea for mercy, no groveling, no last-minute deals. Jacqueline Marceau had simply done what had to be done.

Chapter Twelve

Time 2137LT:

The task of disposing of Quinto's body proved to be more of a chore than Jacqueline had bargained for. The oversized Armenian weighed well over 350 pounds and his bulk proved difficult for Chen and her to handle. Once again, to confuse the authorities and further convolute their trail, Tonu Hon had insisted that it be made to look like a robbery when the body was finally discovered. Jacqueline removed the man's watch, wallet, and keys. Then she destroyed the files concerning the Kaman. In the end, both she and Tonu Hon realized that whichever agency was assigned to investigate the case would ultimately put the pieces together—but every delay, every impediment, bought them more time.

The body was then dragged into the hangar, a crate of aircraft parts was opened, the parts removed and carefully stacked, and Quinto's body was placed inside. Chen was given the task of resealing the container, and when he was finished the two returned to Quinto's small office to wait for word that the President's helicopter was preparing to leave Camp David.

Jacqueline tuned to the ATC channel on the G-A radio to monitor the air traffic inside the Washington National control zone, and tuned the small black and white television to a local news channel.

Then, the two returned to her car, opened the trunk, and removed the fully assembled grenade launcher with the night-vision attachment and the five rounds of 40mm ammunition. Chen was instructed to store the weapon in the cockpit of the Kaman, secure it, and return to Quinto's office. When he did, he found Jacqueline smiling.

"In our country," she explained, "everything is accomplished in great secrecy. In America it is different; the American penchant for wanting to know everything that is happening when it is happening works in our favor. The American President Colchin has been holding talks with the Czechoslovakian President over the weekend at his Camp David retreat. The talks were scheduled to conclude earlier this evening. It is customary for each of the leaders to make a statement at the conclusion of their talks. The media, as usual, will cover those statements, and then the President will be flown directly to Washington General Hospital. When the President begins to make his statement we will be ready. By the time his flight arrives at Washington General, we will be waiting."

Chen Po nodded, folded his hands, and waited.

Jacqueline felt a sudden rush of heightened excitement. Each thread of Tonu Hon's carefully woven plan was coming together, and in a matter of hours now it would culminate in the death of the leader of the most powerful nation on earth. It would be a glorious day for Mao Quan.

For Chen there appeared to be no such evidence of restlessness or excitement. He lit a cigarette and meandered casually about the small office, only occasionally glancing at the television. Jacqueline wasn't sure how well he comprehended what she was telling him, and she decided instead to devote her entire attention to the ATC frequency and the television. From time to time she did glance at her watch, growing increasingly more annoyed at the wait.

Bogner located Joy in the crowded VIP lounge adjacent to the heliport at Washington General. She was still going over the questions she intended to ask Colchin when she looked up. Bogner could tell by her expression she was piqued with him for hanging up on her.

Bogner pointed toward a far corner of the room. "Over there."

"Is that an order, Captain?" she snapped.

Bogner took her by the arm.

"Tobias, what the hell is going on?"

Bogner held his index finger to his lips. "Keep your voice down and listen."

Joy waited. She was frowning. "This better be good."

"Has the President's chopper left Camp David yet?"

Joy shook her head. "Not yet. They just informed us, Havel and Colchin are getting ready to make their statements. We've got a direct feed and the camera will cover both men. The Press Secretary advised us that each would make a brief statement, no more than three or four minutes, and then Colchin would wait until Havel's flight leaves before he boards the chopper to come here."

"What's the flying time?"

"Less than thirty minutes. Now, *you* answer some questions for *me*. What the hell is going on?"

"We're doubling security."

"They always do when—"

"This is off the record. Okay? Less than three hours ago we located 5A's mole, the one that's been feeding info to Mao Quan's hit squad. We also know she's been pumping one of the staff here at the hospital for information. When we went through the files in her office, we discovered that she was paying more than passing attention to the fact that Colchin was being flown in to Washington General following his meetings in Camp David."

"And you think . . . ?"

"What I think is there's damn good chance someone's going to make an attempt to assassinate Colchin—here, tonight. Packer knows, Jaffe knows, and Gerhardt has his Secret Service people combing the whole damn hospital looking for anyone that doesn't belong here. This entire wing is sealed off. We're going through every patient's room, every closet, the food service area, every waiting room, and everywhere else we can think to look."

"A bomb?"

"A good bet, but no sure thing. So far they've proved they're fairly adept with all the standard terrorist toys. That's why I want you to get out of here."

Joy looked at her former husband in disbelief. First she smiled, then she frowned. "You're kidding. The biggest damn story of the year may be unfolding right in front of our eyes and you want me to just pick up my things and walk away from it?"

"Look, Joy, you saw what happened at the World Trade Center and the Federal Building in Oklahoma City. Bombs don't discriminate. If 5A has planted a bomb in here, it'll nail a lot more victims than just the President. I don't want anything to happen to you."

"What happens if you don't find the bomb? Better yet, how do we know there even is a bomb?"

"We wave the President's flight off."

"You better be damn sure there's a bomb before you pull a stunt like that. From where I'm standing, you don't have much time. Colchin is on a tight schedule. If you're wrong . . ."

Out of the corner of her eye, Joy could see orderlies beginning to move the small handful of sixth-floor patients toward the elevators. Then she caught sight of a uniformed officer with a dog. "And just for the record, Tobias, I appreciate your concern, but I'm not leaving—and neither is my camera crew. We're not about to turn our backs on a story with this kind of potential."

"Damn it, Joy, this is no time—"

"You want me to go but you're staying. No way. I'm just as concerned about you." She was still frowning when she heard one of the camera crew call out to her.

"Havel just concluded his remarks. We got it all on tape. If you want to go over what he said before the President gets here, you better review it now."

"If we don't find that bomb," Bogner reminded her, "we may clear the building."

"Dammit, Tobias, you don't even know if there is a bomb."

For David Colchin, standing in the uncomfortable glare of a bank of television lights, what had been for most of the day little more than a discomfort in his chest had now become a gnawing and persistent pain. Twice during the Czechoslovakian President's remarks he had winced perceptibly, and on one occasion had actually clutched at his side.

Virginia Martin, his long-time confidential secretary, standing less than ten feet from him and watching him intently, leaned forward and whispered to his aide, "Chet, I think the President has a problem."

Hurley tried to mask a quick smile. "You

wouldn't happen to be talking about Havel's statement, would you?"

"Not Havel, Colchin. Did you see him wince?"

Hurley nodded. "Yeah, I know. I talked to him about an hour ago. He says he thinks he may have a touch of the flu."

Virginia Martin shook her head. "I've been around that man for twenty-seven years, and I'see him stand up and give a thirty-minute speech with a fever that would have killed a horse. If he's acting like that, he has something really wrong."

Chet Hurley stepped discreetly back into the small crowd of reporters and aides, worked his way to the back of the room, hurried down the hall, and finally into the glare of lights where Colchin was waiting for his Czechoslovakian counterpart to conclude his answers to reporter's questions. "Mr. President?" he whispered.

Colchin inclined his head toward him.

"Virginia said she saw you wince a couple of times. Are you all right?"

David Colchin's face was flushed, and beads of sweat had formed on his forehead. "Virginia is worse than my mother," he said. As he said it, he reached for Hurley's arm to steady himself. "The problem is, she's right. That last jolt got the best of me." He glanced at Havel and then down into the crowd of media. The Czech leader appeared to be enjoying the glare of the spotlight as he finished his answer to a particularly involved question.

"Buy me some time," Colchin whispered with a

grimace. "See if the Press Secretary can find a way to discreetly cut off the questions."

"Will do, Mr. President," Hurley said. Because he had already started to move away, he was unaware that David Colchin had again winced in pain.

Bogner was the last one to arrive. The entire cadre of security people had been hurriedly assembled in a small room off the main corridor on the sixth floor. Jed Gerhardt of the Secret Service, with Packer and Jaffe standing next to him, had already started.

"All right, gentlemen, this is when we earn our pay. The hospital's security staff, not to mention everyone and his brother with a clearance, has been over every nook and cranny of this wing with a fine-tooth comb. Bottom line, no bomb. We can't even find a suspicious-looking package. In addition, Phil Hannon of WG's security staff says his people followed every procedure and for all practical purposes, he has had this wing pretty well sealed off for the last forty-eight hours.

"I see Toby Bogner of ISA just joined us. He's the one that thinks the 5A people are the ones behind all of this. I'll have him bring us up to date on what he knows and then we can make a decision."

Bogner elbowed his way to the front of the room and stood next to Gerhardt. "There isn't a whole lot more I can add to what you already know. Earlier today we discovered the identity of a woman known to be feeding information to a 5A terrorist group headquartered off the southwest shore of Cuba. We spent several hours combing through the woman's files. At this point we can definitely tie her to the assassination of Senator Crane, and we have strong evidence she is connected to the bombs that were put on board Secretary Dunning and Undersecretary Swelling's planes. There's more, but we haven't had time to put a ribbon around it."

"Same one responsible for the shooting at Saint Patrick's this morning?" someone asked.

"In all probability," Bogner said. "When we went through her files this afternoon, we found copies of several newspaper articles, all highlighted, which mentioned the fact that the President would be checking into the hospital at the conclusion of the talks with Havel at Camp David this weekend."

"What makes you so sure we should be looking for a bomb?" someone asked. "Senator Crane was shot with a high-powered rifle."

"Guns, bombs . . . like I said, we didn't uncover anything," Gephardt reminded them. "My people tell me this place is clean, unless we've got some suicide bomber walking around with a bomb strapped to their back."

"So what's our next move?" one of the security people shouted.

Another voice in the back of the room asked, "Does 5A know we're on to them?"

Bogner held up his hand. "We don't know what 5A knows, except to tell you that our mole has disappeared. There's no trace of her."

There was a murmur of voices as Packer pulled Bogner aside. "We're running out of time, T.C. Gephardt's people are convinced the place is clean. Like he said, they can't find anything that would indicate there's been a breach of security. But if we're going to call off the President's flight, we better be letting them know at Camp David."

"Dammit, Pack, something's coming down. I can feel it. I can taste it. I can smell it."

Bogner could tell Packer was reluctant to call the shot. "You know David Colchin as well as any man alive, T.C. You know what he would expect you to do. If you tell me to cancel that flight, I'll see that it's canceled. Colchin's the one who put me in charge of this damned 5A mess, and you're the only man in the room that knows what you saw in those files."

"Dammit, Pack, if we call this one wrong, we could have a dead President on our hands."

"If you cancel and nothing happens, every damn one of our critics will say the terrorists beat us at our own game and we'll open ourselves up to every screwball that wants to mail in a threat against the President."

Bogner turned away and walked over to the only window in the room. It was snowing again, not hard, but enough to coat the ground with a sheet of wind-blown white powder. "I say we tell the President to hold off."

"How long?"

"Until we're damn certain nothing is coming down."

Time 2212LT:

The images on Julie Simon's television were little more than a blur when the program she was watching was suddenly interrupted:

This is an NBS news bulletin. Jay Arnold reporting. Less than ten minutes ago President David Colchin collapsed during a press conference being held at the conclusion of talks with President Vaclav Havel of Czechoslovakia at his Camp David retreat in Maryland. To get further details on this story, we switch you now to our correspondent Jody Gorman at Camp David.

The screen showed a dark-haired young woman holding a microphone while she squinted into the harsh glare of the camera lighting.

That's right, Jay. It was exactly two minutes after ten when President Colchin stepped to the podium here in the main room at Camp David to give his impression of how talks had progressed with President Havel.

The President, in fact, was still congratulating the White House press corps when he suddenly bent over, clutching his chest, and dropped to his knees. Press Secretary Bill Moreland and White House Aide Chet Hurley were first to reach him.

Doctor Philip Hart, the President's personal physician as well as one of his most trusted advisors, had been invited to Camp David for the weekend of high-

level talks with President Havel, and was expected to accompany the President to Washington General Hospital later tonight.
Less than two minutes ago, a White House spokesman informed those of us gathered here that the President was in a great deal of discomfort, and Doctor Hart was at his side.

The scene switched back to the NBS studio, then desolved into a split screen, enabling the viewer to see both Jay Arnold in the studio and the reporter on the scene.

"Did anyone notice anything about the President that would have indicated he was not feeling well?"
"I've talked to several of the people who were here most of the weekend, Jay, and they indicate that the President did look tired and that he did not make his usual three-mile morning jog around the grounds here at Camp David either day."
"Have there been any other indications that the President . . ."

Julie Simon finished her drink, stood up, turned off the television, and staggered into the kitchen. She watched the snow fall for several minutes before she picked up the bottle of bourbon, now nearly empty, and poured the last of the contents into her empty glass. At the same time she continued looking out the window at the snow starting to accumulate in the courtyard below.

The pain, she had decided, had reached the unbearable point, and it was futile to try to assuage it. She opened the door to the cupboard over the sink and took out another bottle, this one smaller but full of the little blue tablets the doctor had given her to help her sleep. She emptied the contents into her hand, hesitated no more than a couple of seconds, and scooped them into her mouth like so many candies. Then she finished her drink.

For a fleeting second there was regret at what she had done, but then there was the sense of freedom, the comfort of tranquility, and even accomplishment. She would, she knew now, in only a matter of seconds, erase the pain and disappointment, ease the burden of guilt, be transported beyond the bitter loneliness of . . .

She weaved her way into the bedroom carrying on intimate conversations with the ghosts of a lifetime of failure.

There were porch swings and parties, school dances and walks down by the lake at her parents' summer home. More than that, there were people who smiled and held out their arms to her. She heard music, sweet music—and church bells, and hymns, and the pounding of hearts, hers and Richard's. There was the sweet breathless pain of climax—the moan of fulfillment, the clinging—and finally the nothingness.

When Julie Simon closed her eyes, the nightmare she had called life slowly evolved into the finality of her death.

* * *

When Bogner walked out of the briefing room, Joy was waiting. "Have you heard?" she blurted out.

Bogner stared back at her. "Heard what?"

"Colchin collapsed at the press conference with Havel."

Bogner was stunned. "He did what?"

"He collapsed. It happened on camera with millions of people watching. He started toward the microphone and suddenly keeled over. Phil Hart is there with him. There hasn't been any word yet on what happened. We're waiting for word to come down the line. We've got a patch back to the studio so we can pick up an anything that happens."

Bogner, still unnerved, followed her into the VIP lounge where the camera crew was waiting. "Hey, Joy," someone shouted, "over here. CNN says it was a heart attack."

Joy wormed her way through the twenty or so people in the room until she could see the television. "CBS and NBC have crews there too," her cameraman informed her, "but CNN broke it."

"Where the hell were we when the word came down?" Joy grumbled. "One of the biggest stories of the year is popping right under our nose, and all we can do is sit here and watch."

Bogner was still watching the CNN reporter when he felt a tap on the shoulder. It was Packer; he was frowning. "We just got a call from the Secret Service people at Camp David. They confirmed what CNN is saying. The President has had a massive coronary. He's critical. Phil Hart is with him. They're loading Colchin aboard the chopper right now—and they'll get here as soon as possible."

"Did you tell them what—?"

"Hart says they don't have any alternative."

"The hell they don't. What about—?"

"I'm afraid we have another problem; Washington International, Bolling, Andrews, and two weather stations south of the Beltway are all reporting icing. Two weather stations in Virginia are reporting heavy icing. At this point, they've run out of options. They're coming in."

Clem Shock was a frugal man who was celebrating the fact that he was completing his twenty-fifth year as a member of the Creighton police department, and his seventh as a part-time security guard at the Creighton airport.

Two jobs had become a way of life for the forty-eight-year-old father of four, and as he reminded himself repeatedly, if a man wanted a career in law enforcement, it took two jobs to pay the bills.

Now, with a thin sheen of ice coating the windows of the tired old station wagon he drove when he was on airport patrol, he pulled into the parking lot of Quinto Aircraft and got out of the car. There were two cars in the parking lot, and as far as Shock was concerned, that meant there was a darn good chance that Quinto had the coffeepot on.

He stomped his way into the vestibule of the tiny building, brushed off the snow, and looked around. "Quinto here?" he asked.

"He stepped out," Jacqueline Marceau informed

him. Then she added, "He went to get something to eat."

Shock glanced back out into the parking lot. "His car's still here. Must've gone with someone, huh?"

Jacqueline turned her chair away from the radio and stood up. Chen Po Lee was standing in the hall leading to the hangar. Shock nodded in his direction and started for the coffee. "Gettin' nasty out there," he said. "Gets any worse and Quinto can close up. You folks might be smart to get on the road too. Looks like the ice is gonna' make the driving treacherous before this night is over."

Jacqueline moved out from behind the counter. "Is Mr. Quinto expecting you?"

Shock took a sip of coffee before he answered. "Naw, I saw the lights on and his car was still here. Figured I get myself some coffee and warn him he left his floodlights on over the doors to the hangar. That old skinflint is tight as the bark on a birch; if he left his lights on I knew he'd want me to turn 'em off."

"Mr. Yen will be happy to turn them—," Jacqueline started to say, but Shock was already waving her off.

"No problem, I know right where the switch is. He's left them damn lights on before. I'll just slip on back there and shut 'em off. Then I guess I'll wait until he comes back—ain't nobody millin' around the airport on a night like this. Besides, I wanted to talk to him anyway—my oldest son is looking for a part-time job. Maybe Quinto can use him."

Jacqueline glanced back at the flickering black-

and-white television set; the word "Bulletin" had appeared on the screen. Under the circumstances, it was only reasonable to assume it was further information on the condition of the President. The unexpected arrival of the middle-aged security officer was something she hadn't bargained on, and given the deteriorating weather conditions, she knew he would question them if they tried to take off now.

Clem Shock had already set his cup down and started for the hangar when he heard the woman's voice. It was measured, firm, perhaps even a little disturbing. He turned to look back at the woman.

"While your devotion to duty is admirable, officer, I fear that it is likewise most unfortunate. You see, through no fault of your own, you have stumbled into a situation that is more than either of us bargained for. Under the circumstances, I seem to have no choice. Mr. Yen and I have a very important engagement—a matter that is quite urgent actually."

Shock, still perplexed, would have asked the woman what she was talking about, but he never had the opportunity. Jacqueline fired twice. At close range, the two shots sounded like firecrackers. The first bullet tore through the man's jacket and burrowed a hole in his chest. The second, higher and decidedly more devastating, burned a tunnel into the area just above his ribs on the left side. The protest the security officer managed to cough out was too brief to be intelligible and too muted to be heard. There was a slightly theatrical manner to the way he slumped to his knees, still staring at Jacqueline. The expression of utter disbelief remained right up to the moment when he toppled face first to the floor.

Chen started to bend over the fallen man, but Jacqueline stopped him. "Leave him," she ordered. "There isn't time." She pushed Chen toward the hangar. "Now we will have to hurry."

"Icing—very dangerous," Chen protested.

"This may be our only chance," Jacqueline said. "It's a risk we will have to take. As soon as we have confirmation that the President's helicopter has left Camp David, we will take off."

Time 2232LT:

(copy) NBS . . .

> *This is Jay Arnold reporting from the NBS newsroom in Washington.*
> *We continue to monitor the reports coming out of Camp David.*
> *Shortly after ten o'clock this evening, President David R. Colchin suffered a massive coronary while preparing to make concluding remarks following two days of meetings with Czechoslovakian President Vaclav Havel.*
> *Less than fifteen minutes ago, Press Secretary Bill Moreland informed the press that President Colchin's personal physician,*

Doctor Philip Hart, had released the follow-
ing statement:
"President Colchin has suffered a heart at-
tack. He is alive but is suffering a great
deal of discomfort. Plans are being made to
transport him by helicopter to Washington
General Hospital."
NBS'S Jody Gorman indicates several
weather stations in the area are reporting
icing conditions at or near flight mini-
mums, but because of the President's con-
dition, the decision has been made to take
the President aboard the helicopter and
leave as soon as conditions permit.

Bogner and Packer, along with a handful of others, continued their wait just inside the corridor
leading to the east wing doors to the Washington
General helipad.

Miller, still out of breath from sprinting the
length of the building, told them, "We're monitoring the ATC frequencies, and the tower at Andrews
confirms that they have WI-GC clearing a flight corridor for the President. They're rerouting everything."

"What about the weather?" Bogner asked.

"It's holding, but just barely. I called the weather
detachment at Andrews. They say it could go either
way. A PIREP from a pilot on an AA flight west of
Baltimore just a few minutes ago indicated the temperature at the five-hundred-millibar level was below freezing. The only thing keeping us from a

full-fledged ice storm is the surface temp. The DETCO at Andrews says we've got a fast-moving cold front roaring in from the west. Some of the stations west of here are reporting a ten-degree drop in the surface temperature in the last hour. As soon as that happens, all of this damned ice turns to snow."

"How soon?"

"He thinks it'll be another hour or so, but Hart says they can't wait that long. They're going to chance it."

"Has Gephardt got a direct line to—?"

Miller nodded. "The Secret Service is in direct contact with Andrews ATC in case the ice knocks the communications out at WI-GC. That way we'll know where the President's chopper is at all times."

"Where's Gephardt now?"

"He's got a bank of phones and a radio set up in a room off the VIP lounge down the hall. That way he can talk directly with Colonel Martin, Colchin's pilot in the chopper."

"Marty Martin? Hell, I know him," Bogner said. "We were stationed at Pensacola together. Can Gephardt's people patch me through to him?"

"Can do," Miller said. He led Bogner down the corridor into the VIP lounge, and Gephardt handed Bogner the mike.

"Marty, this is T.C. Bogner. I'm hanging out with your Sunday night reception committee at Washington General. How's the main man?"

"They're bringing a couple of oxygen tanks on

board for him as we speak, Toby. He looks like he's in pretty rough shape."

"What's your flying time?"

"In good weather, something like thirty-seven minutes. But I've got the DETCO at Andrews weather feeding me an obs every five minutes. It looks like we're going to have to bring the Chief right through the worst of this shit."

"Can you make it?"

"This baby is state-of-the-art, T.C. She's got more bells and whistles than a new Buick. Sometimes I think she's smarter than I am. The GC is pumping the de-icer on her now. I've got both engines cranked and a feedback rigged up on the heaters. We're pumping everything this old girl can muster right back up into a makeshift rotor cowling we rigged up under the stabilizer bar. Keeping the ice off the rotor is the big problem."

"Will it work?"

"It damn sure better."

"How's the weather there?"

"Holding. According to Andrews, it looks like there's one bad patch between us and WG. When we get there I'll take her up to nine thousand and try to pick up that temperature inversion. The trick will be bringing her down out of this crud. If we make it, I'll take you up for a spin and you can get a look at this damn icing first hand."

Bogner could hear people shouting in the background, and he could picture the chaos as the President was being brought aboard. Without warning, the memories came flooding back. . . .

He was lying in the mud in a Vietnamese rice paddy, the smoldering remains of his A-6 less than five hundred yards away and a squad of Vietcong soldiers sloshing through the mud looking for him. Overhead he could hear an Apache's rotors drumming the oily blackness, and he could see the sweeping search beam probing the brackish water and blackness in a desperate effort to reach him before the enemy did.

There was the dueling exchange of ground fire and rocket fire: silver-orange, night-shredding ribbons that created a nightmarish web that momentarily illuminated and betrayed the Apache's position.

Then, after a while, there was a silence. Not a real silence, a manufactured one—like the one poachers create before they stab the beam of light into eyes of the kill and freeze it.

Those few minutes became his eternity. Those few minutes when he pulled himself out of the muck, slime, and stench—and crawled into the harness dangling from the belly of that Apache became his yesterday and his tomorrow all in one. He was freezing and sweating at the same time—just as he was freezing and sweating now.

"T.C., are you all right?" Miller's voice was coming at him through some kind of fog.

"Yeah, yeah, sure . . ."

"Did you hear? They're off the ground."

"They made it?"

"They're in the air. We're monitoring the ATC

transmissions and we've got a feed through from the tower at Andrews."

Bogner slumped back in his chair and waited. There was only one problem; this time there was no Apache out there to save anyone's ass. Bomb or no bomb, ice or no ice, the race was on. The President's and maybe a whole lot of other people's lives were at stake.

(copy) NBS . . . 2255LT broadcast
*This is Jay Arnold in the NBS newsroom
with our continuing coverage of the late-
breaking story from Camp David.
At 10:02 Eastern Time, President David R.
Colchin suffered what is now believed to
have been a massive coronary just prior to
speaking to the press. The President was
preparing to make closing marks following
a weekend long series of meetings with
Czechoslovakian President Vaclav Havel at
Camp David.
As the President approached the microphone, he clutched his chest, stumbled,
and fell. The President's personal physician, Dr. Philip Hart, was at his side
within moments.
President Colchin was removed to the
main house at his camp David retreat, and*

after examining the President, Dr. Hart confirmed that President Colchin had suffered, and I am quoting Dr. Hart now, "a massive coronary."

At this time, the President is en route to Washington General Hospital via helicopter, and NBS's Joy Carpenter is on the scene.

Chapter Thirteen

Time 2259LT:

"GC, this is AT 0719, do you read?"

"Affirmative, 0719, loud and clear. You were coming in a little mush-mouthed just after takeoff. What's it like?"

"At five thousand we're experiencing heavy icing, some turbulence. What happens if I take it up to seven thousand?"

"Hang ten, 0719. I've got the Andrews DETCO on the line. I'll patch him through."

Martin continued to scan the bank of instruments while he waited. He glanced over at his co-pilot, Captain Louis Rhymers, and shook his head. Rhymers was holding his hand at a seventeen-degree angle—an indication he was already at 5,800 and climbing.

"This is Major Knight." The DETCO's voice had an almost paternal quality to it. "Andrews. According to our latest obs, we're reporting a combination of sleet and light snow. Pressure continues to drop. Nothing dramatic, but the front hasn't passed through here yet. Surface winds are light and variable. When they kick around to the west they'll pick up in the area of ten to twelve knots from the northwest."

"AT 0719, this is WI-GC. We're picking up something in the zone."

"I hope to hell it's us," Martin grumbled.

"AT 0719, this is WI-GC again. We've got a target in quad seven on the sweep . . . coordinates 09.5-11.5, approaching from the west-northwest."

"I thought this damn corridor was supposed to be cleared," Martin complained. "What's its altitude?"

"AT 0719, the target is holding at five thousand. Course 33.30-33.40—bearing—"

"What the hell is it?" Rhymer said.

"AT 0719, so far we haven't been able to make radio contact. At the moment we're guessing, either some poor bastard is lost up there in this damned weather or we've got us a target with no radio."

"WI-GC, this is AT 0719. We're still picking up ice. We're at sixty-five hundred and the OAT indicates we haven't gained a thing. We may have to bring her back down to five thousand. Where's that damned unauthorized target?"

"AT 0719, this Andrews GC. What's your visibility?"

Martin stared through the windscreen and activated both sweeps. "I've got the heat cranked up and all I'm getting is a damned smear. Nada—zip—read that an official 'damn near zero.' "

"Can you identify anything on the ground? We show you over Multon. We've instructed the field to turn their runway lights on."

"Forget Multon. One of the crew just crawled up here. Hart says the President could be in deep shit if we don't get him to WG in the next fifteen minutes."

Jacqueline Marceau could feel the sweat trickle down the nape of her neck, under her coat, and into the collar of her vest. Twice the Kaman had vibrated violently under the weight of the ice and dropped—each time to the extent that she thought Chen was going to lose it, but each time he had managed to recover.

The only illumination in the cockpit of the struggling Kaman was a bank of red, green, and yellow indicator lights on the panel, and she found herself groping in the darkness for something to hold on to. The chaos in the cockpit was further compounded by the stream of pleas for identification from first one ground station and then a second. The ground-based voices filled the cabin with an incessant and disturbing buzz of flight jargon that, despite her training and familiarity with what they were saying, sounded increasingly bellicose.

Jacqueline had already removed the M136 from the stores area and secured it next to her. It was loaded and ready. Two standby rounds had been strapped into the holder beside her seat.

Once more she heard the plea from the voice that identified itself as WI-GC. "You are in a restricted zone. If you have lost your radio, so indicate by—"

Chen depressed the squelch button and muted the transmission.

"How much longer?" she demanded. She wondered if Chen could hear the element of fear that had crept into her voice.

"Five, six minutes," he informed her. In the pale wash of the colored lights coming from the instrument panel, she saw for the first time the sheen of sweat on the little man's forehead.

Bogner, standing less than fifty feet from where the President's helicopter would land on the Washington General heliport, could feel tiny needles of sleet peck away at his face, and he shivered involuntarily. Within the last ten minutes he had made the journey from the press room and the VIP lounge back to the heliport for Hart's updates. Now, Gephardt was with him. The Secret Service agent was still wired to Andrews ATC, and was monitoring the exchanges between WI-GC and the President's helicopter.

"They still can't establish voice contact with that aircraft coming in from the northwest, T.C."

"Have they got any kind of ID?"

"WI-GC figures either the damn thing is lost and

the pilot has panicked, or his radio is out. Either way, they figure he's in over his head. If the ice don't get him, the FAA will when he gets on the ground."

"Has WI-GC plotted his vectors?"

"If he maintains his heading, he's headed straight for us. According to Andrews ATC, a couple of times he's drifted north, and each time he's corrected."

"Can we tell what kind of an aircraft he's flying?"

Gephardt started to shake his head and stopped. "Wait a minute, I'm getting something from WI-GC. They say they've established radio contact with the target."

Bogner leaned forward to catch the exchange between the tower and the GC unit.

"The target identifies himself as HN-477. I can barely understand him."

Bogner grabbed the telephone out of Gephardt's hand. "This is Captain Bogner. Get me a verification on that HN-477."

"This is WI-GC, say again?"

"Verification on HN-477. Now, dammit!"

"Let me pull it up on the computer, Captain." There was a momentary pause before the voice returned. "Log T7. It's registered to Weitock Hospital Support Services, a Maryland-based outfit. We can't verify it, sir, but she could be coming into WG on an emergency run. If the captain isn't aware, we've got our scanner on. There's accidents everywhere—a bad one on the turnpike."

There it was—the reason—the answer—spat out of a damn bureaucratic computer on an icy Sunday night while most folks had already bedded down for the night. Suddenly what was happening had all the subtlety of a slam dunk—a bolo punch—a wake up call. Suddenly all of the pieces of Mao's puzzle tumbled into place. Bogner looked at Gephardt. "Now I know why we couldn't find that damn bomb—there isn't any."

Gephardt waited. "What the hell are you talking about?"

"I'll explain later. How long will it be before Colchin's—?"

Gephardt was already barking at the WI-GC crew. "Where is he?"

"She should be coming down out of this soup at any minute. From what we see on the scope, Martin has that puppy right over your head. He's close enough you ought to be able to hear the rotors."

Bogner stepped back as AT 0719's landing lights began to materialize, gradually penetrating the swirling clouds of snow and sheets of sleet. Two of Gephardt's men crouched on the perimeter of the pad waiting. To their left, back under the overhang and out of the weather, was the hospital's official reception committee; a battalion of green-and-white-clad medics, nurses, and doctors. Bogner wondered how many of them would be out there if the guest of honor hadn't been the President.

He shouted at Gephardt, "The minute that damn chopper touches down, kill the heliport floods!"

"What for?"

"If I'm right, we're going to get some company."

Colchin's helicopter was still hovering several

feet over the pad when Gephardt's men raced out of the shadows. The ice-crusted Black Hawk lumbered in, yawing from side to side until it pancaked on to the helipad, scattering quarter-inch-thick pieces of ice over the landing area. The forward door had swung open on touchdown, and one of the Secret Service men had already managed to crawl in. Two others, both in green scrubs, were right behind him.

Bogner raced for the Black Hawk, reached up, grabbed the access bar, and swung aboard. He was shouting at Martin and Rhymers. "Kill those engines and get the hell out of here. We've got company!"

Major Marty Martin was still unbuckling his harness when the first round hit. A ball of fire rocketed the length of the Black Hawk's fuselage, and Bogner felt the deck of the cockpit buckle under him. He saw Martin's body spin, arms flailing, lifted up like a toy on fire, slamming against the bulkhead as the acrylic shattered.

Before Bogner could regain his footing, the second round slammed into the already wounded Huey, and he felt the chopper pitch upward, teetering momentarily on its nose, rocketing him forward, then dropping him sprawling back into the confusion in the personnel area. The force of the blast sent him head-over-heels, slamming into the wall of the fuselage a second time, and he felt the hot metal burn though his jacket, searing his back and neck. He tried to push himself up and felt the spongy, soft, violated flesh of one of the medics beneath him. A hole had been gouged in the man's chest. Between his screams the man belched out a thick, steady stream of mucus and blood. Bogner rolled over, instinctively reaching out for the man, even though he knew there was nothing he could do for him.

An electrical panel tore away and dangled from frayed wires directly over his head, crackling, hissing, raining sparks down on him, and the air in the Huey was filled with the acrid smell of burning insulation.

Less than five feet from him he heard his name. Through the smoke he could see Phil Hart. The man David Colchin had once called the only man in Texas he would trust to put him under the knife was slumped awkwardly against a pile of smoking rubbish, half pinned under a section of the firewall between the Black Hawk's flight deck and the President's personal compartment. He was bleeding from the nose and mouth, and his left arm was twisted grotesquely up and behind him. "There!" he shouted. "The President—the President!"

Bogner managed to pull one leg up, then the second. A jagged chunk of the Huey's aluminum skin had sliced a six-inch-long gash in his right thigh. Still dazed, he squeezed his eyes shut in a desperate effort to screen out the smoke. He could hear the fire behind him, and the smoke was enveloping him as he forced himself to start scrambling his way to his hands and knees. Now he could see Hart; the man was pointing frantically to a pile of smoldering rubble just to Bogner's right.

"There—over there—hurry! For God's sake, hurry!"

For the second time, Bogner shook his head. His eyes were burning and his vision was still blurred. The pounding in his head had a trip-hammer-like precision, and at the same time there was a kind of helter-skelter chaos to his thinking. What he could see was little more than a blur. What he couldn't see had all the ramifications of a nightmare. Over there—over there; the words came at him out of a murky obscurity.

He closed his eyes until the burning sensation passed and his vision cleared enough to see what Hart was pointing at.

He braced himself, pushed away, started crawling toward the stack of smoldering debris, and began clawing and peeling his way through shards of hot glass and tortured metal. Then he saw why Hart had been so frantic. The President was trapped, pinned against the Black Hawk's corrugated steel floor-pan by a section of the fuselage. The undercasing had been ripped out, and a broken sled strut had speared a hole in the metal inches from his head.

"Mr. President!" he heard himself shout, at the same time realizing that under the circumstances the formality sounded ludicrous. The only assessment he was able to make was that Colchin's eyes were shut and his head and neck appeared to be violently twisted to one side.

Bogner swung his body around, pulled his knees up, and used his feet and legs like a fulcrum to shove the biggest section of fuselage off Colchin. Then he scrambled to pull off two more pieces. The gurney that had been used to bring the President aboard had collapsed. It was wedged on its side against the bulkhead—but the President was still strapped to it. In some kind of bizarre, almost preternatural stroke of fate, it had kept the bulkhead support from crushing the President.

"David, can you hear me?" Bogner shouted.

There was no response, and Bogner understood the gamble. Colchin had suffered a massive coronary, and now there was a strong likelihood that he had been even further injured in the attack. He slipped his hands under Colchin's shoulders, locked his fingers in the fabric of the President's bloody shirt, counted to three, lifted, and pulled. Bogner heard his old friend cry out in pain. The body hadn't moved. Colchin's legs were still pinned under the twisted beam of the bulkhead, and the gurney straps were holding.

As far as Bogner was concerned, an already bad situation had found a way to deteriorate even further. The fire in the fuselage was spreading, and Colchin had somehow managed to grope his way out of unconsciousness into a state of semi-alertness. Now he could feel the pain and sense the danger.

Bogner grunted, and tightened his grip. "Help me, you pampered son-of-a—" Suddenly he realized he had heard the President mutter some kind of unintelligible response. Colchin's effort had come out as little more than meaningless fragments

uttered by a man experiencing nearly unfathoma-
ble pain. But Bogner knew the man, and he knew
the main man was telling him to get on with it.

Bogner fumbled around in the smoke until he
found a piece of jagged metal, and used it to cut the
nylon straps. On the third attempt, he felt the President's body slide grudgingly toward him. Colchin,
grimacing in pain, was finally freed from the buckled bulkhead support.

Bogner leaned forward, inched his way under the
body of the President, and lifted. He heard Colchin
cry out again, but he managed to pull his knees
back under him, and struggled to his feet with the
President hanging over his shoulder.

There was a wall of burning insulation between
them as he turned toward the access door. Beyond
was more rubble from the crash—most of it on fire.
Bogner staggered toward the opening, tightened his
grip on Colchin, clawed his way through the wreckage, felt the fire sear his face, and leaped to the deck
of the helipad. When he hit, his legs buckled, went
out from under him, and the two men went sprawling. When he landed, he looked up and he could see
the President's body. People were rushing toward
him.

Bogner seized the first thing he could find, a piece
of the Huey's tail gear, held onto it, and realized he
smelled aviation fuel. It was pooling around him,
and again he forced himself to his feet. He looked
up into the sleet, and the Kaman was less than fifty
feet above him. Now he could hear the uneven
thumping of the Seasprite's ice-crusted main rotor.

It was out of control, no longer able to maneuver under the increasing weight of the ice. He heard someone scream that the chopper was coming down, and he tried to leap out of the way. He could feel himself sliding along the ice-coated surface of the helipad, and then he heard the Kaman slam to the deck, part of it landing on the still-burning Huey. Then, as if in a nightmare, the entire helipad became a sea of twisted metal, fire, and confusion. There was an explosion, followed by another, and Bogner saw a figure leap from the Kaman, on fire. The man was screaming, his arms and legs flailing at the flames as he hit the deck of the helipad. The man ran, and Bogner saw him plunge over the side of the six-story building into the ice-cloaked darkness.

Then he saw the outline of a figure with a rocket launcher. Somehow that figure had managed to emerge from the smoke and rubble of the Kaman, leap from the wreckage, and drop to one knee. The figure brought the rocket launcher up to its shoulder and aimed it in the direction of the overhang over the access doors where the hospital staff was still working over the fallen President.

For Bogner, the next few seconds became a slow, all-but-paralyzing excursion into a bad dream. He tried to move quickly, but it took him an eternity to roll over, scramble to his knees, grope for his automatic, pull it from the folds of his jacket, release the safety, aim, and fire. Before he was done he had squeezed off three rounds.

The figure with the rocket launcher pitched backward, and momentarily lay motionless against the landing skid of the Kaman. Somehow Bogner clawed his way to his feet and started toward the fallen terrorist. He had taken no more than three steps when the fire reached the aviation fuel. In those next terrible seconds a searing ball of blue-orange flame erupted, there was a chain of violent explosions, and the deck of the helipad shook beneath him. The aviation fuel from the two choppers ignited, and there was suddenly a wall of thick black smoke separating him from the inferno. The shock wave from the blast slammed into him and propelled him backward, ricocheting him against the brick wall of the hospital. The wind went out of him and he crumpled to the deck, desperately searching for air to fill his lungs.

This time there was no way for him to claw his way out of his pain. He could feel the curtains close as the cloak of galling, plaguing hurt blotted out all attempts to hold on to whatever it was he was holding onto. The spiral began, the escape from reality becoming a reality, a blessing. He plunged down and down into a surreal world that shut out everything on the surface and transported him back into a protective womb—and total darkness.

6 Nov: Time 0717LT:

Bogner began the long, slow, agonizing climb out of the well of unconsciousness. There was a gradual assault on his senses. He was aware of a starchy stiffness, an antiseptic odor, a realization of being encumbered, and finally, a myriad assortment of aches and pains—none of which were well defined, all seeming to blend into the general kind of anesthetized lethargy brought on by painkillers.

For several moments he floated in and out of his surreal world, holding on, letting go, drifting on a plateau somewhere between two wholly unacceptable universes, neither of which he was prepared to commit to.

Somewhere, on one of those worlds, he heard voices—unintelligible, murky, indistinct, and disconnected sounds. As near as he could determine, those voices were talking about him. Finally, one of the voices seemed to separate from the others and became clear. It was soft and cool, maybe even colored with a tinge of concern. He filtered through the gauzy layers of muddled thought, and finally came up with a name. Joy. The voice sounded like Joy.

With one eye open now, he realized that it was all darkness. When he opened the other eye, he determined there was more of the same. There was pressure against the eyes, and he closed them again.

His mouth was dry, but he was able to form the question, "Who's—who's there?"

The question triggered footsteps, all seeming to come toward him. Then he heard someone say, "T.C., this is Pack. Can you hear me?"

"Where's—where's Joy?" he asked. "I heard her voice."

"She'll be here any minute now," Packer assured him.

Bogner was suddenly aware of the pounding in his head: the roar, the confusion, the bewildering combination of baffling images—and strangely, a rancid odor, that of heavy, oily smoke. "Where—where the hell am . . . ?" Bogner's voice faded before he finished.

"Don't try to talk," the voice cautioned. "If you can move your right hand without too much difficulty, and you can understand me, wiggle the fingers on your right hand."

Bogner tried it, and it worked. It was easier than trying to form and connect thoughts and words.

Packer moved in closer. Bogner was sure he could hear the man breathing. "T.C., you're in the burn unit at Washington General. The doctor says everything is going to be fine—it's just going to take a few days. Understand?"

Bogner moved his hand. He found a way to force the disjointed words through the bandages. "The—the . . . What about—the President?"

"Alive—and I wish I could add well. But I can't because he isn't. About all I can tell you is that he's hanging in there. He's in the ICU, just one floor above you. He's pretty well banged up, but not any worse than you are. He did have a coronary, but the doctors say they have that under control."

Under the bandages, Bogner squeezed his eyes shut. Even with his eyes shut, the image of the carnage on the helipad was still there. "Do—do we know—know what happened?" he asked.

"We're still putting the pieces together," Packer said. "Apparently the Kaman was masquerading as an emergency run. It ignored the restricted corridor broadcast and followed the President's chopper in. They were taking a helluva chance. They must have wanted this shot at the President pretty bad. They made us pay a helluva price—and they paid one themselves."

Bogner managed to get out one word. It was a question. "Quinto?"

Packer nodded. Then he realized Bogner couldn't see the gesture. "Jaffe sent Rickozy out there to check it out. Rooster found Quinto's body stuffed in a parts crate in the warehouse. He also found the body of a local policeman in Quinto's office. Both had been shot. The Kaman Seasprite is gone. As soon as that mess up on the roof cools, we can start sorting through the pieces."

"What about the one with the grenade launcher?"

"A woman. That's all we know. There isn't a helluva lot left of her what with the fire and all. Eventually we'll get an ID, but it'll take a while."

Bogner heard Packer's voice fade until there was no longer anything there, and he slowly migrated back into his drug-induced purgatory where one gray blended easily into another.

Packer watched as Bogner's labored breathing became less strained and he drifted into that artificial kingdom where painkillers do their job.

* * *

Packer saw Miller coming down the hall. He was smiling. As he approached, he handed Packer his notes from the briefing. "Jaffe has all the information he needs. He has the address of the contact point in Bunche Park and he knows about the arms shipments to De Pinos Aquiero. As for the others, we had a bit of luck this morning. The emigration people picked up Cabandra Marti boarding a plane for Mexico City. He's in custody."

"We lucked out on this one," Packer said.

Miller nodded. "Jaffe says his people in Cuba can take care of it. He says within forty-eight hours, Tonu Hon will wish he'd never seen Cuba."

"What about Park?"

"I don't think his connections can bail him out this time."

Packer had just started through Miller's hastily scribbled notes from Hurley's press conference when he saw the nurse walk out of Bogner's room. "The captain is awake," she said.

Packer walked down to the waiting room and signaled to Joy. "Your turn," he said. "He's awake."

Joy Carpenter walked into the darkened room and moved to the side of Bogner's bed. "They tell me my ex-husband is in there somewhere under all those bandages." She smiled.

"Present and accounted for," Bogner managed to reply. His voice was raspy and weak.

Joy bent over the side of the bed and kissed him on the forehead. She could smell the singed hair and burnt flesh—but it was the only place on his face that wasn't covered by swathes of gauze. As she straightened up, she slipped something into his hand.

"Can you feel that?"

Bogner tightened his fist. "What is it?"

"Two airline tickets to Jamaica."

R. KARL LARGENT

RED SKIES

THE TECHNO-THRILLER THAT OUT-CLANCYS CLANCY!

A trainload of state-of-the-art Russian ICBMs sets out from Kiev to Odessa to be disarmed. But all that arrives in Odessa is a shipment of ineffective missiles. Somewhere a switch has been made...and whoever is responsible now controls a fearsome arsenal powerful enough to ignite a nuclear conflagration.

The stolen missiles are just a piece in a deadly plot concocted by Russian hardliners and their Chinese counterparts—a plot that threatens to end with all-out war. With time running out, Commander T. C. Bogner has to use all the high-tech resources at his disposal to prevent the delivery of the missiles—no matter what the cost.

___4301-7 $6.99 US/$7.99 CAN

LADY OF ICE AND FIRE
COLIN ALEXANDER

Colin Alexander writes "a lean and solid thriller!"
—*Publishers Weekly*

With international detente fast becoming the status quo, a whole new field of spying opens up: industrial espionage. And even though tensions are easing between the East and the West, the same Cold war rules and stakes still apply: world domination at any cost, both in dollars and deaths. Well aware of the new predators, George Jeffers fears that his biotech studies may be sought after by foreign agents. Then his partner disappears with the results of their experiments, and the eminent scientist finds himself the target in a game of deadly intrigue. Jeffers then races against time to prevent the unleashing of a secret that could shake the world to its very foundations.

_4072-7 $5.50 US/$6.50 CAN

WAR BREAKER
JIM DeFELICE

"A book that grabs you hard and won't let go!"
—Den Ing, Bestselling Author of
The Ransom of Black Stealth One

Two nations always on the verge of deadly conflict, Pakistan and India are heading toward a bloody war. And when the fighting begins, Russia and China are certain to enter the battle on opposite sides.

The Pakistanis have a secret weapon courtesy of the CIA: upgraded and modified B-50s. Armed with nuclear warheads, the planes can be launched as war breakers to stem the tide of an otherwise unstoppable invasion.

The CIA has to get the B-50s back. But the only man who can pull off the mission is Michael O'Connell—an embittered operative who was kicked out of the agency for knowing too much about the unsanctioned delivery of the bombers. And if O'Connell fails, nobody can save the world from utter annihilation.

_4043-3 $6.99 US/$7.99 CAN

Dorchester Publishing Co., Inc.
P.O. Box 6640
Wayne, PA 19087-8640

Please add $1.75 for shipping and handling for the first book and $.50 for each book thereafter. NY, NYC, and PA residents, please add appropriate sales tax. No cash, stamps, or C.O.D.s. All orders shipped within 6 weeks via postal service book rate. Canadian orders require $2.00 extra postage and must be paid in U.S. dollars through a U.S. banking facility.

Name_____
Address_____
City_____ State_____ Zip_____
I have enclosed $_____ in payment for the checked book(s).
Payment <u>must</u> accompany all orders. ☐ Please send a free catalog.

KNIGHT HAWK

PAT O'CONNELL

The F-15 Eagle fighter is the U.S. Air Force's most effective weapon in aerial combat. Fast, maneuverable, equipped with cutting-edge technology and the latest military design specs, the F-15 is designed to be virtually unstoppable. But suddenly one has to be stopped at all costs, for the unthinkable has happened—America is being attacked by one of its own super-fighters, flown by a top U.S. pilot.

No one can penetrate the security surrounding the heavily-guarded F-15s—except an Air Force captain who has been taught to fly them better than anyone else. Armed with years of flight training and intimate details of U.S. military defenses, one pilot sends shockwaves from the Pentagon to the White House by commandeering a fully loaded F-15 and taking off on a decidedly unauthorized mission—to attack New York and Washington.

___4253-3 $5.99 US/$6.99 CAN

THE PHALANX DRAGON

TIMOTHY RIZZI

"Rizzi's credible scenario and action-filled pace once again carry the day!" —*Publishers Weekly*

After Revolutionary Guard soldiers salvage a U.S. cruise missile that veered off course during the Gulf War, Iran's intelligence bureau assigns a team of experts to decipher the weapon's state-of-the-art computer chips. But fundamentalist leaders in Tehran plan to use the stolen technology to upgrade their defense systems. With improved military forces, they'll have the power to seize the Persian Gulf and cut off worldwide access to Middle-eastern oil fields.

Sent to stop the Iranians, General Duke James has at his command the best pilots in the world and the best aircraft in the skies: A-6 Intruders, F-16s, MH-53J Pave Lows, EF-111As. But he's up against the most advanced antiaircraft machinery known to man—machinery stamped MADE IN THE USA.

_3885-4 $6.99 US/$8.99 CAN

Dorchester Publishing Co., Inc.
P.O. Box 6640
Wayne, PA 19087-8640

Please add $1.75 for shipping and handling for the first book and $.50 for each book thereafter. NY, NYC, and PA residents, please add appropriate sales tax. No cash, stamps, or C.O.D.s. All orders shipped within 6 weeks via postal service book rate. Canadian orders require $2.00 extra postage and must be paid in U.S. dollars through a U.S. banking facility.

Name_____

Address_____

City_____ State_____ Zip_____

I have enclosed $_____ in payment for the checked book(s).

Payment <u>must</u> accompany all orders. ☐ Please send a free catalog.